BRINGING MORDY HOME

MIRIAM LUXENBERG

Bringing Mordy Home

ISBN: 978-1-60091-865-0

Tfutza Publications
P.O.B. 50036
Beitar Illit 90500
Tel: 972-2-650-9400
info@tfutzapublications.com

First serialized in Hamodia under the same title.

Edited by C. R. Soloveitchik
Proofread by C. Scarr
Cover design: Aviad Ben-Simon
Layout: Deena Weinberg

Distributed by:
Israel Bookshop Publications
501 Prospect Street
Lakewood, NJ 08701
Tel: (732) 901-3009
Fax: (732) 901-4012
www.israelbookshoppublications.com
info@israelbookshoppublications.com

Printed in Israel

Distributed in Europe by:
Lehmanns
Unit E Viking Industrial Park
Rolling Mill Road,
Jarrow, Tyne & Wear NE32 3DP
44-191-430-0333

Distributed in Australia by:
Gold's Book & Gift Company
3-13 William Street
Balaclava 3183
613-9527-8775

Distributed in S. Africa by:
Kollel Bookshop
Ivy Common
107 William Rd, Norwood
Johannesburg 2192
27-11-728-1822

Distributed in Israel by:
Tfutza Publications
P.O.B. 50036
Beitar Illit 90500
Tel: 972-2-650-9400
info@tfutzapublications.com

Images in the book courtesy of Freepik.com (and kjpargeter).

BRINGING MORDY HOME

MIRIAM LUXENBERG

To my dear, brave,
tenacious mother
May you be comforted
on the loss of your
husband of 63 years

CHAPTER 1

1987

Waking up in general, and on that Tuesday in particular, was such an ordeal that Devorah Landau wished she could skip it and go straight to lunch. Despite a regular exercise routine, she often woke up achy, and sometimes her knee was locked so tightly it took a full five minutes to bend it enough to get out of bed.

But even with all the discomfort, and almost against her will, she inevitably woke up cheerful, unless she'd been plagued by bad dreams during the night. Then she'd awake confused and chagrined, checking with her husband on the details of her nocturnal escapades and wincing at his report. She never really knew what they were about, but they always ended the same way, with her shouting "Help!" until Aharon woke her up.

Today she beat the alarm clock by twenty-three minutes, aggravating her to no end. The only thing worse, in terms of waking up, was getting woken up by a child who was already in crisis mode. In that case she'd have no time to pull herself together, and if her knee was locked she would have to roll out of bed, which would have been comical if it was not so agonizingly painful.

Marrying at twenty-six, while latish, was still young enough to let her blend in with her earlier-married peers, but the combination of the inevitable aging process and parenting small children could be challenging.

She had promised herself she would never be one of those people who complain, but it happened, and then it would pass. That was one of the advantages of being an older parent. You learned to roll with the punches.

The good news, that day, was that she was up before the kids and her knee was limber. Aharon was already up and out, and she stared at his neatly made bed with fondness. Being a bachelor for thirty-seven years hadn't been all bad. He'd spent the time well, turning himself into a *mentch*. By the time they married he was a ready-made husband, no assembly required. She'd given it a moment's thought, "intermarrying" with a chassid, and realized instantly that she'd be a fool to pass him up, and she hadn't.

She washed her hands and rose to greet the day.

Forty-five minutes later, Devorah was virtually unrecognizable. She was dressed, fully made-up, and her *tichel* was tied to perfection. She preferred a wig, but in her business, selling high-end head coverings, her headgear was her calling card. Aharon didn't mind, and she wore something different every day.

Tuesday was pancakes. She was structured, and her kids almost always knew what to expect on their plates on any given day. She'd recently switched to whole-wheat flour and was happy to see that the kids hadn't seemed to notice — which was not the case when she'd tried to do the same thing with the challah.

Of course, Aharon had accepted the change with his usual graciousness, but when she noticed that his "Um, um, delicious" had seemed more scripted and less authentic than usual, she discreetly switched back to white. She learned from that experience that *oneg Shabbos* also applied to children.

She was in the middle of flipping the second batch of pancakes, which were disappearing at an alarming rate between her hungry twelve-year-old son and her own incessant noshing. When the doorbell rang mid-flip, the not-quite-cooked pancake ended up dripping off the spatula and sticking to the stovetop.

As she grabbed a towel to wipe it up she saw Ephraim Baruch head to the foyer to open the door, and he got away before she could stop him.

It could be anyone these days.

Since Aharon had "made it" relatively big, life had become a little scary, even though they'd been careful to refrain from making any major changes in their lifestyle.

They had both agreed on this: no fancy cars, no vacations, no renovations.

What had given them away was that they had started paying full tuition for all the children, a moral obligation they refused to play games with.

"It's the mailman!" Ephraim Baruch shouted. He always shouted.

Devorah looked at her watch.

"He has a letter! He's asking for you!"

Using the same towel to wipe her hands as she had for the doomed pancake, she ended up with sticky hands. Hoping she looked normal (despite her attention to her appearance, breakfast took a toll on her grooming on pancake days and she often had to redo some or most of it), she finally made it to the front door.

"Good morning," she said brightly, her voice going up a little on the "ing," as if to ask what he was doing there so early.

"Registered letter for you. Came in through our 'Rush' service," holding out the envelope as if she needed proof. "Sign here."

He held out one of those swipers like they had in the supermarket and a pseudo-pen, and as she signed she saw that she'd left little pancake smears behind. She was holding the envelope by two fingers and was just about to open it when she heard a bang and a shout from the kitchen.

"What happened?" she gasped. Even after five kids she still startled at every thud.

Ephraim stood abashed in front of the stove, his back to her. Pancake batter covered the entire stovetop.

"Rena said she was hungry."

Devorah nodded understandingly — she'd long ago abandoned any other approach toward her exquisitely softhearted but incredibly complicated child — and set about tending to the problem itself. She dumped the letter into the *milchig* drawer, which doubled handily as a junk drawer, intending to get to it afterward, whenever that would be.

Now and then throughout the day she reminded herself about it, that she had to fish it out of the drawer and open it. A registered letter could mean something, or it could mean nothing. There were so many strangers in their lives now that it was hard to sort the wheat from the chaff.

But it wasn't Devorah who opened it, and it was a good thing. Later that day, as Aharon was frantically searching for his car keys just a few minutes before minyan, he realized the keys were not in their usual place.

He headed straight for the junk drawer, pulled it out hard and watched as the drawer sprang free from the rollers supposed to be keeping it in place (another thing that needed fixing; Aharon kept a running mental list). He managed to keep the drawer upright, so the contents didn't spill out on the floor, but just like in a Baal Shem Tov story, the white envelope flew up and practically smacked him in the face.

One look at the return address told him all he needed to know: It was time to come clean and tell Devorah the truth.

CHAPTER 2

L ike his wife, Aharon Landau had a unique appreciation of the good in life and knew how easy it was to take it all for granted. Devorah knew this because they spoke about it all the time. They could not get over the fact that they had finally found each other after so many years of searching.

"One thing I knew about my wife was that she'd definitely be *tzanuah*," he'd crow, "because it took me so long to find her!" There was no particular reason why they'd been left behind in the race to the chuppah. They were both healthy, average-looking, and from good families. Aharon had two income streams, the public one as a sought-after kashrus inspector and the hidden one that very few knew about. If it weren't so lucrative it would be embarrassing.

It all started on a business trip to India in search of the origins of a certain exotic seasoning blend that contained six separate spices. He ended up at a farm far out in the country. Hospitality is practically dogma in India, and the idea of not being able to serve the Jewish American was painful for the host and his family. After much discussion, it was determined that he could be served raw, uncut, unwashed (he'd do the washing himself) fruits and vegetables in wicker baskets, and Aharon would provide his own plate and cutlery, which he always carried on him in any case.

One of the delicacies served, among what seemed like hundreds, was an oddly shaped food that Aharon could not identify. When he inquired about it he was told it was called a truffle, a type of mushroom that grew beneath the ground and, as he later discovered, a good one could fetch up to $5,000 on the exotic-food market.

Devorah had tried one — once. It tasted like dirt mixed with garlic and tree bark.

Over time, through family contacts, the farmer set Aharon up as the sole Indian truffle supplier for the entire East Coast of the U.S., which included hundreds of restaurants and hotels. He'd branched out to market a few other exclusive items, which he stored in a locked cold room down in the basement, and it was like having the proverbial pot of gold in their very own home.

So there was no concrete reason it had taken so long to find each other, but it had. By some miracle, as time passed and Aharon had navigated through the lonely years, he never lost his focus.

He had gone to work every day in the hotel kitchen he presided over, spent an hour or two in the evening filling truffle orders, and the rest of his time learning, until two things happened simultaneously:

He met Devorah and his father died just a few weeks later, right after they had announced their engagement. It was as though his father had been waiting for Aharon to get settled before moving on to the Next World.

It was a bittersweet time in Aharon's life, but as the pain and grief eased, life became mostly sweet.

One of the ways he translated his intense feelings of gratitude into action was a zealous commitment to spending quality time with his wife and children. He took the children on an outing, rain or shine, every single Sunday, Devorah's presence optional, at her discretion.

Aharon was smart enough to know that at his age — not so much younger than some of his kids' classmates' grandfathers — he was never going to be one of those rough-and-tumble fathers. His own father wasn't and he grew up fine, but he still tried to overcome some of the natural distance to make the outings enjoyable. Plenty of treats and souvenirs helped his efforts greatly.

In that sense the outings were more grandfatherly, but no one seemed to mind. And even Ephraim Baruch, once he'd accepted that his Tatty just wasn't the type to go out in the backyard and throw a ball around, looked forward to their weekly safari. Aharon had also insisted on a "standing date" with Devorah every Tuesday night. Sometimes she really didn't feel like going out and there were times when she was just dead tired. But Aharon was enthusiastic and indefatigable, and the truth was that once they were out of the house she always enjoyed herself. Aharon was thoughtful and generous; she could tell he gave great thought to where they would go and what they would do, even if it was just getting ice cream and sitting on the boardwalk. Sometimes they sat in the car as he played her a new song he knew she would love. He knew how to make it all work.

That's why she was surprised when, that fateful Tuesday, she found him distant and quiet.

The only time he'd behaved that way in the fifteen years they'd been married was when he had to tell her something bad, unpleasant or troubling, that he knew would upset her.

She knew he kept a lot from her; he was so used to managing on his own that he would simply forget to share what was on his mind or to tell her about pertinent business events. Nevertheless, there were things she had to know. He had been robbed at gunpoint in the parking lot of the supermarket late one evening and had neglected to mention it until two cops had shown up at the door to let Aharon know they'd caught the guy. Devorah had learned to wait until the story eventually came out, but he was so quiet now and it was taking so long for him to get started that it was making her nervous. She waited as long as she could and was just about to speak up, when he finally broke his silence.

"I have something to tell you," he began.

"No kidding," Devorah said lightly. "You think I don't know that? The quieter you are, the longer the story, too, so I guess this is going to be a full-length novel." But he neither smiled nor returned the banter.

Now truly nervous, Devorah attempted to fill the oppressive silence. "Well, anyway, I'm glad you're not a schmoozer like some of those men I see on Shabbos morning who just seem glued to the sidewalk in front of the shul, while their poor, hungry wives—"

"Devorah," Aharon cut her off. Now she knew it was something big. Aharon never interrupted her when she was speaking, even if she was just prattling.

"Devorah, you're not going to like this."

"Just tell me," she said, all trace of bantering leached from her voice.

CHAPTER 3

I t was already 11:15 when Yitta Landau started to worry. Aharon's mother, Yitta, had taken over all babysitting responsibilities once Ephraim Baruch had reached the age where Devorah and Aharon could no longer hire young teen-age girls to babysit their brood. Yitta loved to do it, to give the kids dinner, tell them stories, and make up songs with them. When Yitta was there, everything was under control.

And besides, her nights were too long now, had been for the past fifteen years, so what better way to fill the time?

Yitta enjoyed her Tuesday night shift; it gave her something to look forward to. She would often join the Sunday excursion as well but, like Devorah, her attendance was optional. They knew, and were unfailingly considerate about it, that she preferred to go home no later than 10:30. Aharon would drive her home and come in for a few minutes, and this brief period alone with her only son was precious to Yitta. She tried calling both their cellphones, and when Aharon picked up the second time, she could tell immediately that something was the matter.

"What's wrong?" she asked.

"Nothing, Ma. I'm here with Devorah. We'll be home soon."

"You're late."

She didn't mean to sound querulous, but sometimes it happened. As the years had passed and Aharon still hadn't found his *bashert*, although she never gave up her rock-solid belief that he would one day be married, that didn't mean she wouldn't sometimes feel frustrated and take it out on him.

She cried when he finally moved into his own apartment, and brought him cooked meals every single day until he politely, respectfully, begged her to stop, explaining that he really needed to learn to cope on his own. But that was exactly why she brought the food — because she didn't want him to become so self-sufficient that he no longer felt the need for a wife.

When he married Devorah her worry about him did not abate 100 percent. Devorah knew how to cook, which wasn't something you could assume these days. But when she discovered that Devorah knew how to shine shoes like a professional, she breathed half a sigh of relief, knowing her son to be in relatively good hands. She breathed the other half only after Ephraim, Maya and Rena had made their appearance.

"I know, I'm sorry, Ma, we got caught up. We'll be back soon."

"Please, not too late, okay, Aharon?"

"Okay, Ma."

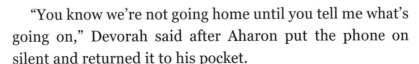

"You know we're not going home until you tell me what's going on," Devorah said after Aharon put the phone on silent and returned it to his pocket.

"I know." He took a deep breath. "I know...but now I feel pressured."

"I'm very sorry about that," said Devorah, "but you'll just have to step up the pace. I'm waiting."

"Okay," he said, stroking his beard nervously. "It's about Mordy."

"Who?" Devorah's response was pure reflex, and she realized what she'd said only when she saw Aharon's puzzled expression.

"Mordy. Mordechai Yitzchak Hakohen Landau." Their firstborn. It was the last thing she expected Aharon to say.

"What about Mordy?" she asked sharply.

The letter was burning a hole in his pocket. He considered, one last time, sheltering her from the truth, keeping it to himself as he had done so successfully all these years, allowing the wheels of her life to turn smoothly. But she had to know the truth now, and he knew it. He removed the envelope slowly from his coat pocket and handed it to her.

"What's this," she asked, "and what does it have to do with Mordy?"

Her voice was cutting, but it wasn't anger — it was fear. She struggled to hold on as she was blown back through a time tunnel, the calendar pages flipping back thirteen years, four months. Even the mention of his name could send her reeling...

———————◦———————

1973

She was lying supine now, in the hospital bed, while Aharon sat in a hard metal chair at her side, learning from a *sefer*, his unique *niggun* trickling into her ear. She rose from the deep, deep pool of anesthesia she was submerged in, thrashing her hands and feet, holding her breath, until her head broke through the surface of the water and fresh air hit her face.

She inhaled deeply, but instead of the warm, briny air she was expecting, there was a harsh, pungent smell that pierced her eyes and the soft places of her face and felt like the burning prick of a dozen tiny sparks hitting the tender skin on the inside of her nose. She closed her eyes again and slept, and when she woke again, Aharon was still there, but now he was a rumpled remnant of his usually well-dressed self. Aharon was meticulous about his appearance without being obsessive. He was accustomed to bringing his shirts to the laundromat to be washed and ironed, his suits to the dry cleaners (though she still shined his shoes), as he did not want to overburden her, which she appreciated. Except for a prolonged bout with the flu, she had practically never seen him at anything less than his tidy best. She knew where she was now. She recalled hearing an incessant ringing in her ears, and the feeling that she was sliding down a weird sort of a tunnel. She had called out to Aharon that something didn't feel right, and that was the last thing she remembered.

She looked up now to find a clear plastic bag half-filled with blood and another, larger bag filled three-quarters with murky fluid, both hanging from an IV pole at the side of her bed.

"Where's the baby?" she asked, groggy but focused.

Aharon had shifted in his chair. "He's in the nursery. They'll bring him in soon," Aharon said, although he knew very well that they would not.

CHAPTER 4

Devorah started to feel chilly, unsure whether it was from a drop in temperature or the shock of hearing Mordy's name. The only time they said it out loud was when they were alone, on his birthday, quietly wishing him well. Aharon would recite *Birkas Kohanim*, Devorah would answer amen, and they would return his name to its hiding place until the following year.

She had opened the envelope. She had read the contents. She had gotten the gist. But there were so many pieces missing she didn't know where to start.

"I thought he was being taken care of by that family — you never even told me their name."

"He was with the family," said Aharon. "And then he wasn't. They couldn't take care of him anymore."

"Why not?"

Aharon considered those five days spent deciding what to do as some of the worst of his life, and he thanked Hashem every day that it was he who had taken the call. Devorah had taken the children to visit her parents in Cleveland. She had moved to New York as an older single for *shidduchim* and, while she joked that she'd stayed in New York for the pizza, the real reason was that she'd be happy anywhere with Aharon and there was no reason to uproot him.

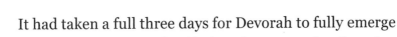

It had taken a full three days for Devorah to fully emerge from the anesthesia, as they'd given her a massive dose due to the great emergency, and she'd run a high fever afterward from an infection. Whenever her eyes opened, she would look at Aharon beseechingly, aware that something was wrong but not knowing what it was. But he could not reassure her. Thirty-seven years of keeping things to himself could not be undone in a day, and the words clogged his throat like cotton. Late in the evening of the third day, she sat up in bed, fully alert, and demanded something to drink.

He ran to the nurses' station and told them Devorah was awake and asked them for some juice. The nurse poured out a cup from a refrigerator behind the nurses' station and followed Aharon to Devorah's room.

"Have you told her yet?" she asked.

"No."

Nurse Wanda stopped in her tracks. "I don't understand you people. Why don't you just tell her the baby was still-born?" Aharon winced at the harsh language. "That's what most folks would do. She never has to know," the nurse continued, "and you wouldn't be the first person to leave a baby in a hospital and not look back."

He recoiled in shock; the thought had never once entered his mind, but now, like an arrow to its target, it sank in. It would be so much easier — he'd have to ask his *rav*, but how could he ask such a question without appearing heartless?

"Think about it," Wanda said. "It's the right thing to do." And she handed him the cup of juice and walked back to the station.

———————●———————

They still hadn't brought the baby in from the nursery, and it was only after Devorah started shouting and didn't stop that they hustled her into a wheelchair and pushed her to the nursery. She'd smiled at Aharon mischievously as they advanced down the hall. "Sometimes you just gotta yell!" She'd been giddy with excitement about seeing her baby.

There had been some talk of showing her a different baby until she was stronger, but Aharon realized that whatever he tried to hide now would resurface, and not in a good way. He could keep things under control if he was as honest as possible now, but that didn't mean it would be easy.

Devorah, still unaware of the gravity of the situation, allowed her eyes to roam the rows of babies in the nurs-ery and wonder which one was hers. It was only when one nurse, the lower half of her face covered with a mask, came and stood behind one of the bulky incubators toward the back of the nursery that she realized that the child cocooned within was hers.

The nurse struggled to wheel the bulky incubator closer to the viewing window, but Devorah had already caught sight of the baby. She froze for a moment, but immediately calmed down. He was her baby and she loved him instantly. (Later that day she would insist they move the incubator closer to the window, which was no small task, but it was better than arguing with the ferocious new mother.)

Aharon watched her carefully, gauging her reaction. When her eyes softened at the sight of the baby, his filled with dread.

"Cleft lip? Cleft palate? We can handle it," Devorah said, tears of happiness filling her eyes. "Isn't he beautiful?" Aharon made eye contact with the masked nurse who was shaking her head sorrowfully. The nurse knew there would be trouble ahead; she'd done her duty and warned him. If he hadn't known better — and Aharon did know better, even though they'd been married only a little more than a year — he'd think Devorah was in some twilight land of denial. What he saw in her eyes now was grounded in reality, but why was he surprised? This was why he'd chosen her from all the others. The look in her eyes was real love, a mother's love, and he shouldn't have expected otherwise.

"It's not just the cleft palate, Devorah," he'd said gently. The baby was covered with a warming blanket so she couldn't see the deformed limbs underneath.

She'd turned her head partly toward him, unable to take her eyes off the baby. "So what?"

"So...?" Devorah asked as she handed the letter back to Aharon.

"There were problems," he said. "The foster father... wasn't, uh, good with Mordy, and Mordy was too much for the foster mother. It got complicated."

"When was this?" asked Devorah.

Aharon cringed. This was going to hurt.

"Twelve years ago. It took some time to get it sorted out. They gave me a week to decide what to do with Mordy, whether we should bring him home or try to find another family..."

Stay with him, Devorah ordered herself. *Don't make this about you. He's your husband. He's also suffering.*

"Ephraim was just born then. You were after birth. You were...do you remember? You were in no condition to...I didn't know...there wasn't time...I asked a *rav* what to do. He answered. I did what I had to do." Tears were spattering from his eyes like raindrops, she'd never seen anyone cry that way, and if she weren't about to step into a cauldron of pain she'd have marveled at it.

She took a deep breath. "Okay. If I look back, I will turn into a pillar of salt. What can we do now?"

CHAPTER 5

Aharon had taken the time to compose a timeline so that he could speak coherently and answer Devorah's questions, so while he wasn't surprised that she was focused on the future, he'd thought she needed to know the details of the past. "What good will it do me, or you, or Mordy?" she replied when he offered to tell her what he knew. "Your mother is waiting for us to return home, and I feel pressured. We can talk about it another time. I just want to know where he is now and what we can do for him."

Even after Devorah had seen Mordy's less-than-perfect newborn body, her devotion hadn't wavered. She asked repeatedly when they could all go home, and each time received another vague reply. Even after Aharon had explained that the baby would have to be hospitalized for a long time, long after she herself was discharged, she was prepared to settle in and wait for that day to come.

The official diagnosis, besides the cleft lip and palate, was cerebral palsy, a patchwork term for brain damage occurring at birth or shortly after. The doctors said that cleft palate and cerebral palsy often occurred together.

Aharon had listened and taken notes, but all he wanted, at that moment, was to have his father standing by his side. His legs were trembling, his normally perfect handwriting nearly illegible, and he wished he could feel his father's arm around his shoulders, holding him upright and keeping him steady. He felt, at that moment of utter aloneness, the loss of his father all over again.

Nothing in his life as a single man, or even as the newly married man that he was, had prepared him for this moment. He supposed there were other events in life that could catapult a man so suddenly into adulthood — as he thought losing his father had been for him — but this was much worse, because it not only hurt him. It would also hurt Devorah.

And if his flesh-and-blood father could no longer hold him, Aharon was forced to go straight to the Source.

He'd nodded at the doctors, considered the options, sought advice, and made some preliminary decisions, while having one of his most troubling questions finally answered. During his life as an older single, he'd tried not to dwell on the why of it, why he'd been left behind. Now he understood that this child, his *bechor*, needed a mature thirty-eight-year-old father, and Hashem, Who watches over all His creations, had sent him one.

Meanwhile, Devorah haunted the nursery, begging for a glimpse of their baby and being granted her wish for a few moments every two hours, until Aharon would come and lead her away.

One day, he walked her out to the hospital garden and settled her on the chilly wrought-iron bench while he sat across from her, hunched over, his hand covering his mouth. It was the first time she'd seen him make that gesture, but she hadn't known then what it meant.

"Devorah," he'd started off gently, sweetly, "our dear child..." — and he shuddered, for although the baby was clearly a pure *neshamah*, Aharon was struggling with his feelings — "You must understand," he began again, "that even when our son leaves the hospital, he will not be ready to come home with us."

"What do you mean?" she'd asked. "We can manage."

"*We* can," said Aharon, "but he can't. His needs are too great for us to care for him at home. We must send him to specially trained people to care for him until he is well enough to come home."

He cringed at his lie; according to the doctors, even if the infant survived, he would never be able to come home.

"That's ridiculous," said Devorah. "Who is better suited to care for him than his own mother?" They'd discussed the matter over the next few days, and while Aharon had known Devorah was tenacious, he was now to learn how persistent she could be. She simply refused to capitulate to the inevitable, and while his heart ached, he couldn't help but admire her strength.

Eventually Aharon was forced to call in auxiliary forces — *rabbanim*, Devorah's parents and siblings, an old friend — and while it had some effect, in the end they'd had to basically pry the baby out of her arms.

And Aharon knew the truth — the baby was not going to specially trained experts; he was going to a volunteer foster family. He also knew that the family was no more qualified than they were but he, and those who loved them, could not support starting out their family with such a burden on their shoulders. There seemed to be no choice.

"Why them and not us?" she'd wailed. There were no tears — those came later — only fierce determination. It was only when she was forced to accept defeat that the tears had finally come.

"What happened after he left the foster home?" Devorah asked, the words breaking the silence in the car like a rock smashing through a closed window.

"I told you, you were at your mother's house with Ephraim Baruch, exhausted, everything finally catching up to you when the Children's Bureau called to tell me they needed to move him."

The name on the letterhead, Ravensfield School for Mentally Challenged Children, still sent chills down Aharon's spine. He'd never visited the place, but he'd heard stories. He'd heard the stories but sealed his ears until he couldn't hear them anymore, and then he stopped asking. He let Devorah believe Mordy was safe and sound when he really had no idea if it was true.

"It's the only option," the agent had told him on the phone. "There's nowhere else to place him." Those he'd consulted had agreed with the agent, and Aharon did what he'd been told he had to do. He knew he had acted in good faith, but like Devorah, if he looked back he would simply drown in the deep waters of the past. They had no choice now but to walk straight ahead.

And as the letter stated, the school was closing. They'd been given a second chance. The question now was what to do with it.

CHAPTER 6

Yitta Landau picked up on the tension the moment Aharon and Devorah walked through the door, but she had learned the hard way that if they had anything to say, they'd say it together, and only when they were good and ready.

Aharon greeted his mother, and after a few moments of small talk went to retrieve her coat from the closet near the front door. He would usually stand there and wait for her while she gathered her things, gave Devorah a brief report on the children, and said good night before she appeared in the hallway. Tonight, though, the routine took a surprising twist.

"Aharon," Devorah said suddenly, "you must be exhausted from such a long, hard day."

Before he could reply that no, he was not particularly tired, she forged ahead. "Let me drive your mother home tonight."

If the brief scene were an opera, the music would now be crescendoing ominously. Aharon glanced at Devorah and asked carefully, "Are you sure, Devorah?" and she replied, "Absolutely." Yitta was perfectly capable of reading between the lines, and headed stoically toward the front door, prepared to accept whatever was heading her way.

———————◦———————

The night was chilly. Devorah preceded her mother-in-law down the front walk toward the car. She opened the door for her mother-in-law and settled her into the front seat.

In their pursuit of understatement, their van, while new, was a modest seven-seater that suited the salary of a kashrus supervisor but less so that of an exotic-food mogul. But that was nobody's business.

Yitta wished that Aharon and Devorah lived according to their real means and frequently said so, but Aharon would just nod and smile and make light of her comments. ("No can do, Ma!" he'd joke.) They both knew he spent money freely where it counted, supporting her and making sure all her needs, and many of her wants, were met.

Devorah sat down in the driver's seat, pushed the seat forward, and buckled the seat belt, but then freed herself from the shoulder strap. She feared somewhat irrationally that if the car stopped short she would be garroted. This habit bothered Aharon terribly, not only because she was putting herself in danger and setting a bad example for the children, but also because of how upsetting it must be for her to have such a morbid fear.

Usually, whenever they drove together, Devorah would play one of her mother-in-law's favorite CDs, but this time she did not. Silence held for the first few minutes, until Devorah took a deep breath. Yitta recognized that deep breath. *Here it comes*, she thought.

"Before I tell you what's going on," Devorah began. ("And before Aharon gets to tell me," Yitta filled in the missing words silently, wondering if they had planned this discussion together or if Devorah was breaking protocol) "...and I will tell you, I have some questions I need to ask you first." Devorah trod carefully now over this bed of nails. If she broke down too soon she wouldn't find out what she needed to know.

She would never forget her mother-in-law's one and only visit to the hospital after Mordy was born. They hadn't known each other well then, and for Yitta, Aharon's choice of a wife after fifteen years of searching was disappointing. ("For this he waited such a long time?" she'd complained to her husband. His soft reply often echoed in her ears when she was missing him most: "Every wife is worth the wait.")

Yitta had rushed in, laden with packages for Aharon's comfort: two freshly ironed shirts, clean socks, and a few loaves of still-warm, apple-and-nut-filled kokosh cake that Aharon would have been happy to exist on indefinitely.

She had brought a bag of oranges and, puzzlingly, a head of cabbage, which was, she had informed Devorah, "to dry up, you know, the milk. I hear it's very painful. Of course, we didn't do that back in my day. We all nursed our babies," as though Devorah had chosen not to nurse.

She had stayed a short while in the room until Devorah couldn't take the tension any longer and feigned sleep. Yitta had then turned to her beloved son, and Devorah could hear the horror in her voice.

"Aharon! I peeked in on the baby before I came to the room. He looks terrible! What are you going to do?"

"I don't know, Ma," he'd whispered. Devorah heard his voice catch. "I'm really frightened."

"I can't imagine what you must be going through. What do the doctors say?"

"Not much, they just imply that he won't live long enough to cause any problems. Devorah wants him home."

"Oh, no," Yitta had said. Devorah could hear the steel beneath her voice. "Under no circumstances. You cannot bring that baby home no matter what Devorah wants. It's no way to start a family!"

Perhaps sensing that Devorah was in fact awake, Aharon had arisen wearily from the chair he was sprawled in and escorted his mother out of the room. He couldn't stop his mother from talking, but he could protect Devorah from hearing what she had to say.

———◦———

"First of all, how much do you know about Mordy?" Devorah asked Yitta Landau now. "How much has Aharon confided in you?"

Yitta took a deep breath. It had taken a long while to build the fragile peace between them, and rocking the boat now seemed foolhardy. On the other hand, now that the subject had come up again, there was no telling what Devorah might do.

"It was a terrible situation, just terrible," she began. "The bottom of his face looking like someone had taken a hatchet to it—"

"It was a cleft lip. You know that," Devorah interrupted her.

"Okay, I know, but it was awful. And his arms and legs so twisted—"

"Cerebral palsy. Not the end of the world."

"Today it isn't, maybe. But when he was born there was no treatment for it, for any of it. No one knew what to do."

"I knew," Devorah said.

"You did not," Yitta countered. "You couldn't have."

"I would have learned." Devorah took a sharp breath and Yitta's heart plummeted. "I would have figured it out." Too upset to drive, Devorah pulled over to the curb.

"What are you doing?" asked Yitta with concern. Devorah rarely acted erratically.

"We got a notice today from the place where Mordy's been all these years, as I'm sure you already know." She did.

"It's closing, and they want to know what we want them to do with Mordy."

"You cannot bring him home!" The words were out of her mouth before she could stop them. "It's too late."

"It isn't too late...it's never too late!" Devorah found herself averring. And that's when Devorah realized she knew *exactly* what she was going to do.

CHAPTER 7

The moment she got home, after practically being held hostage by her daughter-in-law, Yitta called her son, who was already half-asleep, to warn him about her unusual encounter with Devorah. As devoted a husband as he was, he felt a jolt when his mother repeated their conversation.

Aharon stood up from the sofa where he'd been dozing while waiting for Devorah to return home, and moved to the kitchen to make himself a cup of coffee. He drank it straight black, lukewarm from the faucet, and chugged it down in a few gulps. "What did she say, exactly?" he asked, once he felt lucid again.

"She was ranting and raving — you know how she gets (He did not know. He had never seen her "rant and rave" in all their years of marriage), asking me what you told me and what I knew, insisting she could have taken care of your son on her own. She was so upset she even pulled the car over in the middle of our conversation, going on about how it was never too late. And then she looked at me with a gleam in her eye."

Yitta stopped to take a breath and realized she still had her coat on. "I didn't take her seriously, of course, but I thought you should know so you won't be taken by surprise. She was just upset, but still...better safe than sorry."

Little tremors. That's all this was, Aharon thought. They'd get Mordy settled somewhere, and the whole thing would die down.

"Don't let her talk you into doing anything crazy...." Yitta was obviously holding back much more than she was saying. "Do you hear me, Aharon? I mean it."

He heard the car pulling up in front of the house. It wasn't a long drive, but he didn't want to be on the phone when Devorah came in. "Whatever happens, it will be a decision we make together, not something I'm talked into, okay?" When his mother didn't reply, he continued, "I appreciate your calling, Ma," he said. "And the babysitting is a lifesaver. I have no words to thank you. Good night now."

He was just closing the phone when Devorah flew into the house. "We're keeping him," she said. "Whatever it takes. He belongs at home, with us."

Aharon turned to face her and she could tell that he'd already spoken to his mother. She must have really scared her. "It's 1987, Aharon! It's not like when he was born, when no one knew what to do with these kids. We'll get help. We'll figure it out. Right?" While Devorah was taking off her coat, hanging up her bag, putting her keys and glasses on the table next to the door, he poured boiling water into a glass mug and dropped a tea bag into it ("What can I do?" she'd asked when he questioned her insistence that hot drinks must be drunk in glass cups. "I'm a throwback. I'd stick a sugar cube between my teeth if it was socially acceptable.").

He placed the mug on the table, and they sat down opposite each other.

"Make a *berachah*," he said gently.

"It's too hot. I'll wait."

He nodded and sat quietly for a moment, weighing carefully what needed to be said next, but she spoke first. "You're not even willing to consider it," she said, her voice low and a little hard. "I can tell just by looking at you."

"That's not what I was going to say. Please, don't rush me. This is important and I want to make sure that I say everything right, the way it needs to be said."

She backed down immediately. "Of course, Aharon. I'm sorry. Take your time." She wrapped her hands around the mug.

"Believe me, Devorah, if bringing Mordy home would make you happy I would do it in a heartbeat. But there is a lot you don't know, that we...I...never told you."

The lies had folded in on one another, a set of matryoshka dolls of deception, one leading into the other until the truth was a small kernel buried beneath layers of falsehood. It had all started with the bris. Devorah had been forced to leave the hospital after a three-week stay — she'd developed an infection and was given a ten-day course of antibiotics, so she'd bought herself some time. She had worried that she wouldn't see her baby again. Aharon remembered how she had looked that day. She had fought for the baby until the last moment, and when she finally realized she had lost, that she was leaving the hospital without him, she simply crumpled, and he'd had to insist that she be taken down in a wheelchair. If he hadn't just seen it on his mother's face after his father died, he might not have recognized Devorah's expression as she was wheeled out of the hospital. Grief had carved such deep lines into her face that for a moment he was frightened that her face would stay that way and never recover its youth. Even now, he could see ghosts of it around and beneath her eyes when she was tired or worried.

She had assumed that the baby would be leaving the hospital shortly after her own departure, even though she had been told otherwise, and even before she was discharged, she had started talking to Aharon about the bris.

"You'll take care of it, right? You'll make sure?"

He had nodded each time, even going so far as to discuss names with her. It was a long time before Mordy was in any condition for a bris, but Devorah was so anxious about it that after she'd been home about three months, Aharon told her they'd made the bris, that he'd given the name Mordechai Yitzchak after his father as they'd discussed, and it was the first time he'd seen her relax since the birth.

"It's the least we can do for him," she'd said, "if we can't raise him." Devorah was nearly his own height, but she'd looked so small that day, curled up on the couch, the iron rod of fierce defiance that had been keeping her going melting before his eyes.

It took seven months of relentless badgering of every *mohel* in the city until one of them would even look at Mordy, another two months before the bris actually took place, and still another two months for the baby to recover. Aharon was so worried that Devorah would find out the truth that he bought a beeper, telling her he needed it for work but in truth needing it to accept return calls from the *rabbanim*, *mohalim*, and doctors with whom he was in constant contact.

His father was no longer alive to be *sandak* — a bitter blow, as Aharon had often imagined standing beside his father, wrapped in tallis and tefillin, both of them bursting with *nachas* at this continuation of their male line. His father, Aharon was sure, would have understood, and he felt orphaned all over again, naming the baby after his father — the only thing left for him to do.

He had hesitated, wondering if he should save the name for a healthier baby as his mother had asked, but knew that his father would be honored to have this baby named after him. He gathered a minyan of strangers and passed out the *kibbudim* randomly, choosing the oldest as *sandak*.

But as he glanced down at the tiny broken body, strapped onto a padded board to keep him stable, the baby boy's eyes caught his and gazed at him knowingly with solemn trust. It lasted only a moment, and by the time the bris was over Aharon had convinced himself that he had only imagined it, but the heart knows what it knows, and it never lets you forget it.

CHAPTER 8

Aharon was still talking to Devorah, her tea long-forgotten, finally unburdening himself of the memory of those terrible days, forgetting that when a person unburdens himself, he is simultaneously shifting the burden onto someone else.

"All I can say in my own defense," he said now, sorrowfully, "was that I did the best I could for everyone, including Mordy."

He had just finished saying those words when a voice piped up from the other door to the kitchen.

"Who's Mordy?" said Ephraim Baruch, taking a 7-Up from the refrigerator and sitting himself down at the table to join them. They kept a ready supply of the soda available for him after he agreed to drink it instead of caffeine-containing colas.

He looked over at his mother.

"Why are you crying?" Then at Aharon. "What happened?" Aharon and Devorah had long ago devised a signal — she would touch her right eyebrow, he would brush his left shoulder — to remind and encourage each other that while Ephraim Baruch tested their boundaries, they were an experienced team of "border guards."

"How're ya doing, tzaddik?" said Aharon. "Long time no see." He was tired; it was, as he said earlier, the best he could do.

"I just saw you this morning," Ephraim said. He stood up then, took a few things from the fridge, and cut up a plateful of fruit. He put it down on the table, intending to put it halfway between his parents, but was unable to stop himself from pushing it closer to his teary-eyed mother.

Aharon let his eyes flick quickly to her right eyebrow — *Should we tell him?*

A slight turn of the head from her — *Not yet.* Not without thinking it out first. The signals went unnoticed by the normally eagle-eyed Ephraim as he listened to his mother's *berachah.*

She knew she had to eat from the plate, accept his gesture respectfully and keep praise to a healthy level. A child shouldn't be overpraised, she and Aharon had decided together. The apple slice she chewed and swallowed barely slid past the lump in her throat.

"Everything's fine, sweetheart," she said now. "It's late, after a long day."

Ephraim wasn't suspicious and, they'd learned, never intentionally chutzpadik; he was just doing the math. "You and Tatty usually come home very happy on Tuesdays," he said simply.

"That's true," said Devorah. "But most rules have an exception." She had to step very carefully here — too much information and he'd demolish it with questions, too little information and he'd become unsettled.

"But, really," she repeated, "everything is fine." She put her hand over his for emphasis and took another apple slice. He'd cut them the perfect length and width.

"Who's Mordy, though?" he asked again.

Aharon didn't need a signal to know that it was time for him to step in. There wasn't an actual reason to pull out the secret weapon, but this situation could become volatile if not handled correctly. They were both too wound up and emotional. There was one thing Ephraim could not say no to, and Aharon offered it now.

"We can speak about Mordy another time..."

"Promise?" said Ephraim.

"No. Possibility."

"Okay."

"Meanwhile" — and now Aharon walked over to Ephraim's chair and pulled his son's long legs out from under the table and rested them on his knees — "climb up."

The game had started years ago, when Ephraim was small. He would hold his father's hands and start climbing up from his knees all the way up to his father's head. Ephraim's face lit up, and he looked over at Devorah uncertainly. Could he leave her?

She nodded lovingly, and Ephraim grabbed his father's hands. He climbed up to Aharon's shoulders and turned himself around, he'd learned to balance himself from years of *simchah* dancing with his father.

He raised his arms up and, from down below, Aharon could feel the boy fill up with himself and his vigor, reigning over the small principality that was their dim kitchen.

"'Night, Mommy," he called over his shoulder, bending carefully, arms out and low in front of him like a surfer, to avoid the door frame. Devorah whispered good night and watched her menfolk leave the kitchen, both of them her comfort and her blessing, each in his own way.

While she was sure Ephraim had other purposes for being brought into this world, she knew that one of them had been to comfort her. He didn't even know he was doing it, it was just the way he was created. The plate of fruit was just a small example — he didn't have to think to himself, *Oh, I'd better do something nice for Mommy.* It just poured out of him, and it was usually exactly the right thing.

Devorah's mother often said that you don't get every *nisayon* in life. Hashem throws in plenty of freebies and Ephraim was one of them. And he'd been born at the right time as well. Another mother might have found his quirky mind, intense personality and frenetic energy unsettling, but not her. After the empty silence Mordy had left behind, she'd take any child, any way he was handed to her. The more noise, mess and action, the better, and Ephraim filled the space perfectly. She and Ephraim were truly a match made in Heaven. And Aharon. You think you know a person. She remembered very well that period of time he had been speaking about. Every moment that passed without Mordy having a bris was a black hole, and she had, indeed, been merciless, believing that if she did not make it happen, no one was going to bother.

She'd had no idea how much pressure she had put on Aharon — the thought had not crossed her mind for even a moment that Mordy was too weak and unstable for a bris, and that no *mohel* would dare attempt it.

She knew their marriage was unique, so she rarely discussed it with others except to express her gratitude that she had found a soulmate with whom to build a family. She quietly wondered about the lives of her friends, how they were still, after years of marriage, keeping parts of themselves hidden from their families.

Having Mordy so early in her marriage had exposed her essence in such a way that there was little left to hide. There was no mystery, no layers to unravel or unfold. It had all spilled out of her at once.

Another woman might be angry at her husband's deception — and according to him, this was just the tip of the iceberg. Who knew what other revelations were lying in wait?

But Devorah was determined. From that moment on, she was taking their marriage out of the equation. No matter what happened next, their marriage could not and would not suffer.

CHAPTER 9

The next morning — Wednesday — Aharon and Devorah, while being perfectly cordial, had circled each other like prizefighters. There was a huge elephant in the room, so big that it was difficult to know where to mount the attack.

She knew Aharon: First stop for him was always *da'as Torah*, and that was why she'd waited so long to find the right one to marry. Like Eliezer asking to be shown a sign that Yitzchak's wife would be the one to offer to water the camels, she'd waited to hear the magic words, and once she'd realized where Aharon's priorities lay, she knew he was the right one for her.

They could go to their *rav* and roll out the whole story, and more than likely — although the *rav*'s replies were never predictable — he would ask, "So what exactly is your *she'eilah*?"

Devorah was sure he didn't need them to tell him; he wanted them to clarify it for themselves. She knew her question very well: "Now that circumstances have changed, may we bring him home?" But she did not yet know where Aharon stood, because, he claimed, she could not make such a major decision when she did not have all the facts.

He didn't understand that mothers don't always need *all* the facts.

As the children began their day, riding away in their carpools, Devorah waited for Aharon in the kitchen, sweeping crumbs and rinsing breakfast dishes. She poured herself a second cup of coffee and looked through the mail. Aharon finally came home a moment before she was ready to give up.

She got up to serve him the omelet she'd kept warm, but he shook his head sadly. "I haven't davened yet."

And that was when Devorah realized two things: First, that they were in deeper waters than she'd thought, and second, it's harder to suppress a gasp than one might think.

"I'm sorry," she said, meaning it. "I see how hard this is for you."

"Devorah," he said, wrapping his *peyos* tightly around his fingers, "you know I would do anything for you. Anything."

"I know," she responded.

"But I don't think I can do this. I don't think we...I...I don't think I can bring Mordy home."

His body language communicated his sincerity very well, but she refused to acknowledge the words. "Oh, come on,

Aharon. We haven't even discussed it yet. We don't even know what's involved."

"*You* don't know."

"Here we go again," she said, softly. "More secrets. I don't know how many times I have to tell you. I do not need to know *every single thing* that happened."

"You may not need to know, but I need to tell you."

If it hadn't been such a fraught moment, she'd have excused herself and gotten up for a piece of paper and a pen, because this was another question for the *rav*. If Aharon did need to unburden himself, did it necessarily have to be to her?

"I kept information from you all these years because I was advised it was the correct thing to do, and I believe it was. But if we are going to 'move ahead,' as you keep saying, then it's not fair *to me* if you only know half the story. There might — no, there will definitely — be things you'll find upsetting, and I don't want you to blame me. My hands were completely tied."

Tied wasn't even the word for it, he thought. Shackled, chained, manacled. Aharon didn't fully understand why he was pushing to make a full confession if Devorah was willing to let him off the hook, but he knew it would backfire eventually if he didn't tell her everything.

The past was a moving target, shifting direction and perspective every time you looked at it. It wouldn't be long before Devorah would start connecting the dots and the bitter facts of Mordy's life would be revealed.

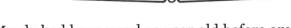

Mordy had been nearly a year old before anyone started talking about discharging him from the hospital. No one had expected him to survive that long. He'd outgrown the cribs and nursery equipment, and the pediatrics department did not want him. But once the subject took hold, all anyone could think of was getting Mordy out.

"He's taking up a bed that a truly sick child might need," the hospital administrator had said to Aharon earnestly.

"What am I supposed to do with him?" Aharon had asked, bewildered.

That was when the Bursteins stepped in. They knew about Mordy from their son, one of the *mohalim* Aharon had been in touch with. They urged their son to tell Aharon that they would be willing to take Mordy in and care for him. They were a middle-aged couple with all their children married and still energetic.

Aharon did meet with them, but he couldn't see in them what he believed it would take to care for Mordy. They were soft and placid as yielding dough, and Aharon thought Mordy needed someone tougher, stronger, and maybe even a little fierce (like Devorah, he had to admit) to raise him.

But the pressure was mounting, there were no other options, and against his better judgment, he approved the arrangement and the Bursteins registered with the Children's Bureau.

He didn't know why he was surprised that they requested a hefty monthly payment above and beyond the medical expenses. Surely the Bursteins would have to cut corners elsewhere, they said, and they were right, he had no argument. Cleaning help, a newer, more reliable car, big enough to hold Mordy and any equipment he needed, eating out in restaurants to save time on food preparation that could be spent caring for Mordy — the list was lengthy, but Aharon said yes to everything. And they did try. Martin and Fanny

Burstein started spending time with Mordy at the hospital, but Aharon could see that their enthusiasm had already started to wane even before they took him home.

It wasn't long before he began getting messages from them through the Bureau that it was not going well. Mr. Burstein, it turned out, had never intended to be involved with child care. He fully expected his wife and the various aides they employed to do all the work.

Fanny had tried her hardest, using every ounce of her strength, but without a mother's natural love to cushion it, Mordy's utter helplessness was too much for her. She grew depressed from the internal conflict — she was a good person, she wanted to succeed — until her children insisted Mordy be "given back."

And that was when Aharon's nightmare had begun.

CHAPTER 10

T here hadn't been many options available for children like Mordy. There were a few private institutions, and had Aharon known about them at the time, he would have moved heaven and earth to ensure that Mordy had a place in one of them. When the agent from the Children's Bureau had called to tell him he had five days to decide what to do, the only option he'd been given that day was the Ravensfield School for Mentally Challenged Children. He was unaware that the agent received a commission for every child she sent there.

The phone call had coincided, to the day, with Devorah's visit to her parents. Just as Aharon had returned from dropping her off at the airport, the phone rang. Ephraim's birth had been nothing like Mordy's. He had come into the world smiling, looking around with clear eyes as if he wanted to get to know everyone in the room. His face shone, and it was hard to look away from him.

But it had been that very luminescence that shook Devorah to her core. After the shock of giving birth to Mordy, Ephraim's beauty had opened up the dark room where Devorah had stored her feelings. The contrast of light and darkness had been simply overwhelming, and it was in caring for Ephraim — feeding him, diapering him, rocking him to sleep, the normal routines of a new mother and baby — that she began to fathom all she had missed out on with Mordy.

When she had held Ephraim, she realized she'd never held Mordy, not even once. Never fed him, never bathed him, never done all the motherly things every baby needs, and she hadn't even known what she was missing. She hadn't known what it was to be a mother, and the realization was an empty pit she had unwittingly stumbled into.

Her reaction had startled all of them; Aharon had been lulled into a false sense of security when Devorah seemed to have bounced back from the ordeal, so watching her fall apart after Ephraim's birth was even more confusing. And poor Ephraim — after a few short weeks in the sun, he had succumbed to his mother's sorrow and began howling in sympathy.

Aharon, unaccustomed to asking for help, had resolved to handle the situation on his own, and for a while he did. Devorah grew adept at masking her pain, but nothing helped Ephraim — babies are expert at seeing through masks — and he was inconsolable.

Aharon had been sure it would pass, but after three months, it finally dawned on Devorah's mother that every single time she called, the baby was screaming so loudly that she could barely hear her daughter, whose voice had become suspiciously whispery.

Devorah had politely refused her mother's offers, which grew more and more insistent, to come to help her or have Devorah and Ephraim come to her, until finally, with Aharon's exhausted blessing, Tzivi Greenblatt hopped on a plane, swooped in, and whisked daughter and grandson back to Cleveland. It had been three months of intensive TLC, at which both Greenblatts excelled, and by the time she had sent them back home, Devorah and Ephraim were almost as good as new. All Devorah had done during that time was sleep, nurse the baby, and eat, not to mention spending hours cuddling and bonding with Ephraim. Aharon had joined them for most Shabbosos and returned to New York early Sunday because he did most of the work for his truffle business then.

Tzivi knew exactly when to advance and when to retreat. Nothing needed to be voiced — she instinctively knew what was needed and when. Breakfast and lunch were ample, nourishing meals, lots of milk in the morning, and meat every afternoon. Tzivi had racked her brains to duplicate her daughter's childhood comfort foods. Most of them had been poorly executed mishaps concocted before Tzivi had learned her way around the kitchen.

She'd hardly been able to suppress a smile when Devorah had cooed at one brunch offering, "Wow, Mom, you still make the mac and cheese just the way I like it!"

"I hope not," she replied good-naturedly. "Lumpy, and

without properly folding the hard cheese into the cream sauce the way I do now!"

"It must be the love I taste," said Devorah.

Supper was salads, fish, and fruit. Water and apple juice were poured and served on the hour, with freshly squeezed lemonade on request. Soft music played throughout the house, the sheets and blankets were clean and soft; her mother changed them every day.

Tzivi bathed Ephraim and sang to him, then returned him to Devorah diapered and dressed in pajamas. Her father placed books and magazines he thought she'd like in strategic locations where he knew she'd find them. The Greenblatts were marvelous healers; patient, attentive, soft-spoken. There was no mention of Mordy at all, even though it took days for Devorah to finally stop weeping.

But even the most luxurious accommodations can lose their charm. One day Devorah had gotten out of bed and knew that she was okay again. Her strength — both physical and emotional — had returned. Ephraim was plump and round-cheeked, filling out his stretchies and smiling toothlessly to one and all. There were no strangers in Ephraim's world.

The day finally came when Aharon was able to bring them home. Mother and son were the best of friends by then, and while Aharon felt a bit left out, he was so happy to see his wife and son restored that he easily put his own feelings aside. But like his wife, he too was adept at masking his thoughts. While Devorah was resting and healing, Aharon had been tossing and turning without cease ever since that first call had come in from Mrs. Carolan, the agent for the Children's Bureau.

"Mr. Landau? Ay-ron Landau?" Her voice was hoarse and deep, heavy with smoker's cough.

"Speaking," Aharon had replied naively, unaware of the hurricane heading his way. He held the phone under his chin as he extricated himself from his coat, having just returned from the airport.

"This is Mary Jo Carolan calling from the Children's Bureau about your son."

Aharon had been momentarily confused. Why was somebody calling about Ephraim? Had they broken a law by sending him out of state?

"My son?" he echoed.

"Yeah," Mary Jo replied. "Murray. It's misspelled here."

Aharon didn't bother to correct her, he was recovering from this verbal blow to the solar plexus. He sat down without intending to, clutching the phone with a sweaty hand.

After the bris, Aharon had convinced himself that the matter was settled, that the whole *parshah* of Mordy, despite Devorah's delayed reaction, was behind them, and the future would be tranquil.

"What about him?" he said, trying to compose himself.

"The foster family you placed him with — the Bursteins?"

"Yes, he is with the Bursteins."

"Well, they're sendin' him back. They can't handle him. Whaddya want us to do with him?"

CHAPTER 11

DR. JEREMY COHEN

I t had been many long, exhausting years, but the past few had been particularly draining. Evaluating patients and struggling to get them all placed into safe environments had taken all my energy. Sometimes it felt like everyone else on staff had abandoned ship before all the passengers had disembarked, but I'd been warned about that before I even set foot inside this place.

Working at Ravensfield was not my first choice, or even my last. It had been nowhere on my radar during my residency until one day the chief resident, Dr. Tim Kelly, called me aside and told me to meet him in the cafeteria. This was unheard of — Kelly was known to be an ogre, and some of us suspected he even lived in some kind of lair.

But I was not easily intimidated. My father, a fighter pilot in World War II, had taught me to stand my ground by the time I was twelve, and he included a few tips on psychological warfare in case, I suppose, I was captured by the enemy and had no weapon. Still, this training had been useful throughout my life, whether holding my own in the schoolyard , defusing gang fights between the Jews, Italians, and Irish who lived in our neighborhood, or clawing my way into college and med school.

So, in the general scheme of things, Dr. Kelly was small potatoes as far as I was concerned, not to mention that he reminded me of some of the Irish boys I used to fight.

He must have picked up on my unflappability because as far as I knew I was the only one so summoned, and I appeared on time in the "caf." I wasn't surprised to find him already waiting — he was meticulous and would have found a way to show up even if he was in the middle of a crisis.

"Sit," he said, pushing a cup of coffee my way. I tasted it and realized he knew exactly how I took it, and I suppose that didn't surprise me either.

"An opportunity has come up," he began. "It's not for everyone, but it *is* for you."

He went on to describe Ravensfield, how it was in desperate need of a doctor with excellent qualifications as well as a compassionate spirit, who would be willing to act independently even if it went against hospital policy.

"Why would I need to do that?" I asked. I realized I was missing some crucial piece of information.

"It's not a regular hospital."

He was a better judge of character than I had suspected, and I was sure he'd taken a good look at my file as well. He knew I would agree without a moment's hesitation.

"The pay is low," he said, "but room and board are included, so that should cut down on your expenses. I'll accompany you to your interview."

I looked at him questioningly, wondering why he would do that, but as I was about to ask, he rose from his chair and was gone before I could get the words out of my mouth.

The following week, Kelly picked me up after rounds and we drove off to Ravensfield in his car. He seemed to know the way very well — another piece of the puzzle. We arrived and pulled right up to the main entrance, and he was out of the car and through the door before I had even stepped out of the car.

We walked through a small corridor, the walls lined with pleasant photographs of its landscaped grounds. My brief look around before being herded into the office gave truth to the artwork — whoever designed the place knew what they were doing.

I wouldn't have known the difference if my mother hadn't been so keen on gardening. She started digging into the earth during the war, when housewives were encouraged to plant "Victory Gardens." James H. Burdett's *Victory Garden Manual* (I learned the whole thing by heart, as it was always open on the kitchen table) was distributed to every home, and my mother took it to heart, most likely because my father was away at war.

Her interest in landscaping extended beyond the manual, though, and that's how I knew how well Ravensfield was designed. From the photos on the wall I could tell that each sight line, each sunrise and sunset, each tree and hedge was meant to maximize the beauty of the place.

Kelly walked ahead of me down the hallway and stopped at a closed door at the end of the hall. He opened the door without knocking and gestured me to enter behind him.

"This is Jeremy Cohen, the one I was telling you about," said Kelly.

The man behind the desk rose to greet me. He was short and dapper, with slicked-back salt-and-pepper hair and a thin moustache above his lip. He wore a pristine white coat with his name on a tag over the right-hand breast pocket: Dr. Robert Boyer.

"Nice to meet you," I said, taking his outstretched hand and shaking it firmly. One of the things my father taught me was to pay careful attention to a man's handshake, and I was not impressed with Dr. Boyer's. His hand was clammy and soft.

Dr. Boyer was just as busy taking my measure as I was his. I had seen him flinch slightly at the mention of my name, which led me to conclude that Dr. Boyer was not fond of Jews. It didn't bother me one way or the other — I was applying for the position of doctor, not rabbi, and in any case, religion was not a factor in any of my decisions. My parents are first-generation Americans, much more interested in making a living and sending me and my brother to college than going to temple and lighting candles. Two of my mother's siblings had married non-Jews as well.

"My colleague Dr. Kelly speaks highly of you," said Boyer. "What brings you to a place like Ravensfield?"

It was a loaded question, but I was ready. I bombarded Boyer with questions. He finally acknowledged that

Ravensfield was in fact a hospital, although some would say a dumping ground, for the physically and mentally disabled, both children and adults.

"I appreciate the challenge, sir," I replied formally. "And I'd like to be of service to these individuals."

"It's not going to be easy," he countered. "You'll need a strong stomach, and nerves of steel."

"Not a problem," I answered.

I saw Boyer look at Kelly and nod, as though confirming something they'd spoken about earlier.

I didn't care. The more I heard about this place, the more I was interested in being a part of it. Something inside me was waking up, something I didn't yet know about myself. All I could think, at that moment, was that I belonged at Ravensfield almost as much as the patients.

CHAPTER 12

JEREMY

I t wasn't long before I received word, both from Dr.
Boyer by mail and from Dr. Kelly in person, that I'd been
hired by Ravensfield, effective as soon as I finished my
residency. Those few months in between were a strange,
twilight time, and if I knew then what I know now I wonder if I would have gone through with it. What was wrong
about hanging out a shingle somewhere, working as a GP,
earning a nice living, doing rounds at a hospital once a day?
Plenty of men like me were doing exactly that, marrying,

starting families, buying Cadillacs and starter homes on Long Island. But I wasn't built that way, and I suppose everyone — my family, my friends, and my colleagues — knew that. I was always out of step, going left while my peers went right, but fortunately going straight when the occasion demanded it.

I had always been drawn to extremes, insisting on waiting in front of the lions' cage to hear them roar instead of going to the petting zoo like all the other kids. My father would stay with me the whole time, quiet and patient, while my mother took my brother around to see the other animals. My being drawn to work at Ravensfield rather than choosing a more pedestrian existence didn't surprise anyone too much.

I'd originally wanted to be a psychiatrist, not because I was particularly interested in the human mind, but because it was the most demanding of the medical professions. You first had to qualify as a doctor and only then could you become a psychiatrist, and I was intrigued by the challenge.

But that dream only lasted until I took my first class in genetics and became fascinated with DNA. I couldn't believe how much information is stored in our microscopic genes and chromosomes, and how much of who we are depends on the trickled-down dominance of our ancestors' traits. It grabbed my narrow little mind and blasted it wide open. Nevertheless, once Dr. Kelly waved the challenge of Ravensfield under my nose, my plan to become a genetics researcher faded away and I followed along where he led like a little puppy.

I arrived at Ravensfield in my old tan Chevy with a couple of suitcases in the trunk. My mother sent along food as though I were going on safari and would not be near any food source for months. Unlike Kelly, I knocked politely on Dr. Boyer's office door, and when he opened it he seemed surprised to see me. I felt a jolt of panic — had he forgotten he'd hired me? — but both he and I recovered quickly. He offered me his clammy hand, which I shook reluctantly, and after briefly welcoming me, led me out of the building and on a tour of the grounds. He claimed he needed a bit of fresh air and was happy to take me around himself.

I was still largely clueless about Ravensfield. I knew only that it held a diverse population of people with physical and mental disabilities. And even though I was a doctor, I didn't really know what that meant. So, when Dr. Boyer asked me if I had any questions, I blithely replied, "Not particularly. Patients are the same everywhere."

Dr. Boyer looked at me strangely, but held his tongue.

We walked around for quite some time, but did not enter any of the buildings. Dr. Boyer pointed them out as we walked by, spouting facts and figures, but we didn't interact with any patients. I thought then that he wanted me to adjust to the place on my own and experience my own first impressions privately, but I know now that he knew I'd bolt once I saw the cold and impersonal way he handled the patients.

He told me I would be in charge of caring for children, which was fine with me — medicine was medicine. But, said Dr. Boyer, the children were not all in one building. They were placed in different units around the hospital and were frequently transferred from one ward to another, so I'd have to keep track of their whereabouts and check up on every young patient at least once a week.

Then we stopped at my car to pick up my suitcases. He did not offer to carry one of them, and I followed him to the staff housing carrying both myself. I was relieved when we reached the lobby and he told someone there to see that my suitcases were taken up to my room. Dr. Boyer left me then, with instructions to appear again the following morning in his office.

I inquired about my room and was given a key. I went upstairs and found my suitcases waiting outside the door. Accustomed to my share of dingy university housing, I was shocked to find myself in what looked like an upscale hotel suite. It was beautifully decorated with pretty artwork on the wall, thick curtains covering the windows, a small kitchen/living room, and a nice-sized bedroom.

I later discovered that a grateful parent had endowed the staff living quarters. The money would have been better spent on the patients, in my opinion, but I was in no position to complain.

Once I unpacked and ate some of the food my mother had packed for me, I donned my white coat and stethoscope and set about acquainting myself with the patients hospitalized at Ravensfield. I headed for the building directly across from the dormitory.

Stepping into the lobby for the first time was an experience I will never forget, and I don't even know if I can describe it properly, because it went so far beyond words. There was no recognizable order, but it was not a madhouse in any way. Patients were sitting on chairs, standing, lying around on couches. There was some muted crying, some whispered talking and hushed giggling, some involuntary movement of arms and legs, yet there was overall an otherworldly stillness.

The impression I had of that first, astounding tableau pierced right through me and has never left me.

I looked around, wondering where to start, and my gaze fell on a little boy, who looked at me through the bars of his crib as if he'd known me all his life.

CHAPTER 13

JEREMY

I was drawn magnetically to this child's large, brown, happy eyes. His eyelashes were so long I could practically have curled them around my little finger. His face was terribly deformed, with an untreated cleft lip and palate marring his features in total incompatibility with his glowing face.

Although I could see at a glance that there were many children in desperate need of attention, still, I had to start somewhere, so I walked over to this child's crib. I was intercepted by a nurse or nurse's aide — I hadn't yet learned to tell them apart — who tried to turn me toward the needier cases.

"Don't bother with that one," she said. "He's hopeless."

"Really?" I replied. "It doesn't seem that way to me."

"Trust me. The kid can't walk, can't talk, just babbles all day at the top of his lungs and drives us crazy. And he stares at us through the bars. We have to feed him his meals and he makes such a mess that we draw straws to choose who gets the chore. Sometimes," she added conspiratorially, "we just skip it."

My stomach lurched when I heard that, but I hid my reaction. I didn't want to make enemies so early on. "I'll keep that in mind," I murmured, but nevertheless continued walking toward the child's crib.

Up close I could see that he was in a bad way. There was no chart attached to his crib, as is standard practice in every hospital I'd ever worked in, containing the patient's medical history. His chart, I soon discovered, was kept under lock and key in the nurses' room and was extremely skimpy. In any case, I like to get a look at a patient before I read his chart. There is so much to see from mere observation.

As I approached the crib, I noted his slack limbs, and I saw that the only part of him that he could raise was his head. His hair was shorn to the scalp (to ward off lice, I was told) like the other patients', but his eyes told me the real story. There was definitely somebody at home in there.

"Hello, there," I said loudly, in case he had auditory issues, which often happens with kids with a cleft palate. "How are you doing today, little guy?"

His smile lit up his whole face and I had the feeling that if he could raise his arms to me he would have. He garbled a few sounds, gibberish really, but I thought I could sense an underlying order. Then I told myself I was imagining things. I patted him on the back and moved on, but his eyes stayed with me throughout the day.

It was ironic that I'd been assigned to pediatrics, because I had little interest in treating children. The only babies I'd ever held were during my brief stint in neonatology, and I'd managed to avoid pediatrics completely by a deft bait and switch with one of my colleagues that slipped under the radar of the hospital.

Although I'm not squeamish — I wouldn't have gotten very far as a doctor if I were — kids turned me off. They were hard to keep clean, they were invariably uncooperative, and their shrill voices shattered my nerves. My few encounters with ailing children had unnerved me and left me with no incentive to specialize in pediatrics, but I willed myself to overcome my aversion because I really wanted to work at Ravensfield.

But the joke was on me, because I came to discover that the practice of good hygiene in the hospital was far below the level of anything I'd seen until then. There were shortages of everything, the patients were showered mostly in groups once a week, and many were either not toilet-trained or were incapable of caring for themselves. There was one nurse and one aide for each department, which were all overcrowded. Many members of the staff were well intentioned and conscientious, but just as many were not.

I discovered all of this simply by making it my business to visit each ward every day. It took me weeks to locate all the children, as they were placed everywhere. I was never sure I got around to them all, and I wondered why there was no dedicated children's ward. I made myself a familiar figure, speaking with the other doctors and nurses, keeping the conversation light but digging for information at the same time.

My colleagues, though, had learned to be circumspect and revealed little, and I quickly realized I was on my own.

I also spent time talking with the patients, both children and adults, and developed the habit of stuffing my pockets with candy and little toys to hand out. While many were unresponsive, a few of them could hold a conversation, and they enjoyed the company. As I spoke with them, I observed their eyes, the condition of their skin, their nails, and the way they smelled. Each different odor told its own story.

When I could, I also looked at their feet, silently preparing detailed treatment plans as we chatted. I noticed that the more "with-it" patients were in better condition, either because they knew how to take care for themselves or the staff simply found it easier to work with them.

I tried not to judge anyone; the work was grueling and there was a high turnover, making it hard for the patients to develop rapport with anyone except one another. But I surely had my work cut out for me, and I was determined to improve conditions one step at a time.

It wasn't long before my out-of-step behavior was reported to Dr. Boyer, and I was called into his office for a talk. He lit a cigarette as I entered, and I stood back as the nasty odor filled the room.

"Sit down," he said. It sounded like an invitation, but I knew it was a command. I was at a disadvantage because of the smoke, and I struggled to hold my breath and pay attention at the same time.

"How are you finding it here?" he asked. "Are you settling in?"

"Very well, thank you," I replied. "It's an interesting place."

"That's one way to put it." Dr. Boyer smirked. "I hear you are getting acquainted with some of the patients and asking all kinds of questions. Why are you doing that?"

I realized I was on shaky ground, so I tried to tread lightly. "I'm just trying to familiarize myself with the hospital as a whole. I like to see the big picture, and I enjoy talking to people."

"Be that as it may," Dr. Boyer replied, "this is a hospital, not a coffee shop. Your job is to keep track of the children and make sure they are not suffering from contagious diseases, infections, or broken bones. That is your only job. Am I making myself clear?"

Was he ever.

"Of course, sir. I understand. I'll try to mind my own business from now on."

My business being, of course, taking the best care of the patients that I possibly could. But he didn't need to know that. Not yet, anyway.

I was just getting started.

CHAPTER 14

RAVENSFIELD
SCHOOL FOR MENTALLY CHALLENGED CHILDREN,
1987

Dr. Cohen, tell us what's going on," said Aharon, more harshly than he meant to. "Why is the hospital closing after all this time?"

Jeremy gazed at the couple sitting across from him. He'd seen this combination before: one of the two looking determined to get to the bottom of things, and the other one resigned. He wasn't surprised when the determined one took the lead.

Jeremy shook his head. "It's hard to explain, but I'll try. About six months ago, there was a huge scandal at one of the other...ah...facilities...like this one, but it was in much worse shape."

He'd learned, after speaking with parents and relatives of the patients, to avoid the words mental institution. It nearly always aroused an angry, often hysterical reaction, and while this couple seemed stable, you never could tell. It was best not to risk it.

"A reporter burst into that hospital with a film crew without warning or permission and captured some terrible images on camera. He was in and out before they could stop him, and the film was aired that very evening on the nightly news broadcast, raw, without any editing.

"Well, as you know, a picture is worth a thousand words, and there was no way to undo the damage. The families were outraged, and there is still a massive class-action suit pending. The result was that all the public facilities in the city have been forced to close. You must have heard about it. It was in all the newspapers." Devorah and Aharon looked at each other, realizing they were going to have to reveal some important facts about themselves.

"We don't really read all the newspapers," Aharon said, not venturing to add that to the best of his recall the local Jewish weekly they did read hadn't covered the story. "Believe me, had we known about it, we would have become involved." He winced as he said that because he knew Devorah hadn't known about Mordy's true situation at the time. "The first we heard about it was the letter we received in the mail." He pulled it out of his jacket pocket and held it up for Jeremy's inspection.

Before Jeremy launched into his practiced speech, he couldn't help challenging what they had just told him.

"What do you mean, you don't read newspapers? Everyone reads newspapers."

"We're...uh...Jews..." Aharon began.

"So? I'm also a Jew, and I read plenty — as much as my schedule allows, anyway." This was a painful admission — he had been so caught up in his work that he had so far never found time to marry and start a family. That left him way too much free time on his hands, even with his total involvement with the patients. Aharon took a deep breath. They were there to talk about Mordy, not to give a lecture on religious Jewish practice to a clueless doctor. A man like Dr. Cohen, had he applied his skills and intelligence to the Jewish community, could have been a tremendous asset. Instead, he chose to criticize their self-imposed insularity. Any other time, he would have pursued it, but not now.

"Be that as it may," said Aharon, "we are here to discuss our son Mordechai."

"Mordechai? His name is Murray. Murray Landau." Jeremy stared at them suspiciously. Something didn't feel right.

"He was obviously assigned that name by the hospital. His name is Mordechai, after my father."

"Well, I'm going to continue to call him Murray, if you don't mind," said Jeremy. "It's easier on the tongue."

"Actually, we do mind," said Devorah, to Aharon's dismay. Hadn't she been listening? There was no point in arguing with this doctor.

"Anyway," Aharon interrupted, earning him a wounded look from Devorah, "what happened after the exposé?"

"The Department of Mental Hygiene went into all the state hospitals and investigated," said Jeremy, "and the court ended up closing all the hospitals at once." Because they were his beloved Murray's parents, he refrained from going into more detail. Their hospital wasn't nearly as bad as the one exposed, but they got swept along with all the others, leaving 200 of their patients with nowhere to go.

Jeremy had worked hard to protect Murray and make sure he had whatever he needed. He'd been accused of favoritism countless times, but what could he do? The boy had captured his heart. He yearned to tell his parents all about their son and the many gifts he had discovered the boy had, but he didn't feel it was appropriate now. He first had to guide them through their shock at the upsetting news.

When Dr. Boyer learned about the scandal, he had gone livid with rage. "How dare they?" he'd ranted. "After all the hard work we do to make sure our patients are well cared for! How dare they lump us in with those other places!"

But there was no way to "unsee" those painful film clips, and they were all judged guilty. Dr. Boyer insisted on calling a press conference proclaiming for the record both his innocence and his outrage, even though he knew there was nothing he could do to stop the closing. His main concern was protecting his reputation, and he had demanded that Jeremy stand behind him. By that point, though, Jeremy had already tuned Dr. Boyer out.

"What do you recommend we do?" asked Devorah. "What are the options?"

Aharon looked away. During the past few weeks he and Devorah had engaged in a fierce battle of wills but had not reached a decision. He had spent hours trying to convince her that it would be an insurmountable task to care for Mordy at home.

There was little information to be had; parents would hide their special children in back rooms, foster homes, and other secret places, while the wealthy could afford private institutions. Books on the subject hadn't been written yet, and the doctors Aharon had spoken to fourteen years earlier said it was out of the question to bring "children like this" home, as it would be a waste of time and money. After being notified that Ravensfield was closing, Aharon and Devorah had discussed the matter endlessly, raising their voices and then lowering them, careful not to say anything hurtful that could not be unsaid. It was the first real rift in their marriage, and it threatened to tear them apart.

But this was all before Devorah met Mrs. Mirsky. And once Aharon heard what she had to say, he feared his case was as good as lost.

CHAPTER 15

Mrs. Chana Mirsky had appeared on their doorstep one day, ostensibly to purchase a hat from Devorah's home business. Devorah accompanied her into the private salon in the back of the house, firmly closing the door so her client would feel secure in her privacy while trying on the hats. Chana gave a few cursory glances around the room, and then faced Devorah.

Devorah eyed the tall, elegantly dressed woman standing before her wearing a fashionable *sheitel* and tasteful jewelry and judged her to be in her early fifties. Devorah wondered why she was interested in buying hats when it was clear that the woman probably hadn't worn a hat since she was a little girl walking to school on a cold day.

"I hope you don't mind," the woman said, "but I am here under somewhat false pretenses."

"What do you mean?" Devorah asked quietly.

"My name is Chana Mirsky. I understand that your husband has been going around asking certain people about their children with special needs," she said. Her voice was soft but Devorah could detect an undertone of both joy and determination.

"He has?"

Devorah knew Aharon was desperate to find support for his resistance to bringing Mordy home, but she hadn't realized he would go that far. Even now, after all these years, he was reluctant to discuss the subject openly.

"We're a close-knit group — in fact, we have an informal support network and get together from time to time. As I'm sure you can imagine, we don't really publicize it, but we are sort of like partisans trying to defeat the system."

Devorah gestured to the older woman to sit down in one of the plush chairs Devorah had insisted on when she designed the salon. Comfort and pampering were high on her list of professional priorities. She had turned on the Krupp's Brewmaster she kept on a specially designed shelf, and now poured some coffee into two cups. "Milk? Sugar?" she asked.

"Black."

"Black? Okay." Aharon was the only one she knew who took his coffee black, but she knew better than to question her clients about anything, even phony clients like this one. Her job was to listen, support and encourage, and ultimately convince them to buy a hat. It was much harder than it looked, but she enjoyed it immensely. She discreetly loaded her own coffee with milk and sugar and sat down across from Chana.

"I had no idea," said Devorah. "He's a good man and—"

"I don't need to hear your story, sweetie — not yet, anyway — and only if you really want to tell me. I'm here to tell you *my* story.

"Twenty-two years ago, I gave birth to a beautiful baby boy. He was my sixth child, and I thought I knew everything there was to know about having children. But Ruvy came with a little surprise attached, what I now know to be an extra chromosome. He had something called Down syndrome."

"Down syndrome?" asked Devorah. "What is that? I never heard of it."

"Not many people have," said Chana. "Someone noticed it in the 1800s, I think, but it wasn't officially diagnosed or studied until 1959. I was really on my own."

"What about your husband?"

"I was widowed when I was expecting the baby."

"Oh, I'm so sorry," said Devorah.

"The truth is that I was so busy with Ruvy that I didn't have much time to mourn. I pay for that sometimes, when the ache of missing my husband washes over me.

"Anyway," and here she leaned over to pat Devorah on the arm, "I had this baby and I had no idea what was wrong with him. All I could see was something strange about his tongue, his face was a little flat, his eyes a different shape from those of my other children.

"At first I ignored it, certain he'd grow out of it. But instead of growing out of it, he grew *into* it."

"What do you mean?" asked Devorah.

"Other things started to become noticeable. The tiny head in proportion to the rest of his body, the short neck... but it was only when he was three years old and still lying flat on the floor that I was certain something was wrong.

"I ran around from doctor to doctor, from hospital to hospital, and no one could give me any useful information. The only advice I was given was to 'put him away' and get on with my life."

Devorah froze. Those were the exact words she'd been told when she was fighting to keep Mordy after his birth. *Put him away*, like he was a coat thrown over a kitchen chair, waiting to be stuffed into a closet.

Chana noticed Devorah's expression. "I guess that comes as no surprise to you," she said dryly.

"So, what did you do? Where did you end up sending him?" Devorah asked.

Triumph burned in Chana's eyes. "Nowhere. I kept him home with me."

"You did? How?" Devorah said, her heart pounding. She needed to hear this. She had known deep down that it was possible, and here was her proof.

"The same way I kept my other children home. He's mine and I love him. Some of my other children were frustrating to raise, but I didn't dream of sending them away because of it! It's true Ruvy was a handful — two handfuls, plus — but I knew he belonged with me and his brothers and sisters.

"In a way it was a blessing that my husband passed away before Ruvy was born, even though I still miss him terribly. He never would have allowed me to keep Ruvy."

"But how did you do it? How did you raise a retarded child on your own?"

She could feel Chana bristle at that.

"Can we use the word *special* instead? Or *gifted*, as in 'a gift from Hashem'? 'Retarded' has such a negative connotation, even though it seems to be the official term."

"I'm sorry," said Devorah. "I didn't mean to—"

"Of course you didn't. I'm not rebuking you, I'm just trying to educate you. But in answer to your question, Ruvy was about ten by the time he was officially diagnosed, but I was already way ahead. I didn't need a label slapped on him to know what he needed. I scoured the city for the right program for him, and one fine beautiful day I found one.

"There was only one drawback."

CHAPTER 16

The program I found for my Ruvy when he was five was in a public school in Queens," Chana Mirsky said. "At first I didn't know what to do. *What? Send my son to a public school? Never!* So now I was not only getting flack and pressure to send him away to foster care or an institution, but also not to dare send him to public school.

"'What does he need school for? He wants a drum, give him a drum. He wants a ball, give him a ball. And besides, how are you, a young widow, going to manage with him at home?'

"I knew it was a risk. Part of me wanted to believe that they were right, but the other part of me really wanted Ruvy to have more. I wasn't expecting him to turn into a genius...I just wanted him to learn the most that he was capable of, have more structure than I could give him by myself and, to tell the truth, to give myself a little breathing room during the day. He was — and still is — a delight, but he was a handful and a half as a child.

"I must have gone to that school a dozen times to check out the staff, the atmosphere, the other children, the special program. They were more than willing to work with me and respect our religious needs. I had a list a mile long and they accommodated it, even when new staff replaced those who moved on. And even though he encountered so many different people, he was still 'my Ruvy.'"

Devorah listened intently, her eyes misting from time to time. She wondered if Mrs. Mirsky had always been so strong and decisive or if circumstances and experiences had made her so. Either way, she was a force to be reckoned with.

"Don't misunderstand — I didn't force the issues, but I was persistent, beyond what I imagined I could be. As I said, the pressure on me was immense, and I didn't have my husband to shield me, but I had unbelievable *siyata d'Shmaya* all along the way.

"Of course, I did my best to keep the relationship pleasant. I baked hundreds of cakes and cookies for the staff, brought them nice things to decorate the classrooms, sent *mishloach manos*, wrote little thank-you notes all the time. Somehow it worked."

"Where is Ruvy now?"

Mrs. Mirsky looked at Devorah in surprise.

"He's at home."

"You *never* sent him out? Isn't he a grown man by now?"

"Why would I do that? He has a job, he works, comes home and eats, just like any other person."

Devorah looked up through the skylight she had installed in her salon because she was a bit claustrophobic. Aharon had been wonderfully empathetic and generous about it. Although he was careful with their money, he had ordered an especially beautiful skylight rather than a plain one. That was Aharon, through and through.

Mrs. Mirsky now recited a *berachah acharonah* and stood up to go. Devorah picked up Mrs. Mirsky's fine cashmere coat from the chair where she had carefully laid it down and held it open to help her into it. It was, perhaps, an old-fashioned gesture, but her grandmother had always done this and Devorah had always admired it, so she took on the custom herself.

"Don't misunderstand," Mrs. Mirsky said again, and Devorah wondered if that was something she had to say a lot. "I'm not telling you what to do with your son. I'm just telling you what *I* did. Everyone has her own story, knows her own strengths. If you want to speak to others, I can introduce you to both those who kept their child at home and those who sent their child away.

"Meanwhile," she concluded, placing her soft hand around the curve of Devorah's cheek, "remember this: Your son has only one mother, one person who will fight for him, and that, my dear, is you!"

Devorah returned to the salon and closed the door, even though she knew the children were waiting for her to come serve their supper. She sat down, leaned back in the soft chair, and let Chana's words wash over her. She inhaled them, tasted them, ran them through her mind one by one.

She stared at the darkening sky through the domed skylight overhead and, as though she could see the path somewhere out there, she imagined walking with Mordy down the road of his life. She wondered whether she would have the strength for it, especially if Aharon withheld his support.

As if she had summoned him by her thoughts, she heard a light tapping on the door — one, one-two, one-two-three, their own personal signal so she would know it was not one of the kids knocking, clamoring for attention. She stood up to let him in.

"Hi," she greeted Aharon in the doorway. "How was your day?"

They had an unspoken agreement that he did not enter the salon (except to make repairs) and she stayed out of the "truffle room." But now he did something unusual: He came all the way into the salon and closed the door gently behind him.

"I heard about your client. What was that all about?" he asked, careful to keep his tone neutral.

"Ladies' stuff," Devorah replied lightly. "You know."

Aharon's right hand immediately began stroking his beard and covering his mouth and his left now rubbed his ear as well.

"Devorah—"

"Aharon, it'll be all right," she said. "However it turns out, it will be okay." She walked past him and out the door. "Let's go out to eat tonight," she said over her shoulder. "It's Tuesday! We haven't been out on a 'date' in ages. Let's call your mother. I'm sure she'll be happy to hear we're back on our dating schedule so she can come to babysit and see her grandchildren."

———————◦———————

As they waited for Yitta's taxi to arrive, Devorah pondered her conversation with Chana Mirsky one last time, determined to put it out of her mind temporarily and give Aharon her full attention.

CHAPTER 17

Ephraim Baruch moved closer to his grandmother as she sat reading on the couch. Yitta knew Aharon and Devorah were loving, affectionate parents, but as the kids got older, the parental hugs and cuddling naturally lessened.

But they were still heat-seeking missiles, and a bubby at rest was the perfect target for a stealthy snuggle. Ephraim was a squirmy kid, and even if he had wanted more hugs from his parents, he probably wasn't able to sit still long enough to fill his quota. Yitta pretended to ignore his current proximity so he wouldn't feel self-conscious.

"Bubby," he declared, "something strange is going on in this house."

Yitta put down her book — *Victory Garden*, one of the best books she'd read in a long time — and turned to look at her beloved grandson. She knew exactly what he was talking about but decided to let him roll it out like a rug at her feet. Once she heard what he was thinking she would try to come up with a good answer.

"What do you mean?" she asked.

"Don't play possum with me, Bubby," he said, smiling so she knew he was not being disrespectful. He had learned the expression from her and, having no idea what a possum was but liking the sound of it, he had adopted it as his own. "You must know what I'm talking about. Mommy and Tatty are acting strange — s-t-r-a-n-g-e!"

They laughed together, because Aharon and Devorah used to spell out words so the kids wouldn't understand. When he was little, they had spoken in Hebrew, then after that, Yiddish, then finally spelling out words, but Ephraim Baruch outwitted them every time. "We're going to have to learn Chinese," Aharon had said one day, only half-jokingly.

Yitta nodded in agreement. "They haven't spoken with you recently?" she asked carefully. She did not want to think about the trouble she would be in if she inadvertently — or not — spilled the beans, but neither could she keep things back from this precious boy.

Ephraim smiled smugly, sensing he was making head-way.

"Well," he said, "if you mean, 'Did you daven Maariv?' or, 'Why did your *rebbi* leave a message to call him right away?' then I guess so. But you know they never get upset about those things. They know that I know that I need to daven Maariv and that I'll do it eventually. And my *rebbi* is always calling about something, and they don't get too upset about that either.

"But I can tell they're worried, and I wish they would just tell me what it was instead of me letting my imagination run away with me."

He took a deep breath and looked up at Yitta with those green eyes of his — Aharon's eyes exactly — the long lashes making shadows on his face.

"I'm scared, Bubby."

Yitta wished the couch would open up and swallow her, right then and there. That would scare Ephraim, all right, and she wouldn't have to respond to his truly heartfelt plea. A young child picking up on tension in the house will start sucking his thumb again or pick fights with other kids, but an older kid will worry, really worry, almost like an adult — or maybe even more. The pendulum swung back and forth. Yitta was not able to decide: Should she tell? Should she not tell? Should she excuse herself and call Aharon and ask him what to do? Back and forth, the pendulum swung. Ephraim's eyes were getting damp. The clock was ticking away.

Yitta took a deep breath.

Aharon and Devorah were at their go-to coffee shop, the one they went to when they were not in the mood for new experiences. They really liked the coffee there, and the carrot muffins were out of this world. Along with a big salad, it was a perfect meal — for Devorah. Aharon bore it stoically and would snack on salami later.

"So, what are you having?" he asked jokingly, just to lighten things up, knowing perfectly well what she'd order.

"I think I'm going to wing it," she said, "and order the bran muffin with walnuts."

For some reason he thought she was joking now, because she always ordered the same thing. So, when the waitress arrived, and he ordered the carrot muffin for her (he loved ordering for her, she also liked it — it made her feel protected), she clucked in annoyance.

"I want the bran muffin, I told you," she said.

"Really?" he replied. "You were serious?"

The waitress had looked back and forth between them, waiting for the standoff to end.

"I'll have the carrot muffin, please, the Greek salad, and the iced mochaccino," she said.

Devorah turned her head to stare out the window. This was not going the way she had thought it would. Sometimes the privacy and one-on-one face time worked very well for them, and sometimes it just didn't. Since when were they so off, so on the wrong page with each other?

"What's up, Debs?" he said. Wrong move. She was in no mood for another one of his little jokes.

"Please don't call me that."

The table between them might as well have been an ocean.

"Devorah, I—"

"You know what?" she said, interrupting him. She heard what he was saying even though he hadn't said it yet. "I'm not Mrs. Mirsky, first of all, and second of all, I don't even know what we're dealing with here. I only just found out the hospital was closing three months ago!

"I...I...I put Mordy on the back burner of my mind, a small flame under the pain, a tiny, tiny flame. Suddenly it's become a bonfire!" She was not able to stop herself now. "We don't even know who Mordy is now, or what he looks like. Can he walk? Can he talk? What happened with his cleft palate? We know nothing!"

Aharon lost his composure then for just a second, just one second, and that was all it took. "They fixed it," he said, his words galloping miles ahead of his mind.

Devorah had stopped her tirade in mid-flow. "What do you mean, they fixed it? How do you know that?"

Now what do I say? Lie and feel guilty? Tell the truth and feel guilty? The lies were adding up faster than he could keep up with them. What was this doing to their marriage? Everything was crumbling down around him. He was crumbling.

And the pendulum swung.

CHAPTER 18

Aharon and Devorah were both reeling — as much from Chana Mirsky's story, which Aharon had finally gotten out of Devorah, as from the letter from Ravensfield and Yitta's perfidy. Telling Ephraim Baruch about Mordy had been an inexcusable breach of trust. To her credit, she called them immediately afterward to tell them what she'd done, but it had been more because she was concerned by Ephraim's reaction than because she felt guilty about it. "He was worried," she had tried to explain. "He asked me straight out. Was I supposed to lie to him? I didn't tell him much anyway, and I don't think he understood the implications."

Ephraim had in fact understood very well, and when they returned home from their dismal date, Ephraim was waiting for them with a barrage of questions.

Worse, though, was his emotional state. Despite his towering intelligence and his many idiosyncrasies, he was a sensitive boy. He was less upset about not being told he had a brother than he was concerned for Mordy himself, locked up in a hospital with no family around him.

"How could you do that to him?" he had cried. "He's all alone there!" Aharon and Devorah had been unable to answer him. They themselves hoped that the meeting today with the doctor would clear up some of the mystery. Devorah had been determined to charge in and demand to see Mordy, but they had so far been stymied by Dr. Cohen's long explanation about the mental hospital scandal and the reason for Ravensfield's closing.

But now Devorah had had enough. "Dr. Cohen, I appreciate hearing all this, but I must insist you take me to see my son. From what I understand..." Here she darted her eyes toward Aharon, who looked right back at her. It would be much easier to avoid her gaze, but Aharon knew that to retain her respect, he had to keep his head up. "...I understand that my husband has seen Mordy, albeit a number of years ago, but I have not."

Jeremy Cohen nodded. Sometime before, Murray (as Jeremy unapologetically continued calling him) had gone through a period where his cleft was continually getting infected. It was hard to control, and Jeremy had decided that the kid had taken enough antibiotics. The cleft had to go. He had approached Dr. Boyer for permission to operate and had been flatly refused.

"If I agree to have this one's lip fixed, I'll have to have that one's cataracts removed, and once I do that—" Boyer had begun.

"I get the point," Jeremy had interrupted, and he had stormed out of the office.

Salvation had come from his old colleague and mentor, Dr. Tim Kelly. Jeremy had found him one day inexplicably roaming the halls in one of the Ravensfield buildings, and a lightbulb flashed on in his head. He had invited Tim back to his quarters in the staff dormitory and served him a hot dinner, knowing that he, like Jeremy himself, had not yet married. Jeremy had explained the situation, told him a bit about Murray's case, and took Tim over to see the patient after they had finished eating. Tim had also been taken in by the boy's appeal.

A short time later, while Dr. Boyer was away on his yearly vacation, Jeremy had whisked Mordy over to Tim's hospital and back again before anyone was the wiser. By the time Dr. Boyer had seen the surgeon's report, there wasn't much he could do about it.

In fact, it was Tim who had insisted on getting permission from Mordy's father before operating, and Jeremy had balked. "You know I can't do that," he'd said. "There's been no contact."

"Well, make contact," Tim had replied bluntly, "or else I'm not operating. I want to help you, but not at the expense of the kid or my own career."

Jeremy had had no choice but to track down Murray's father and, after a difficult conversation, had received Aharon's permission to operate.

So Aharon knew, at least, that the cleft had been repaired, and had told Devorah as much in the car on the way to the hospital. He had even confessed to her that when he gave his permission for the operation, he had gone to the hospital late at night and seen Mordy.

He had expected to see that Mordy had grown in the intervening years, but still he had been surprised at the transformation from baby to preteen. Aharon had seen a fine-featured, sweet-faced boy without a cleft, sleeping peacefully in his bed. He'd left quietly, thoughtfully, and with an ache he could not name or explain.

Tim had done an excellent job and Mordy recovered quickly. Jeremy had come every day to examine him and make sure the palate was healing properly. By the time the swelling had gone down, Jeremy could see what he had known all along was underneath the unappealing surface. Although he had been reluctant when Dr. Cohen had requested his permission to have the operation, Aharon was grateful now that the cleft had been fixed. It would be a lot easier for Devorah to handle, and he was glad he had agreed to it.

Jeremy now took a deep breath. This was always the hardest part. "Mrs. Landau, I understand your urgent need to see your son—"

"And I'm sure you *don't* understand," Devorah shouted. Everything leading up to this day — the recent discussions with Aharon, finding out about Chana Mirsky's son Ruvy, Yitta disclosing the long-kept secret to Ephraim, Ephraim's reaction — all flared up and out, all at once. "You have no idea."

She stood up and turned to Aharon. "You seem to know everything. Which building is he in?"

"Mrs. Landau, I must insist—"

"Insist all you like," she broke in. "After I see my son."

Jeremy stood up so he could look the frenzied mother in the eye. "The only way I can allow you to see him is if you agree to resume guardianship. Otherwise I'm obligated to turn him over to the state. It's best for the child if there is continuity of care. Meeting family members can be harmful to his welfare."

Devorah's laugh was bitter and grated on Aharon's ears.

"You have got to be kidding me." She took a deep breath to calm herself, as she realized that if she did not cool down, she really wouldn't get to see Mordy. The place was huge, she would never find him on her own. She sat down and looked at her husband.

"Well, Aharon," she said softly, ignoring Jeremy. "It looks like we've reached the moment of truth. What's it gonna be?"

CHAPTER 19

Devorah's ultimatum hung like a damp blanket over the room, absorbing all sound and making the air heavy and hard to breathe. Jeremy was the first to recover. He wasn't a husband but he was a man, and the look on Aharon's face was enough for him to jump in and try to rescue the poor fellow before he drowned.

"My apologies," he said. "I didn't mean to come on so strong. I was simply explaining policy, but at this point, with the facility closing and everything up in the air, we can be a little more flexible. If you're willing to take responsibility if something goes wrong, I don't see any harm in making a short visit to Murray now, and we can speak again afterward."

Devorah nodded with satisfaction. "That wasn't so hard, now, was it?" She turned to look at Aharon. "I'm sorry," she said, ignoring Jeremy again. "I didn't mean to put you on the spot like that, but I also kind of did."

"It's fine," said Aharon, rising from his chair. "I understand. Let's go see our son, okay? Lead the way, Dr. Cohen."

They set out down the winding path to the children's wing. Jeremy had worked long and hard to gather the children into one building and keep them together so he could care for them properly. He had realized that while Dr. Boyer eventually got word of everything that occurred in the sprawling grounds — with the help of reliable informants — he didn't always notice changes right away. When Jeremy had started moving the children one by one into the small building on the outskirts of the property and moving the adults out, it had taken a while for Dr. Boyer to realize what he'd done.

Jeremy wasn't a maverick or a rule-breaker — he respected systems and procedures and chain of command, but not when it came to these special children. While all the patients in Ravensfield were helpless in one way or another, the children were the most vulnerable. As the years passed, he had grown more and more protective of them and was willing to go to bat for them even if he was penalized for it. Dr. Boyer was not about to fire him; despite his frequent misdemeanors, Jeremy was a superb doctor.

As they walked silently through a light drizzle, Jeremy debated whether to give an introduction or just bring them into the ward and let them draw their own conclusions. He had also considered bringing Murray out to his office but decided against it. An electric current seemed to be flowing between Murray's parents that Jeremy could not penetrate. They weren't speaking, but he understood they were communicating with each other fiercely on a subliminal level.

He had already seen a great deal of marital conflict during this process of reuniting parents with children they often hadn't seen since birth or had never laid eyes on at all. He'd witnessed screaming matches, copious weeping, quiet resignation — a whole gamut of reactions. But these two were manifesting a relationship he hadn't seen before. At first he thought they were playing out a standard good cop/bad cop dynamic, but now he realized how hard they were struggling to please each other while disagreeing and this despite some sharp wordplay between them. The father clearly didn't want to bring Murray home, but the mother clearly did. He wondered how they would resolve the question.

"Here we are," he said, opening the wide entrance door and allowing Aharon and Devorah to pass through. He had instituted a few different methods to mitigate the unpleasant odors that permeated the building. Proper ventilation, twice-daily swabbing of walls and floors, and regular vacuuming of carpets, as well as regimented diaper and bathroom routines, had gone a long way toward making the wards more pleasant.

Flowers and plants, placed high up and away from curious hands, made the rooms feel fresh and clean. He hated to see visitors grimace upon entering his domain, and he was happy when the Landaus smiled as they stepped inside.

He had converted the large ground-floor lobby into a gathering place for the children during the day. There wasn't much socializing as many of the patients could not communicate, but they could parallel play or sit on the couches and look at books or play with toys. Jeremy felt a thrill of satisfaction with his improvements whenever he visited the children's building, even if no one else appreciated them. On the advice of Mrs. Mirsky, Aharon and Devorah had brought small toys for the children, and after asking permission from Jeremy, slowly walked around the lobby handing them out and getting some sweet smiles in return.

Mrs. Mirsky had explained that it was good not only for the children, but for them as well. "Giving is getting," she'd said in her pithy way. "It will relax you and open you up to what you see." They had taken her at her word and could see now that she had been correct. They were much more centered and ready for whatever lay ahead.

Jeremy didn't take every set of parents into the wards, but he believed Aharon and Devorah could handle it, and he proved to be correct.

He didn't keep Murray in the lobby for a few reasons. One was that he was prone to colds and bronchitis. His breathing sometimes sounded like a locomotive chugging past, and he often had to be moved out of his room because it disturbed the other children's sleep.

More importantly, though, he had no way to protect or defend himself. While he wasn't paralyzed, he had little control over his limbs. An arm or leg would spasm and shoot out unexpectedly, and if he hit another child accidentally, pandemonium would ensue.

Jeremy tried to treat each patient as an "only child," but like everyone, he had his favorites, and Murray was certainly one of them. He slowed down now as he led the

Landaus down the corridor toward Murray's room. Many of the children had already left the premises, they had either returned home with their parents, moved into foster care, or were sent out of state to other institutions.

"So," he said, stopping once more, this time in front of Murray's room. "Here we are."

"Here we are," Devorah echoed, drying her hands with a tissue she had pulled from her purse.

"Do you have any idea what to expect?" asked Jeremy.

Aharon nodded slightly, while Devorah shook her head. "I haven't seen him since he was three weeks old," she murmured.

Jeremy smiled. "I think you're going to like him." He opened the door with a flourish.

"Mr. and Mrs. Landau," he announced. "I'd like to introduce you to a very special person. Meet Murray Landau, your son."

CHAPTER 20

Devorah braced herself, but when her knees began to buckle, she realized she couldn't go through with it.

The truth came crashing down on her head: She had succumbed to outside pressure and abandoned her child. Who knew what the years here had done to him?

She had examined the faces of the children in the lobby when she handed out gifts, and despite what she was sure were Dr. Cohen's best efforts, they looked pitiful. How much could one man accomplish? No one had ever held these children, kissed and hugged them or sung to them, and no matter how much love and care she poured into Mordy now, she was afraid she would never be able to rehabilitate him.

They stood at the door to Mordy's room. She was about to turn back when she became aware of the strong and reassuring presence beside her. Aharon could feel her hesitation, but he knew they had to go through with it. For Devorah to refuse to see the boy would be disastrous. As for himself, he could barely contain his curiosity. When Devorah turned to look at him, her eyes revealed her panic, and he looked over at her and nodded his head. That was all he had to do, she would know what it meant.

Jeremy observed their silent communication and once again found himself intrigued. He had wanted to alleviate their concerns while they were still sitting in his office, but words would not do the boy justice. They had to see Mordy to believe it.

He opened the door and, startling Aharon and Devorah, burst into the room with a big smile.

"Hey, buddy," he said cheerfully.

"Hi, Dr. Cohen," someone said in a calm, clear voice. They peered into the room to see who had spoken. Dr. Cohen was standing at the foot of an empty bed and there was no one else in the room that they could see.

"Remember those important people I told you about?" Jeremy turned aside as he spoke and now they saw that someone was seated in a wheelchair near the window. "The ones I promised you were going to meet today? Well...here they are... Your parents!" he finished.

The Landaus were shocked. How could the doctor talk that way to a sick and neglected child?

"Come in," he gestured to them, "he's been waiting for you!" Aharon went all the way into the room while Devorah waited in the doorway. Her stomach dropped when Aharon came to an abrupt halt. He was blocking her view of the person in the wheelchair when again she heard a clear voice speaking.

"Hello. It's so nice to finally meet you."

Jeremy smiled broadly. All the years of working with Murray, bringing in a speech pathologist, and practicing and practicing some more, had worked the garble out of the boy's speech. Now his voice was low and steady. It still wavered from time to time, but he had been so motivated and driven to speak clearly that he had continued doing the exercises by himself until his voice was clear enough to communicate.

Aharon turned around to face Devorah with a broad smile on his face. "Come in," he said to her. "It's good."

Devorah walked in with her eyes squeezed shut, so frightened she could hardly breathe.

"Hi, Daddy. Hi, Mommy." Devorah's eyes flew open. She knew that voice — low and slow. Aharon's voice. But how could Mordy be talking like — well, like a normal person?

"Hello, Mordy!" Aharon said, his voice containing a strange note that Devorah had never heard before.

She walked all the way into the room and saw now what Aharon saw: a beautiful teenager with sparkling hazel eyes flashing glints of gold and green and brown, and neatly cut auburn hair. Apart from a slim but noticeable scar on his face, there was no other sign of the cleft lip and palate he had been born with.

He was sitting in a wheelchair equipped with a special head support. His upper body looked normal — fit, even — but his legs were covered with a blanket.

"I don't understand," said Devorah.

"Excuse me, Daddy, but why are you calling me Mordy? My name is Murray."

"What's going on?" Devorah glared at Jeremy. "Who is this boy, Dr. Cohen?"

"He is your son," said Jeremy. If she hadn't looked so distressed, Jeremy would have enjoyed this.

"He can't be. My son is brain-damaged. They told me so at the hospital when he was born," she said.

"It is true that Murray has some brain damage," Jeremy said. "I can't be 100 percent sure, but after studying his medical records, speaking to the doctors at his birth hospital, and conducting my own research, my conclusion is that he suffered something called a 'fetal stroke' during birth, and not cerebral palsy like they told you. I understand the delivery was extremely traumatic, and whether the difficult birth caused the stroke or the other way around, his oxygen was cut off momentarily and he did suffer some brain damage."

Devorah looked frantically back and forth from Dr. Cohen to Mordy, and she simply could not process the words the doctor was saying together with what she was seeing. "Then how could he be...? He seems to be—"

"Mrs. Landau," said Jeremy, cutting short his explanations. "Murray has been waiting a long time to meet you. How about saying hello and talking with him a bit, and we can discuss particulars later? I believe this is what you were demanding a little while ago, no?"

Aharon pulled up a chair and sat down next to Mordy, gazing at his son with awe and wonder. He grasped one of Mordy's hands and held it in both of his. Suddenly Mordy reached up, unashamed and curious, and flicked one of Aharon's *peyos.*

"What are these?" he asked Aharon innocently.

"Murray has had quite a bit of exposure to different types of people during his years here," said Jeremy, "but I don't think he's ever seen an Orthodox Jew."

"Wait just a minute," Devorah said, gripping her purse like a shield to protect herself from attack. "This is all going too fast for me."

"Sit down, Mommy," said Mordy, smiling shyly.

Devorah literally paled. "Aharon, come outside with me for a minute. I need to talk to you." But it was too late. Aharon was smitten. Getting up and walking away was not an option, as far as he was concerned. But he sighed and stood up. He knew he had to do as his wife wished. "We'll be right back," he said, patting Mordy on his shoulder and then his cheek, where he was surprised to feel the beginnings of a beard. "Don't go away."

There was a beat of silence until Aharon realized what he had said and looked mortified. Mordy leaned back against the headrest and burst out laughing. "Don't worry, Daddy," he said, tapping the arms of his wheelchair with his elbows. "I'm not going anywhere!"

CHAPTER 21

Aharon acceded to Devorah's request immediately because she was so distressed. They stepped out of the room to speak to each other in the corridor. The walls of the hallway were covered with drawings and paintings obviously made by the children, interspersed with large, inspirational nature photos and hundreds of Polaroid shots of the children themselves, playing ball, dressed in costumes, holding hands in a circle. Aharon wanted to examine each one of them individually, but Devorah was waiting impatiently.

"What is going on? Is that really our Mordy? How can it be? Did you know about any of this?"

Aharon took a deep breath, determined to calm Devorah down and bring her back to herself. Not only had he never seen her this rattled, but he hadn't known she was capable of it.

"First of all, if you mean, did I know Mordy was so amazing, then no, I did not. I had no idea."

Her throat was filled with hot sand. *Don't you understand? All this time we thought he was just a vegetable. I put him out of my mind, I didn't daven for him, I pretended he didn't exist.*

"And look at him. He could have been with us all this time. We could have had him at home. We could have done it."

She looked up at him, her eyes frantic, her hands clutching her throat. "Aharon, Aharon, I can't breathe."

Aharon helped her to take some deep breaths while he thought about what she was saying. Had all this pain been bubbling beneath the surface all these years? Had her loving and easygoing nature been a mask she had been forced to don to keep the agony at bay?

He looked around for a chair, so she could sit down. He was afraid to leave her and upset her further. Without taking his eyes off hers, he backed slowly down the hallway until he reached a small kiddy chair and brought it over to her.

She sat down hard. "I didn't expect this. I thought he was an invalid and I wanted to bring him home because I had *gaavah*. 'Look at what a *tzaddekes* I am, caring for my helpless child!' But Aharon, he's...alive!"

Of course, he was, but Aharon knew what she meant. Yet where his own reaction had been simple and instantaneous acceptance, hers was ripping her to shreds. He recalled

Jeremy hinting at Mordy's progress, but Aharon had thought he meant more along the lines of feeding himself or taking a few steps.

"But isn't it better this way?" he asked gently.

"Of course, it is, but how do we do this? We're strangers."

"No," said Aharon. "We're family. We've discovered a long-lost relative — our own child! — and we'll embrace him and accept him as we would any of our children." Devorah covered her face with her hands. Where was the brave Devorah of a few minutes ago, fighting for the right to see her child? How was she now hiding from him in the hallway? She was a mother, this was her child! No matter how guilty and torn she was feeling, Mordy came first.

"Okay," she said, struggling to her feet. "I'm ready. Let's go."

"What?" said Aharon. "No, no, we're not leaving yet. I want to stay with Mordy."

She looked at Aharon with a smile, her features returned to their normal expression. "I mean, let's go...back inside. His mama's here."

<hr />

She walked ahead of Aharon and pushed the door to Mordy's room open with the momentum of her whole body, strode eagerly over to her son, and hugged him.

Mordy smiled a huge smile, and Jeremy nodded with satisfaction. "Mordy—" she began.

"Murray," he said.

"No," she insisted. "Your name is Mordy. Mordechai Yitzchak Landau. You were named after your grandfather."

"I have a grandfather?" said Mordy.

Devorah didn't think it was an opportune moment to inform Mordy that his grandfather was no longer alive, so she brushed the subject aside. "Of course! You have tons of family." If she'd known Mordy was so with it, she'd have brought photos along.

Mordy grinned. "I had a feeling I belonged somewhere — right, Dr. Cohen?" He beamed at Jeremy. "I was right."

A tiny flame of rage flared up within Devorah, no bigger than the tip of a match, but it was to grow in intensity as time went on. She watched the easy interplay between the young man and his doctor, and she couldn't help but wonder why, when Dr. Cohen discovered that Mordy was of normal intelligence, they were not informed and given the chance to reconsider their decision.

Mordy had been at Ravensfield for nearly twelve years.

But there was time for that later. Her mind was already compiling a long list of questions for the knowledgeable Dr. Cohen, and he was going to have a lot of explaining to do. Right now, her attention belonged with Mordy. "Mordy," she asked, "do you know anything at all about us?" Mordy shook his head. "Could you call me by my name, please? I know you gave me another name, but I'm used to being called Murray."

"No," Devorah flared, until Aharon stopped her with a look. "Okay, all right, for now." But she knew she was never going to call him by that name. She'd rather call him nothing until he was ready to accept his real name.

The boy went on. "And to answer your question, no. I didn't even know you existed. I knew there was such a thing as parents, but for a long time I thought I didn't qualify because I couldn't walk. I guess Dr. Cohen didn't want to get my hopes up.

"But then everyone started leaving, and when I asked where they were going, Dr. Cohen sat down with me and we had a long talk. That was the first time in my life I heard about you.

"Dr. Cohen didn't know too much about you, but all I cared about was that I had parents. A mother! A father! I still can't believe it. Here you are." He looked then from Aharon to Devorah and finally his eyes rested on Dr. Cohen, as if for reassurance.

"So, what happens now?" Mordy asked.

CHAPTER 22

JEREMY

When Mordy asked them all what was going to happen next, deafening silence met his question.

"What's going on?" he asked, his eyes traveling from face to face. "Nobody has a plan?"

The formerly vociferous and outspoken Mrs. Landau is suddenly struck dumb, I observed, narrating the scene in my mind, *while the formerly soft-spoken Mr. Landau gazes tenderly at Murray.*

"I'm sorry, we haven't really discussed it yet," Aharon murmured. I looked at Murray with raised eyebrows. Murray knows very well that I have a plan and what my plan is, because we've discussed it often. He has been extremely helpful as I've been preparing my proposal to receive government funding for the establishment of a chain of group homes for mentally and physically challenged children under eighteen. There are already homes for adults, but the main option for children is either to remain at home or be fostered.

There's nothing wrong with foster care in my book, but it's not always a viable solution. In my group homes, and hopefully not just in my dreams, I'll have a system of continuous care. We'll work with children so they can be moved seamlessly into adult group homes and grow up with us. It sounded much too ambitious a project to most people I approached, but sometimes it only takes one, and I found that one. Mrs. Genzel is going to fund the entire project, at least until I get it up and running. When I talk to the parents, I mention my homes only as a possibility. I don't want people to think I'm drumming up business, even though I think it would be the best solution for many of these kids. In any case, it won't cost the first few patients anything due to Mrs. Genzel's astounding generosity. She says the idea touched her heart, but she hasn't yet said why. I don't want to pry, I figure she'll open up eventually.

And she has already incorporated the project under the name HOME, an acronym for Housing Options Made Easy. She's already made a huge deposit into a special account she opened.

And my young friend Murray knows all about it.

When Murray was about eight years old, he had finally grown tall enough to be moved from a crib to a bed — and with that he began to change. Suddenly he was much more alert when I spoke to him instead of just smiling vacantly. Then, instead of uttering unintelligible sounds, he'd seemed to be trying to repeat what I was saying.

I was so surprised that it took me a while to realize there were wheels turning inside his head. I'd treated hundreds of children over the years, but this was the first time I'd seen something like this. Either children begin to speak intelligently at a certain age or they don't, because they cannot, but Murray seemed to have been "playing possum" until then.

His sounds became more and more insistent, and I understood that he wanted to learn to speak properly. I didn't think he could, but I had our speech pathologist test him just in case I was wrong. First Mrs. Raymond, the pathologist, checked Mordy's mouth, tongue, and throat. Then she tested his hearing. Finally, she just started chatting with him. I had watched carefully and couldn't see anything positive, but the pathologist had pointed out that even though the child couldn't respond verbally, he was communicating.

She had said his eyes were responding, and that "there's definitely somebody at home in there, trapped and struggling to get out."

She had added, "I am sure his comprehension is excellent, but I see there's a problem with his swallowing. What do you feed him? Or should I say, do you feed him at all? I notice he has a gastric feeding tube. It could be that's one of the reasons his throat muscles and tongue are so weak. He's had no practice whatsoever."

I had been embarrassed. I should have realized that

swallowing was the problem, but I'd been so busy I hadn't given the problem the attention it deserved.

The nurses, or nurses' aides, or whoever drew the "last straw" and was assigned to feed Murray, always had a very hard time because he often choked while being fed. The staff had complained bitterly about it until Dr. Boyer had agreed to have a feeding tube inserted in his stomach and feed him formula.

Mrs. Raymond had demonstrated a regimen of exercises to do with Murray to improve his swallowing so that he could both eat normally and start speaking. She had also provided an illustrated exercise handbook and a box filled with various items designed to help strengthen Murray's mouth and throat muscles and wanted to show me how to use them.

"But aren't you going to be working with him?" I had asked Mrs. Raymond.

She had looked at me as if I were from another planet. "Dr. Cohen, with all due respect, I'm sure you know I am the only speech pathologist on staff here. I have so many patients they are lucky if I get to them once or twice a year. I've already given Murray twice as much time as I give my other patients — more, actually," she had said, looking at her watch and clucking her tongue. "I've showed you the exercises, here is the equipment you'll need, and I wish you the best of luck."

She had turned abruptly and rushed out of the room. I trailed after her, trying halfheartedly to thank her for her time, but she hadn't turned around or responded.

I made up my mind then that if the swallowing difficulty was going to keep him from speaking clearly, I was willing to work with him, help him do the exercises, whatever it would take.

CHAPTER 23

Murray," said Jeremy, smiling to show that he wasn't upset that the boy was simply ignoring his complicity in Jeremy's Plan, "I believe we've discussed My Plan once or twice, haven't we?" Mordy looked at Jeremy as if he had no idea what the doctor was talking about, and that was when Jeremy knew he had lost him. Murray wanted to go home. Jeremy raised his hands in defeat. "Let me explain," he said to the Landaus. "I am planning to open a group home for children who cannot be cared for in their parents' homes. Murray knows all about it. I was hoping he would be coming with me, but I see that was presumptuous on my part. In any case, why don't you spend a few more minutes with your son and then we can sit down and talk?"

Devorah was frozen in place, but Aharon recovered quickly. "That sounds interesting. I'd like to hear what you have in mind, and as you know, we haven't made a decision yet." He looked at Mordy apologetically, hoping to signal to his son that as far as he was concerned, he'd take Mordy home that very minute.

"Well," said Mordy, "I would like to be included in this conversation, seeing that it concerns my future." He smiled brightly, but Aharon could see that Dr. Cohen knew exactly what Murray was thinking.

"I'm sure you would. I would too if I were in your shoes," Jeremy said. "First of all, not to put too fine a point on it, you don't wear shoes." Mordy blushed and raised the bottom of his blanket to prove Jeremy's point. His feet were bare, and his parents could see what terrible shape they were in. His toes were badly misshapen, as were his legs.

"Temporarily," said Mordy. "You know I'm going to get braces. You know I'm going to walk."

Devorah couldn't restrain herself. "Dr. Cohen, how can you speak to him like that? Where's your sensitivity? He's a child."

Jeremy let out a breath. This visit was not going the way he had planned it at all. He gazed out the large window at the beautifully landscaped grounds, wishing he were out there, sitting on a bench. Murray's amazing progress convinced him it would be safe to let the conversation go ahead wherever it led.

Jeremy knew that Murray's brain damage was partial and totally random. He couldn't add figures, but he could spell words. He couldn't walk but he could, with great effort, clap his hands. He could move his features at will to form expressions, but he had a hard time moving his whole head.

He had never known when they were going to hit a wall in his progress, but Murray took it all in stride.

Mordy, however, was not about to sit quietly without putting in his two cents' worth "I'm almost fourteen years old. I can handle it. Dr. Cohen's the best. I know he's only teasing."

Devorah exploded. What was Dr. Cohen trying to pull here? There was no way — absolutely no way — that this could be the same child she'd abandoned in the hospital fourteen years ago. If she hadn't been so distraught, she would have realized that he resembled Aharon and Ephraim. Without their *peyos* and zero haircuts, yarmulkes and the vibrant expressions of those who are born keeping Torah and mitzvos, it was hard to recognize him.

"I demand to know what's going on here right now! Is this some sort of a sick joke?"

Jeremy understood her wrath and confusion and prepared to temper it. She had given away what she believed was a child with no future, who had somehow grown into a handsome, articulate smart aleck. With all the emotion whirling around the room, he was surprised she was still standing.

"Sorry, buddy. Nice try, though," he said to Murray.

"I demand my rights," Murray said.

"Good luck with that," Jeremy replied. Once they got started on the one-liners, they couldn't stop.

"Dr. Cohen!" Devorah was very nearly hysterical. "Please!"

Jeremy gestured for the Landaus to step out of the room with him. "I'm sorry," he said as moved into the hallway. "My apologies. Mrs. Landau, you know very well that this is your son, and the more you deny it, especially in front of him, the harder it's going to be for all of you."

Aharon looked at the doctor sympathetically, then at Devorah, amazed at how the tables had turned so quickly. He understood what she was going through, as much as one person could understand another, even a husband and wife who were as close as they were.

He could feel the shock and guilt radiating from her like a magnetic field. He left her side for a moment to bring over a chair for her. The walls were painted a dull beige, but the paint seemed surprisingly fresh. (He found out later that Mordy had cajoled the head of the janitorial staff into giving his room and the hall a fresh coat.) Aharon pulled the chair over to her but she ignored him, hands on hips, a deadly sign, as he well knew.

"Please, sit down, Mrs. Landau," said Jeremy. "I'll explain everything to you and your husband, but I need you to calm down. Your son may not be a child any longer, but he is still young. Whatever you decide, he'll need your support. We need to get to the bottom of this before I allow you to spend any more time with him. Despite his clever mouth and amazing progress, his condition is not stable. It's important to keep him on an even keel as much as possible."

Devorah sat down finally but could not continue the conversation. She covered her face with her hands, as if the two men weren't there or at least as if they couldn't see her. She especially didn't want Aharon to see her in such a state. She didn't care much about what Dr. Cohen thought — she'd already written him out of their decision-making.

She began to cry. "I can't do this," she sobbed, trying to make as little sound as possible. "No matter what we decide, I'll never forgive myself for not going the other way."

CHAPTER 24

J eremy led the Landaus back into Murray's room.

It was time to move on. Had Jeremy known the extent of the emotional storm he would be party to, he might have planned this meeting differently. He had been so enthralled with Murray's progress and so personally involved in the boy's development that he hadn't considered that the parents had missed out on it completely.

All they saw now was a "finished product," albeit one with still shaking and withered arms and legs, and a head that wobbled on his neck. He hadn't considered how shocked they would be. The Landaus had believed they were going to encounter a totally handicapped child and instead they were greeted by a virtual wunderkind.

Jeremy looked at Murray, who was trying not to stare at his mother's tearstained face. Their eyes met, Murray's full of questions and exasperation. Jeremy reassured him that his parents' shocked reaction was only to be expected.

"Come," he said to the Landaus now, much more firmly. "Let's go back to my office." He spread out his arms to shepherd them from the room, but Devorah wasn't quite ready to leave. She walked over to Mordy's wheelchair and, afraid to touch him, plucked at the blanket covering his legs.

"I'm sorry about this, *tzaddik'l*. I was just so surprised. I'll..." she turned to look at Aharon, "we'll be back soon."

Mordy rolled his eyes at his mother skeptically. "Why do you keep speaking Chinese? What's a *tzaddik'l*, and why are you calling me that?"

Devorah took a step back. Where she had been expecting a sheep, she kept coming up against a lion. And a new panic seized her now. *He doesn't know a thing about Yiddishkeit.* She had envisioned his seamless integration into the family as a silent observer — if that — rather than an active participant.

She was simply on overload. She needed a break.

"It means a very good person," she replied.

Jeremy prodded them out the door.

"Let's go back to my office," he said.

"I think we'd do better with some fresh air. Is there somewhere outside where we could sit down and talk?" Aharon said.

Jeremy nodded reluctantly and led them to a small gazebo on the lawn. He would have preferred the distance of a desk between them, and a place where roles were clearly defined. Sitting so close together made him nervous, but with this couple — this family — none of the regular rules seemed to apply. They all started talking at once, but Jeremy took the lead. "I apologize that I didn't prepare you in advance. I thought you would be delighted."

Aharon was quick to agree. "We are delighted. Don't get us wrong. We're his parents, and which parents wouldn't want to see their child thriving?"

Devorah cut in, impatient with platitudes. "My question is, Dr. Cohen, why weren't we notified? Why weren't we informed that our son was capable of having a relationship with us?"

"Mrs. Landau," Jeffrey answered, "I'm going to be frank with you." He had met enough parents to know that giving them the straight truth was never a good idea, but again, the rules just weren't working. "Let's turn your question around. Regardless of whether he was able to have a relationship with you, which I believe he always was, there was plenty of time for you to build a connection with him. When children are whisked away at birth—"

"It wasn't my fault!" she cried. "I wasn't given a choice!"

Aharon looked away, red patches of shame creeping up from his neck to his face.

"Be that as it may," continued Jeremy, "once the papers were signed, you relinquished your responsibility for him, so we had no obligation to you. Had the hospital not been forced to close, this meeting would probably never have happened, but any involvement on your part during all this time would have been welcomed."

In Jeremy's experience, some families had always kept in touch and visited the children, some did not, and some spoke only with him and did not visit their children.

"I didn't know that it was an option," Devorah whispered.

"He didn't just disappear into a black hole," Jeremy continued. "He was very much alive, and as you can see, he's very socially aware. As he grew older he craved companionship. Luckily, we" — meaning Jeremy himself — "noticed that and we began to work with him. And look at the results! Instead of beating yourself up with guilt and anger, how about reveling in the fact that your son has built up a strong personality and character for himself, not to mention his intelligence?"

Aharon interrupted at this point to turn the conversation to where he desperately wanted it to go. "We are very grateful to you, Dr. Cohen," he said. "Truly grateful. But as Mordy himself said, let's talk about what happens next. Can we just pack him up and bring him home with us?"

"Theoretically, yes, but practically, no, not quite yet."

They clearly had no idea what caring for a child with extensive special needs entailed. He needed a specially designed bed, a custom-made wheelchair (as the ordinary ones they used in the hospital often did more harm than good), a lift to put him in and out of bed once he grew bigger and heavier, feeding machines, sterile equipment — the list went on and on. Health insurance would cover some of the expenses but not all, and that too had to be considered.

They were a long way from bringing Murray home, but the question was whether they were willing to take the first step. "It'll take some time for you to prepare, not just a physical place for him but an emotional one as well. You have other children at home, correct?"

"Yes," Aharon replied. "We have three younger children. Mordy is the oldest."

Jeremy nodded. "It will take just as much time to prepare them as it will everything else. You two have a lot of work to do. We will have to meet many more times before we get everything settled. I can't let him go until you are one hundred percent ready on every level."

Every word Jeremy said was a stone tossed into the Landaus' laps, and the load was growing heavier by the minute. They needed to take this in very small steps.

"Thank you for your time, Doctor," said Aharon, standing up. "We have a lot to think about."

Most parents just walked away at this point, leaving Jeremy to feel that he was little more than a recorded message, as though he had not put his heart and soul into these kids. Where was the gratitude? Where was the appreci—?

Aharon put out his hand for Jeremy to shake. "And thank you for all you've done for Mordy. I know he never would have gotten as far and grown as much without your help and your devotion. Dedication is something money can't buy, but if it could, you would be a rich man. I envy your portion in the World to Come."

Jeremy beamed, pumping Aharon's hand up and down, until Aharon's final words sank in. Words that slipped out of Aharon so naturally landed on Jeremy like a boulder.

CHAPTER 25

JEREMY

Yirmiyaaaah!"

I'm about nine years old, sitting around the large table at my grandparents' house at what must have been a Passover Seder, because when we visited we always ate at the round table in the kitchen. I'm sandwiched between my mother and my father, wedged in so tightly that I can't wriggle out, as they know I'd like to do.

My grandfather was not a large man, but he had a huge voice. His long, thin face and soft features did not prepare you for the roar that emerged from him without any effort on his part — it was his regular speaking voice. He loved to sing, and when he revved up his deep baritone the walls really shook.

"It's time to say *Mah Nishtanah*, Yirmiyahu!" he said, leaning over to me with a hopeful smile. "How about in Yiddish this year, eh?" His eyes were bright, and I hated to see the disappointed look on his face as I mumbled the Four Questions in English.

My mother had tried to teach it to me a few times, and I have to admit that when I heard her say the Yiddish words I burst out laughing. They sounded ridiculous to me. We were Americans — my father was an army veteran and we spoke English. But my grandparents would often speak to my mother in Yiddish. She would always respond in English because she didn't want my father to feel excluded. As it was, he rarely joined us when we visited.

My brother and I would squeeze ourselves into the small space around the table. The table was lemon-yellow Formica, and the chairs were padded with thick yellow vinyl cushions and entombed in clear plastic for easy cleaning. In the summer my legs would stick to the seat until I got smart and started wearing long pants to Papa and Nana's house.

My grandmother would carefully remove an emerald-green glass bottle of Coke from the pantry closet and place it ceremoniously in the middle of the table, smiling at us encouragingly with her lopsided false teeth. Papa would open it with the bottle opener, Nana would place two sparkling clean glasses in front of my brother and me and pour us each a drink. It was warm and a little flat, but we drank it all as though it was medicine.

My mother would sit sideways, and quietly sip coffee as my grandparents looked fondly at us. After the initial greetings, none of us spoke much. My brother and I had kick fights under the table until my mother would give us a look and we'd stop — temporarily.

We'd start getting up to go after about an hour, and it would take another hour to get out the door. My grandmother would start loading things into bags, which my grandfather would dutifully carry down to the car. He didn't mind making two or three trips, while my mother stood there helplessly, mortified that her father was schlepping for her.

"I have two strong, healthy boys here, Papa," she'd say.

"I know. They'll have their time. Let them enjoy," he'd reply, and hustle back upstairs for another load. Finally, the two of them would emerge at the entrance to their apartment building and stand together seeing us off. When they stood that way, it looked like they were one unit, each side waving a hand as we drove off.

My mother would be quiet on the way home. She didn't even get involved when my brother and I would start to squabble, and eventually we got bored and stopped because we couldn't get her attention.

By the time we got home, she'd be back to her normal self, and the whole thing would happen again in reverse. My father would be waiting outside, sometimes still in his work clothes, holding a green glass bottle of ice-cold Coke. He always seemed to know the exact moment we would arrive.

He would greet my mother, give us a big smile, and then, as if it were choreographed, he'd give us the bottle of Coke to hold, open the trunk, and carry the bags into the house.

We'd sit down and eat the dinner my mother had prepared before we left, and by the following morning, our visit to Papa and Nana would be packed away like a winter coat in summer — until the next visit. I wish now that I'd been kinder and more attentive to my grandparents. I stopped going with my mother to visit when I was a teenager, and the only time I saw them after that was when they came rarely to visit us. And when they did come, they'd bring their own food.

My mother would hover in the background, while my father seemed to enjoy the visits tremendously. He would dig in to my grandmother's food as if it were his last meal on earth, and he treated them like royalty.

My father was always very respectful and polite, but with my mother's parents he was lit up, animated, like being with them plugged him into an electric socket that he had no access to anywhere else. I liked seeing him that way, but it scared me too because I didn't understand why he seemed to like them so much but never came with us to visit them.

A few years after my grandmother died, my grandfather got sick and came to live with us. My father took such good care of him, again revealing a side of himself that both fascinated and frightened me.

I remember my grandfather talking about the World to Come a lot during that time. "What's going to be in the World to Come?" he'd moan. "I failed as a Jew. I failed as a father. Look who I have left to take care of me." My father would nod and soothe him until my grandfather calmed down and went to sleep. Dad would turn and find me standing in the doorway, observing the scene, and he'd give me one of his inscrutable smiles.

So, when Aharon Landau started in on that World to
Come business I almost lost it. Was he wishing death on
me? The warmth and goodwill I'd started feeling toward
him froze in place like an ice sculpture. "What did you just
say?" Jeremy asked accusingly. Aharon was still shaking
Jeremy's hand until he roughly pulled it away.

Aharon looked at Devorah, confused at Jeremy's abrupt
mood change.

"I'm sorry. Did I offend you? I was giving you a blessing
that Jews often give to one another, and I am especially
grateful to you as you've been so kind to our son."

"I have no interest in any World to Come," Jeremy
growled. "And neither does Murray, by the way. If you try
to push that stuff on him he just won't stand for it. Forget
about it. And the only world I'm interested in is this one. Do
we understand each other?"

CHAPTER 26

A sudden rainstorm exploded against the windshield on the drive home, and Aharon quickly raised the windows before he and Devorah got drenched. Its unexpectedness had a strange effect, and both Aharon and Devorah burst out laughing.

"Did that just happen to us?" she gasped. "All of that?"

Aharon nodded. "I believe it did. But there was so much happening that it's hard to know just what you could possibly be referring to."

Dr. Cohen's abrupt change in mood had cut the visit short and the Landaus had left with nothing settled. "What was that all about, do you think?" said Devorah.

"I suppose you're talking about my *berachah*? Talking about the World to Come? No idea. I thought he was just an I-don't-care-one-way-or-the-other type of Jew. I was just trying to be nice, and I really do appreciate what he's done for Mordy."

Devorah nodded. "You know, we have to be careful. I know you are used to doing business with all kinds of people, but I keep close to home. How am I going to know when I'm about to set off a land mine?"

The rain settled into a steady patter, drumming on the roof and beating against the windows, shutting out all the outside noise and magnifying inside noise. Devorah's breathing sounded loud in her ears.

"You just answered your own question," said Aharon. "You don't know. You just have to do your best, as you always do."

Jeremy's odd response to Aharon's heartfelt thanks had left them both up in the air until Aharon had quickly got them back on track. "It's been a long day, Dr. Cohen," he'd said, "and as you mentioned, we have a long way to go before we can consider bringing Mordy home. There are many issues we'll need to work out, and we will work them out, one at a time. The main thing is that we work together, isn't it?"

Jeremy had seemed about to calm down thanks to Aharon's peacemaking efforts, but then Devorah had intervened. "Dr. Cohen, we see that you are a wonderful physician — you truly heal! But when it comes to family matters such as Mordy's religious observance, I'm afraid that has very little to do with you. Those issues we will have to work out with our rabbis."

Dr. Cohen had looked as though he'd been slapped in the face. Shock, hurt, anger — the emotions rolled across his face in a continuous loop. Aharon had stepped in front of Devorah, afraid the fellow would lose control and belt one or both of them.

"But since we're on the subject," Aharon said now to Devorah, "why did you say that to him just at that moment?"

"That's what I mean!" Devorah answered. "How was I supposed to know he was going to get so upset? Anyway, I think we're missing a bigger point, don't you?"

"What point?"

"Are you kidding?" She began to imitate Aharon, putting a goofy smile on her face and waving her hand. "'Hi, Mordy!' Like you'd known each other forever. What happened to 'We can't, Devorah,' 'You have no idea how hard it will be, Devorah!' Where did that guy go? I think that's the real conversation we should be having right now."

Aharon tapped his fingers on the steering wheel in time to the beat of the rain. What could he say? Devorah had a point. He had certainly done an about-face, but how could he help himself? His heart simply filled to bursting at the thought of his feisty son and he could feel the blood rushing to his head.

Because the truth was that he'd always known. From the moment Mordy had looked up at him during his bris with those wise, little eyes filled with trust, he'd known that his firstborn had a firm lock on his heart. That moment when their gazes met had returned to haunt him many times over the years. It was a private agony he carried with him that he had never shared with anyone.

What if he had been less of a coward and called the whole thing off? What if he had said, "I'm sorry, there's been a mistake. I'm taking my baby home with me"? What if he had been less afraid of what his mother would say? At that point, there had still been time to turn back, to change their minds. What if he had returned home that day after the bris, holding Mordy in his arms and placing him down gently next to Devorah? What would their lives have been like if he'd chosen to live authentically, to be true to himself and follow the heart that was filling up now with love faster than he could stop it?

Aharon lived in fear that his whole life, ever since Mordy was born, had been just a show; his face, a mask, his marriage — no, not his marriage. That was the only solid factor in all these years. But the rest of it was just a reaction and response to that day. When he had found himself in contact with shady buyers for his exotic foods, he had asked himself if he should sweep it under the rug and do business or turn away and do what he knew was right. If one of the kids tested his patience, he had asked himself what he would do if this kid was Mordy. If they were too loud, he would tell himself, "Better a kid too loud than one making no noise at all." He had held up every decision he made against the decision of that day when he had turned away from his son and turned his son away.

Devorah was unknowingly right — he had known Mordy since forever. Not a moment had gone by since that day that Aharon did not have Mordy in his mind and in his heart.

"Tell me the truth, Aharon," Devorah said. "If Mordy hadn't been so alert and with it, would you still feel the same?"

CHAPTER 27

Anyway," Devorah continued, "I don't know what Dr. Cohen was so upset about. I mean, obviously Mordy is going to be *frum*, there's no question about it. I'm already planning his *upsherin*."

Aharon didn't know if Devorah was kidding about the *upsherin*, it didn't *seem* like she was, but at the moment he couldn't be sure about anything. He wisely chose to ignore it and they managed to arrive home without incident.

They were met at the door by Yitta before they even had the key in the lock.

"*Nu?*"

"Hello, Ma. How are you?" said Aharon.

"How do you think I am? I'm a bundle of nerves. What happened?"

"Will you let us in the door first?" asked Aharon lightly. But it sounded like an accusation and, offended, Yitta turned her back and returned to the kitchen.

Aharon heard Devorah take a deep breath behind him, and he prayed she would stay calm until he could get his mother in the car and drive her home.

Yitta, always a devoted mother no matter the circumstances, had a warm supper waiting for them, for which they were both extremely grateful.

Aharon washed and took a big bite of bread, and before Devorah even sat down he was halfway into the brisket and baked potato.

"Thank you so much, Ma," Devorah said, cutting the meat as she spoke. "It was really nice of you to do this for us."

Yitta had folded both hands in her lap, nodded her head at Devorah, and turned to watch her beloved only son eat. The unbidden thought entered her mind: *If Aharon is my beloved son, what must Mordy be to him?* But she immediately corrected her thinking. *No, the situation is completely different. Mordy's a complete stranger to them, whereas I've raised Aharon from birth. Two completely different things.*

Feeling his mother's eyes on him, Aharon looked up. Much as he wished to postpone the confrontation, he was unable to make her wait any longer. Wiping his mouth with a napkin and crumpling it in his hand, he said, "First of all, thank you. It was delicious, as usual."

Yitta nodded, her face a mask, but despite her impatience she reveled in her son's compliment.

He moved his chair back and took a deep breath. "It was surprising, Ma. Mordy was not as we expected."

"What do you mean?" asked Yitta.

"He...well...I can't describe it... He was just so..." The tears rolled down his cheeks and he wiped them away quickly with the back of his hand. "This is ridiculous, I'm sorry. He was just so...beautiful! You could barely tell there was anything wrong with him."

Yitta sat up stiffly. "What is he saying?" she asked, confused. She turned to Devorah. "Mordechai Yitzchak is an invalid!"

"Yes and no," said Devorah. "And," she added kindly, "even if he were, the name Mordy suits him just fine."

"What are you talking about?" Yitta cried. "Stop with the riddles. Tell me what happened."

Aharon took the lead, explaining to his bewildered mother all that had occurred during their visit to the hospital. Yitta shook her head back and forth, unwilling to believe what Aharon was saying.

"That is impossible," she said flatly. "That child was a vegetable—"

"Ma, please!" Devorah had remained quiet while Aharon was speaking, but she just couldn't handle the epithet. She knew it was a word often used to describe disabled people, but now, after seeing and speaking to Mordy, Devorah could not abide it.

"But that's what he is."

"What he *was*," Aharon intervened. "*If* there was ever anything really wrong with him in the first place."

"Aharon, what are *you* saying now?" said Devorah.

"How do we really know what was wrong with Mordy?

Nobody ever tested him. All we knew was that he went through a very difficult birth, had a cleft lip and palate, and that his reflexes were not normal."

"Don't be ridiculous," said Yitta. "He was retarded. We all saw that."

Aharon wisely dropped the subject. They were all too tired to discuss anything sensibly at the moment. "Be that as it may, that's not what he is now. He's alert, smart, funny—"

"And crippled," Yitta interrupted him. "And barely Jewish! He knows nothing of Yiddishkeit."

Aharon knew his mother was just scared or she'd never talk this way. But he also knew he had to take her home before he and Devorah both lost control.

He murmured *Birkas Hamazon* as fast as he could and stood up.

"How about we head for home now, Mama?" he said softly, invoking the name she'd taught him to call her as a child, when she was upset. It seemed to calm her.

Yitta rose to her full four-foot-nine height. "You can end this discussion now by taking me home, but you can't hide from the truth. If you bring this child home, you are asking for a world of trouble. Mark my words, Aharon. A world of trouble."

Devorah saw them to the door. She waited until the car drove off, and then went back into the house. Her mother-in-law had managed to whisk the few dishes off the table, rinse and dry them in the few moments while Aharon and she were *bentching* and he went to bring her coat.

She hated hearing her *shvigger*'s words, but she had to admit that there was some truth behind them. She really *had* been planning to make an *upsherin* for Mordy, whether they brought him home or not, but Dr. Cohen's words rang in her ears.

"*Don't you dare try that stuff on Murray,*" he'd said, "*he won't stand for it.*"

Maybe he would and maybe he wouldn't. She would have to rethink her strategy. Mordy was a teenager now, not a three-year-old, willing to do whatever Tatty and Mommy wanted, easily persuaded with lollipops.

Devorah's head was spinning — she couldn't stop the thoughts from tumbling one after the other, and she knew that at some point, sooner rather than later, they were going to need some guidance. She didn't want to forget any of the details, though, for who knew what would turn out to be important? She decided to write down everything that had happened.

It took her almost two hours of intense concentration to get it all out on paper, and when she read it over, she was surprised to see in black and white how angry she was, torn between the equally maddening intolerance of both Dr. Cohen and her mother-in-law. By the time she looked up, she realized Aharon was still not home. She knew Yitta liked to schmooze with him when she had the chance, but never for this long. She folded the papers and left them on the kitchen table, meaning to show it and discuss it with Aharon when he got home, but she fell asleep soon after, and didn't hear Aharon come in.

When she went down to the kitchen early the next morning, she was surprised to find Ephraim awake and sitting at the table with Aharon, their heads together and the sheaf of papers spread out in front of them.

CHAPTER 28

Waking up in the morning was the hardest part of Murray's day. He was "put to bed" early in the evening and more or less left to himself until 6:30 the following morning. Often, he would stay up reading or awkwardly doing crossword puzzles (now that his arms and fingers had been strengthened with exercises Dr. Cohen had ordered) or planning chess moves until the middle of the night when fatigue would finally overtake him. Because he didn't move around much — hardly at all — he had extra adrenaline with no way to work it off.

Either way, 6:30 a.m. would arrive no matter how much or little he'd slept. Michael, the nurse, would come barreling in, surprisingly energetic after being on duty all night, and the routine would begin. Temperature, pulse, blood pressure, chest palpitation, catheter check, and limb check for wounds or infection. Then would come the grueling hoist from bed to wheelchair, from wheelchair into the shower wheelchair, and out again, drying, dressing, and back in his special wheelchair for the rest of the day. It was cumbersome, but the two of them had been doing it together as long as Murray could remember, so they more or less had it down to a science.

"'Mawnin', Michael," Murray good-naturedly mimicked the nurse's Brooklyn accent.

"'Mawnin', kid. How'r'ya doin' t'day?"

"Same old, same old," Murray answered.

Murray had picked up some of his vocabulary from the radio Dr. Cohen had insisted on placing in his room when he was still in his crib. The doc had instructed the nurses to leave it on all the time, and even now Murray could repeat whole segments of ad slogans verbatim.

Murray would tell Michael a joke he'd read in the *Reader's Digest* and Michael would guffaw, and before they knew it, the morning routine was finished and Murray was left with a long day stretched out in front of him.

Waking up had multiple meanings for him — his actual waking up in the morning, and his symbolic "waking up," which is how he referred to his emergence from his non-communicating days. His inner life had always been articulate from the time he'd outgrown infancy, but he had had no way at first to take what was inside and bring it outside.

Every day he would raise his eyes and look directly into the eyes of whoever passed by his crib, waiting for someone to focus on him. Most of the time he had been ignored, the nurses were super-busy and the other patients hadn't paid him any attention. Once they implanted the feeding tube, he got hardly any attention at all.

Then one day a man had appeared next to his crib. A tall man in a white coat, with bushy brown hair, big round glasses, and smelling of cherry Kool-Aid. Murray's sense of smell was so powerful that it sometimes made him cry, which he found confusing because he was rarely sad.

For some reason this man — the nurses called him Dr. Cohen — had taken an interest in Murray. According to this Dr. Cohen, Murray had been about six when they'd met and was still being kept in a crib. His arms and legs were almost atrophied from lack of movement, and he couldn't talk or eat, the nurses had reported. His lips sometimes bled. People usually backed away from him at first glance, but Dr. Cohen was different.

At first the doctor had come to see him from time to time, and Murray looked forward to those visits so much that his heart would pound when he heard the doctor's voice. Even if those visits lasted only a few minutes, a feeling of happiness that he didn't know how to define had engulfed him.

One day not long after their initial encounter, Dr. Cohen had stopped at his crib and, as he was about to walk away, Murray had seen him hesitate. "Hey, little guy," he'd said, even though Murray was already six, according to his chart. "Male, age six, paralyzed, cleft lip, with feeding tube..." he'd read.

"Hey, little guy," Dr. Cohen had said, crouching down to look Murray in the eye between the bars. "What's going on in there?" He'd grabbed a chair and sat down, which brought him level with the patient, and somehow the boy intuited that this was probably his one and only chance to establish a real connection with someone. With all his strength, he concentrated all his mental power in his eyes and prayed that Dr. Cohen would see him, really see him — and it had worked.

"Huh," Dr. Cohen had exclaimed in his laid-back way. "How about that?" He'd stayed a few more minutes, speaking softly, asking questions, trying to understand what he was seeing and gauge Murray's responses. He'd lifted the boy's arm, then a leg. While the leg flopped down as soon as he let go, the arm showed some resistance — a slight reflex. Then he'd examined Murray's mouth. Again, Dr. Cohen's eyebrows rose, and Murray was on his way. That's not to say it had been easy, but it had been sweet for Murray. Every day Dr. Cohen brought something new to stimulate him, either physically or mentally, and slowly he had come out of his shell. Then Dr. Cohen had taken him away someplace and fixed his lip and mouth.

And then Dr. Cohen did the most marvelous thing one person could do for another — he'd brought his own mother in to visit. Her warmth, her smell (cinnamon?), became his lifeline. She would read stories to him with endless patience, starting with little nursery rhymes and gradually working up to *Treasure Island* and *Call of the Wild*.

She came in regularly, and Murray knew that Dr. Cohen enjoyed her visits as much as he did, if the amazing aromas coming from her numerous shopping bags were any indication.

And then Dr. Cohen had brought in the speech pathologist, who had diagnosed his untried ability to speak and rec-
ommended getting rid of the feeding tube and showed Dr.
Jeremy exercises to strengthen Murray's mouth and throat
muscles. The doctor himself had worked with Murray a few
minutes every day thereafter, and Murray had progressed
rapidly.

Dr. Jeremy had at first taken the feeding tube as a given,
just because it was there, but then he removed it. It was
Michael who had told him the truth. "Murray was a mess,"
he'd said, "wit' his lip and tongue like that, and he couldn't
lift his head. The food would get stuck in the cleft. No one
wanted to feed him, and he was starvin' a little, I guess, so
they just put the tube in."

"He'd been eating before that? Swallowing?" Jeremy had
questioned.

"Not much, but yeah, some. We were just lazy."

CHAPTER 29

I t had taken years for Murray and Jeremy to accomplish all they had, years of Murray being moved around by Michael, whose bulk was large but whose step was light, who tried to be gentle and for the most part succeeded, even though the procedures Murray had had to endure were uncomfortable no matter how gentle the caregiver.

Murray's life had vastly improved once he'd begun to talk.

And once he started, he did not stop. Anyone and everyone was fair game for conversation, even those who could not answer him. In the early days he'd grunted a lot and garbled his words, and after a few tries, his conversation partner would get frustrated and drift away.

But slowly his speech had cleared, like fog drifting away in the sunlight, until he could be easily understood. At that point his arms still weren't strong enough to propel himself around a lot on his own in the wheelchair, so he'd wait until someone came by and he'd "hitch" pushes to get where he wanted to go.

He'd once even made it outside onto the grounds and sat there until someone finally realized he should not have been there and dragged him back to the ward. Not that it wasn't permitted — he just wasn't allowed to go anywhere alone.

It had been freezing outside on that particular day, but he hadn't cared — it was one of the only times he'd been outside in his entire life. He'd nearly passed out from the cold air blasting into his lungs, and he'd understood then why he shouldn't be doing it alone, but he'd loved it, just loved it, and begged and pleaded to be taken outside whenever possible.

And he so loved to talk. It seemed as though he was making up for all the years of silence. He was so gregarious, so persistent and uninhibited, that he would even get a few words of response from some of the older patients who hardly ever spoke. He'd make his way up to the nurses' station and pester them with questions until he knew where each one lived, what their salaries were, and the names and ages of their spouses, kids, and pets.

Murray had eventually noticed that his wheelchair was getting to be a tight fit and that his pajamas reached only down to mid-calf. He had grown but was still being treated like a small boy.

Dr. Cohen was aware of it but he couldn't solve every one of Murray's problems, so Murray took matters into his own hands. He'd started nagging the nurses, who managed to locate larger pajamas in the adult ward and pass them on to him.

But a proper bed, a real room, and a bigger wheelchair were a lot harder to come by. He'd asked Dr. Cohen if there was anyone he could speak to about it, but Dr. Cohen had only chuckled bitterly. "Yeah, sure, Dr. Boyer would go right along with that."

Murray had taken note of the name and discovered that Dr. Boyer was the director of the hospital and his best bet. He had not been able to write yet at that point, as his hands weren't strong enough, even though eventually he would be able to do that, and even learn to type.

So, he enlisted Mrs. Cohen, Dr. Jeremy's mom, to help him out, and she was glad to do it. Together they composed an extremely eloquent letter to the mysterious Dr. Boyer, laying out the reasons why his natural growth required attention and accommodation.

A month or so later the doctor made a personal visit to the ward, causing a general panic, as the ward was in its typical state of barely controlled chaos and the staff would have liked to make a better impression. Dr. Boyer hadn't even tried to hide his disapproval.

"Who and where is Murray Landau?" he asked the staff. He knew very well who Murray was — ever since he had chastised Jeremy years earlier for paying too much attention to certain patients.

Smiles broke out among the nurses. "Oh, Murray. He's a character," said one.

"He's da best," said Michael, the nurse, nodding his head.

Dr. Boyer removed the letter from his pocket and laid it down on the desk. The head nurse picked it up and glanced at it, burst out laughing, and passed it to the other nurses. "Oh, yes, that's Murray all right."

Annoyed, Dr. Boyer folded up the letter and replaced it in his pocket. "Which room is he in?" he demanded coldly.

The head nurse quickly wiped the smile off her face and replied, "He doesn't have a room. He's in the ward."

The ward was a wide, open area with twenty cribs lined up, ten on each side, and a scattering of children in wheelchairs. Faces stared out through the bars of the cribs like incarcerated prisoners, but most of the gazes held no expression at all.

He walked down the aisle until he came upon a fairly large boy squeezed into a child's wheelchair. He eyed the nearby crib, from which Murray had persuaded one of the handymen to remove the end panel to accommodate his growing legs.

"Who are you?" Murray asked suspiciously, eyeing the doctor's well-tailored suit, pencil-thin mustache, and slicked-back hair. Dr. Boyer kept his distance from the patients for this exact reason: He didn't like intrusive questions.

"I am Dr. Boyer," he'd responded stiffly, "director of this hospital."

Murray immediately regretted his gruff question and had quickly switched gears. "I'm Murray Landau. Thank you for coming to see me."

Murray had seen how shocked Dr. Boyer was at his good manners, clear speech, and now-friendly attitude. A few more moments of conversation, and even the aloof Dr. Boyer had been unable to argue with what he was now seeing.

Dr. Cohen noticed thereafter the changes that were taking place: a different wheelchair, a regular bed, but was too busy to seek an explanation until one day when he went to look for Murray and did not find him in his usual place in the ward.

His heart had stopped for a second — surely he would have been notified if Murray had taken a turn for the worse. His physical condition, while not great, had been stable.

Jeremy had hurried over to the nurses' station, but before he could say a word, they pointed him in the direction of the private rooms at the end of the hall.

"Don't tell me..." said Jeremy. "Did you...?"

"Apparently Murray himself accomplished the impossible," the head nurse had said. "Dr. Boyer came to see him personally."

"Well, how about that?" Dr. Cohen had said, proud to bursting of his protégé.

CHAPTER 30

And so, against her will, Yitta had included *kapitel* 100 of Tehillim in her daily davening, as the *rav* had advised. Along with *Ashrei* and *Aleinu*, the pillars of her life since her dear Mordechai had passed away, she'd murmured the words of the short chapter coldly and without feeling, but never missed a day.

She couldn't formulate what it was she was praying for, so she just repeated the words, hoping they would somehow form a prayer, like the prayer of the shepherd who only knew the *aleph-beis* and so shouted the letters from the hilltops. She had hoped that that would ease her soul.

She hadn't realized until she was sitting in the car next to Aharon as he drove her home, after she'd heard of Mordy's near-miraculous renaissance, that the answers to prayers have a way of sneaking up on a person. She'd said the *kapitel* every single day for fourteen years without an ounce of expectation, her motivation being solely the *emunas chachamim* that her parents, grandparents, and husband had instilled in her, and that was unbreakable.

Not once, not after Devorah had safely recovered from the dangerous birth, not after observing the warm and supportive relationship Aharon and his wife had developed between them, not after the birth of her beloved Ephraim Baruch, grandchild of her heart, and the other — all healthy — grandchildren, and not after Aharon's astounding financial success, not once had she attributed any of these wonderful blessings to that tiny *kapitel* she murmured each day. The forty-four words of thanks, each one a pebble she'd forced from her mouth, had seemed to be a burden, but she now realized it was in fact her greatest blessing. So why should she now be surprised that Mordy had somehow recovered — enough, at least, according to Aharon, to communicate and even make jokes? She remembered the *rav*'s words, that Hashem could contrive a miraculous solution to her dilemma, and He had.

She knew all this, yet she was still determined to fight their decision. Even if her grandson's condition had truly improved, it would still make all of their lives very, very hard if they brought him home. They would become the talk of the town, fingers would point, eyes would roll, tongues would wag, and she could not bear the thought of it. "Aharon, stop it!" she barked suddenly. "You're speaking nonsense and you know it!"

"Mama, I..."

"No!" Even as she spoke she already knew she was wrong. Support him, help him, the voice inside of her urged, but she could not. "A child like that does not belong at home."

Aharon had heard her viewpoint so many times that it almost didn't hurt anymore. He turned his head away from the road for a second and then, before she could rebuke him, he understood.

"You're afraid," he said softly, kindly.

"I'm not," she snapped, but suddenly wasn't so sure. *Am I?*

"I have an idea. Let me take you to see him."

"I will not go," she replied. "I won't set foot in one of those places. Never."

"Just hear me out," said Aharon. He had pulled into her driveway and stopped the car, but instead of walking her in as he usually did, he stayed in the car and kept the motor running.

"No," she said.

But Aharon, his mother's son, was equally tenacious. An idea was forming in his mind, and he wondered whether it would help or make things worse.

"Okay," he said, "then do you mind taking a short ride with me?"

"Where to at this hour?"

"I want to show you something." Yitta wouldn't say no; in fact, this question of Mordy was the only thing they had ever really disagreed on. She knew Aharon did not doubt her love, it was just her understanding that she could not always provide.

He backed carefully out of the driveway, hummed a little under his breath, and the two drove in silence until Aharon pulled up in front of a small strip of stores in another part of town.

"What business do you have here?" she said. She couldn't fathom why Aharon had stopped in front of a Chinese restaurant.

He went around to her side of the car, opened the door for her, and waited patiently for her to emerge. He knew she wasn't old and frail, it was just a way to show her *kavod*. "It's *treif*. I'm not going in. *Ma'aris ayin!*"

"It's okay, Ma," said Aharon. "We'll go around the back. No one will see you." He chuckled a little, as the area was almost completely deserted, and the few passersby would hardly care what an elderly Jewish woman and her son were doing in the neighborhood.

He led her around to the back of the restaurant and in through the service entrance. The strong smell of steaming vegetables (and she hated to think what else) and pungent spices struck her forcefully. Aharon stood by the door, scanning the kitchen until he found what, or whom, he was looking for.

"Mr. Aron!" a voice cried out from inside. A short, broad fellow came bustling toward them. "How are you? I know, no food, no tasting. *Treif. Treif.*"

Ho Yok Weng was one of Aharon's customers, as the exotic produce that Aharon procured was in great demand for Chinese cuisine. He rarely got very close to his customers, he was just cordial enough to maintain a pleasant business relationship. Mr. Weng, however, and his irrepressible good humor and warmth broke through Aharon's carefully woven defenses. He'd visited enough times to know that Mr. Weng was a very special man.

Yitta saw that the restaurant proprietor was walking slightly bent over, and a sort of harness was tied over his clean white apron. Aharon smiled at Mr. Weng. "I was just out with my mother and thought I'd stop in to see how you liked the new shipment of mushrooms."

"Your mother? Hello!" He smiled warmly at Yitta, revealing the absence of several teeth, but the smile was wide and genuine.

It was then that Yitta realized what was odd about Mr. Weng. As he turned to the side, she saw a child of about ten or eleven in a carrier strapped onto his back. The boy's eyes were open but unseeing, dark and milky against a face the color of a stormy sky.

Mr. Weng observed Yitta's expression and sought to assure her. "He's my son. He fell down when he was a little boy and no wake up."

"Why are you carrying him around like that?" asked Yitta, restraining her fury at Aharon for bringing her here and forcing her to see this. "Why isn't he in a hospital?"

"Why hospital?" replied Mr. Weng. "He's not sick. Only his body is sleeping. His heart and soul are awake!"

CHAPTER 31

His mother's silent treatment, so familiar from his childhood, was still ringing in his ears when Aharon walked into his own home. He was anxious to discuss everything with Devorah and was disappointed, but not totally surprised, to find her already asleep. It had been a long, draining day for both of them, and he too was looking forward to a good night's rest.

But alas, it was not to be. He tossed and turned for a few hours before giving up and heading down to the kitchen for a cup of coffee, figuring he might as well start the day already.

If he thought he was going to sit there in solitude, however, he was mistaken. Ephraim Baruch was already seated at the table, still in his flannel pajamas, with his head bent over sheets of paper and a cup of coffee in front of him.

"Good morning," said Aharon casually, as though they often met at that hour of the morning. "What are you looking at?"

Ephraim did not lift his head to answer his father's question, his eyes were locked on the paper in front of him. "I'm not sure," he replied. "I found these on the kitchen table." He lifted up the papers, covered on both sides in Devorah's distinctive handwriting.

Aharon walked over to take a look, then regarded Ephraim with dismay. "Do you always read Mommy's things, Ephraim?"

"No! Never!" he replied. "Well, not never, but usually never. But it wasn't my fault this time. I saw my name and I—"

"Mmm," said Aharon. "It's not right, but I probably would have done the same. So, what is it?"

"Are you allowed to read Mommy's things?" Ephraim asked.

That was a good question. Had they ever discussed it? He had made it clear to Devorah, early on and as nicely as possible, where his boundaries were, but had she ever said anything about it? He couldn't recall. But leaving this on the kitchen table was, in his opinion, an open invitation.

"Um, more or less. We have an understanding," replied Aharon.

Ephraim was skeptical. "Well, if you think it's allowed..."

"Ephraim, I think there is some kind of chutzpah going on here, but I can't quite put my finger on it enough to rebuke you. Just give me the papers, okay?"

Ephraim clenched his lips and handed them over, watching his father carefully as Aharon scanned what Devorah had composed, apparently the night before, judging by the date in the top right corner.

The notes listed, in detail, in tiny letters — which was a hint in itself of her state of mind, as Devorah's handwriting was usually large and loopy — the entire story of Mordy from beginning to end, in a kind of shorthand that Aharon understood perfectly but might have confounded the normally bright Ephraim. She had ended with a list of pros and cons.

Aharon nodded a bit, walked over to the cabinet, removed the glass mug he favored, and poured a cup of the hot, fresh coffee — black and instant — that Ephraim had already prepared measured out for him. Aharon had to admit the coffee tasted much better than coffee from the fancy coffeemaker he had bought Devorah for Chanukah a few years earlier.

He had delayed long enough, trying to figure out what to say, and he couldn't put it off any longer. "So, what do you think?" he asked.

Ephraim looked up at him with his clear, frank gaze. "I don't get it. What's the question?"

"What do you mean?" asked Aharon.

"Well, if it was me, I would really want you to take me home, no matter how happy I seemed to be. How happy can a kid be without his parents? He doesn't even know what he's missing."

Mipi ollelim v'yonkim, thought Aharon. *Out of the mouths of babes... It's all so clear to them.*

"You're right, Ephraim, but sometimes it just isn't that simple. It will be very hard to take care of Mordy, and also, it breaks my heart that he isn't—"

"*Frum*," Ephraim completed the sentence for him. "Tatty, I'm shocked," he said, and Aharon knew that this time it was not with chutzpah but with the honest feeling of a twelve-year-old. "Don't you always tell us that no Jew is ever lost? You've always brought home the weirdest people for Shabbos, and that's what you say. How can you not feel that way about your own son?"

And this is exactly where and how Devorah found them as she stood just outside the door of the kitchen. She had foolishly left her list on the table for easy access so she wouldn't have to go looking for it when Aharon came home. It was not meant to be read without explanation. It looked a lot colder on paper than the way she would have explained it.

Both Aharon and Devorah had the same thought: Ephraim's insight was rather frightening. He had somehow combined the respectable intelligence of both of them and turned it into a supernova of knowledge and understanding that caught them off guard.

She thought Aharon might need some help at this point, so she stepped into the kitchen, pretending she had just woken up.

"Good morning," she said through a conveniently genuine yawn. It was only the start of the day and she was already tired.

"Good morning, Mommy," said Ephraim sternly, in silent rebuke.

Aharon lifted his eyebrows in her direction as though to warn her that she was in for it. Once Ephraim turned his attention to something, he did not let go of it easily.

"Good morning, *tzaddik'l*," she said. "You're up early." She purposely ignored the papers now back in his hands, but he wasn't letting her off easy.

"Mommy, with all due respect…"

Devorah suppressed a smile. They had taught him to say that if he planned to say something in the least bit critical of an adult. *At least our* chinuch *is working, she thought.*

"With all due respect," he repeated, sensing her attention wandering, "I think you are making a very big mistake." He shook the papers in her direction. "And I think Tatty agrees with me."

"Whoa," said Aharon. "Hold on there. Whatever happens, I agree with Mommy, no matter what it is."

Ephraim looked at him, puzzled.

"Never mind," said Devorah. "I appreciate your input, Ephraim, and I admit I made a mistake, leaving this out for anyone to see." She stared at him sharply. "However, this is up to Tatty and Mommy to decide."

She tried to sound convincing, but they both knew that young Ephraim was one hundred percent right.

have an idea," said Ephraim. Devorah rolled her eyes.

"*Tzaddik'l*, I just told you it's up to Tatty and Mommy. We're not taking suggestions."

"I know, but just listen." Ephraim's eyes were shining the way they did whenever he had a brainstorm. They could almost hear the cogs spinning furiously. "Right, Mordy won't become *frum* overnight — well, like, no one would. It's not a good strategy to bring him home and try to do it all at once."

"Nu?" said Aharon, listening intently. It could have been embarrassing, but sometimes the truth came from unexpected places, and he respected that, but still, it was hard hearing it from his own son. Wasn't a father supposed to know best?

"It's almost Pesach." Ephraim rushed onward. "Isn't he an *eino yode'a lish'ol*? How about let's invite him for Pesach? You would do it for anyone else, wouldn't you? If someone called you and said, 'Hey, we have a fourteen-year-old boy with, whatever it is he has, whatever it's called, and he needs a place to stay for Pesach, we'll send a helper with him,' wouldn't you say yes? You would. You know you would. You'd make it work."

He looked eagerly at his father, then turned to his mother, but the two of them were still as statues, shocked into the clarity they had been seeking.

"Step by step," Dr. Cohen had said. Devorah had thought he was referring to the preparations for bringing Mordy home permanently.

But who said they had to do everything all at once? It would be hard enough to arrange everything even for a short visit, but it would not be impossible.

Devorah's eyes gleamed. She looked at Aharon, but he covered his eyes, unwilling to reveal his true emotions while Ephraim was sitting between them. He smothered the urge to hug and kiss his son and thank him with all his heart for offering an excellent solution to a difficult problem, because he was sure Ephraim wouldn't understand his reaction.

"We'll think about it," he said instead. *You are so smart, you are so special, you have such a wonderful heart, how did we merit a son like you?* "Now go upstairs and get ready for yeshivah. It's almost time to go."

"You'll really think about it? I could help. You know I could."

"We know," they said together, and then they laughed a little but didn't say any more until Ephraim left the room.

"That kid," said Devorah as soon as the door swung shut behind him, putting her hand to her forehead.

"Takes after his mom," said Aharon.

"Not," said Devorah. "But he's right, isn't he?"

"He is," said Aharon.

"Okay," said Devorah. "Then yes."

———————◦○◦———————

Despite Ephraim's daily reminders, it was a couple of weeks before Devorah called Dr. Cohen, his harsh words of warning were still ringing in her ears. One morning, before opening her salon, she gave Mrs. Mirsky a call and asked if they could meet.

"Of course, my dear," she replied. Her voice embraced Devorah like the warmest blanket. "Should I come to you?"

"No! I'll come to you." After that first visit, Devorah was careful not to impose on the older woman. "How soon may I come?"

"Anytime. I'll be waiting." Devorah dressed quickly but carefully because, although she knew Mrs. Mirsky would never judge her, the woman's easy elegance made Devorah want to live up to it. After a quick cup of coffee and a bran muffin, she checked her makeup once more and left the house. She'd hardly rang the doorbell when Mrs. Mirsky opened the door wide and wrapped her arm around Devorah's shoulder. Escorting Devorah inside and seating her, Mrs. Mirsky hurried away to bring refreshments, as she did for every guest who crossed her threshold. As Devorah settled herself on the comfortable but classy couch, her eyes were drawn to a large photo album opened up on the coffee table. She leaned forward and very hesitantly picked it up. It commanded her full attention. For of course it displayed pictures of Ruvy at various ages. Baby, toddler, eight or nine, bar mitzvah. She turned page after page, unable to take her eyes off the images of the much-loved and happy boy, raised by a family who cherished him.

"Don't think we have pictures only of Ruvy." Mrs. Mirsky laughed. "Each child has his or her own album. But he is so photogenic, isn't he?" Devorah was loath to reply, because if she hadn't known the whole story she'd have found the pictures of Ruvy off-putting, as the boy was far from attractive. But she could see his mother's love reflected in him, from his neat yarmulke and *peyos* to the beautiful outfits he invariably wore. She was sure Mrs. Mirsky had purposely left the album out for her to see.

"He is," she said eventually, meaning it. "He's lovely."

As if on cue, Ruvy bounded into the house, a huge smile wreathing his face.

"Hullo, Mommy!" he said, throwing his whole being into his greeting. Realizing there was a guest then, he pulled back, but only a little. He smiled at her and said, "We listened to two Avraham Fried discs in a row today!"

Devorah didn't know what to say, but Mrs. Mirsky did. "How wonderful!" she said, as though Ruvy had told her he'd won a million dollars, but naturally and genuinely, not the fake, exaggerated response she herself might have come up with. "You must have really enjoyed that!" They smiled at each other with such warmth that Devorah teared up.

"I made you a nice snack," said Mrs. Mirsky. "It's on the table in the kitchen." She watched as Ruvy left the room, her smile following him as he went.

"Wow," said Devorah. "I think you just answered all my questions." Mrs. Mirsky smiled, but Devorah again took note of how gaunt she was. Despite her positive attitude, surely raising Ruvy alone had taken its toll.

"Uh, we are thinking of having Mordy home, for Pesach. A trial run!" She didn't mention that her twelve-year-old son had given them the idea.

Mrs. Mirsky nodded her head in approval. "That's a very good idea," she said, sounding a little surprised. "A wonderful idea. Nobody says you have to take it all on at once." She left unspoken the fact that she had had the good fortune to raise Ruvy from birth and thus grew together with him.

"Remember, though," said Mrs. Mirsky, reading her mind once again, "my relationship with Ruvy wasn't built in one day." She bent over slightly to look directly into Devorah's eyes. "It takes time. Trial and error. Step by step."

There it is again, Devorah thought, *my new theme song.*

CHAPTER 33

JEREMY

Nice to hear from you again, Mrs. Landau," I said pleasantly. I had been wondering when she would call.

"Thank you, Dr. Cohen. There are a few things I'd like to discuss with you. When would be a convenient time to meet?"

I tried to pin down her tone of voice. In the few times I'd spoken to her, she'd made her state of mind very clear. First the mama bear routine, then she became angry, then scared, then angry again. This voice was a new one. Determined? I wasn't sure.

"Right now is just fine," I replied, wishing I had closed the door to my office. Not everybody had to hear this conversation and, truth be told, if it got heated I didn't want anyone to overhear that either. I wanted to stay coolly professional.

"Oh, okay," she said. She may have been hoping she'd have a day or two more to plan what she should say to me, but if she had already made the effort to call, I figured I might as well make time for her. And truthfully, with the hospital emptying out so quickly, there wasn't much for me to do in any case.

"We were thinking of...actually, um, bringing Mordy home for what you might call a trial run."

I sat up then, immediately on the alert. "What is that supposed to mean?" I asked. I did not want Murray tossed around like a ping-pong ball.

She hesitated. "Don't you think it would be better if we spoke in person?" she asked, clearly sensing my hostility.

"No, let's talk now," I demanded. "When you say 'trial run,' what would that entail?"

"Well, as I'm sure you know," she said, "we will be celebrating Passover soon. It's when we commemorate the Jews leaving Egypt."

"Excuse me," I interrupted, rather rudely. "I don't need a Jewish history lesson. I know what Passover is. But what does that have to do with Murray?"

"Well," she said again, "as I'm sure you also know, Passover is eight days long—"

"No, it isn't. It's two nights, two Seders," I said.

"No, it is really eight days," she said evenly. I could tell she was nervous, though. "Two *Sedarim*, uh Seders, then some days in between that are like half-holidays, where we spend time together, go on outings, that sort of thing, then two more days of holiday at the end.

"It's a nice, festive time and we think it will be a good time for Mordy to join us. We would all be home and relaxed, and I think he would enjoy himself and we could sort of get to know each other — as a family."

I sat back in my chair, but I was listening carefully, turning over what she was saying in my mind. One part of me was bristling. I had warned them about the religious stuff, even though I knew it was not my place, but I couldn't help it.

On the other hand, my rational mind knew very well that this was an excellent, even brilliant, idea. Passover was a good time for what she called a trial run — not too heavy, and I could tell Murray beforehand about the bread thing and all that. He'd be able to handle it.

And I don't have to tell him it's an important religious holiday, I can just tell him it's something Jews do, like Thanksgiving. They always make a big deal about Thanksgiving here, so he'll get the idea. That would work. Yes, that would work. The answer was yes.

"Dr. Cohen? Are you still there?"

"Yes, I'm sorry. I'm here. I was just considering the idea, and I think it could work. But as I said before, it would still require a lot of planning and preparation. Are you ready for that?"

"Whether I am or not is irrelevant. I'm prepared to do whatever is necessary for Mordy to have what he needs. I was wondering, though, since we won't have much time for training, would it be possible to send an aide with him, someone who is familiar with his care?"

Another good idea. They had obviously given this a lot of

thought, but I couldn't very well send big Nurse Michael to spend Passover with them.

Then the perfect solution occurred to me.

"I don't think we'd have any aides available, but if it's okay with you," as if she would say no, "I can accompany him myself."

I tried to hide my reluctance, remembering those Seders at my grandfather's house and how I hated them, but I knew I was the only one who could make this happen. I wanted Murray to have a good, decent life, and if it meant rejoining his family, I wasn't going to do anything to hold him back.

Then again, if I myself got an intimate look at the Landau family, I could tell whether or not they were fanatics he needed protection from.

Mrs. Landau had grown awfully quiet. I imagine that she too was mulling over the situation and trying to decide if my being there would ruin the whole thing.

But a mother is a mother. "I see," she said. "That would solve the problem, wouldn't it? We wouldn't have to worry about Mordy's health and safety, knowing you were there. It's a good idea. Yes, okay." She waited a second before saying — begrudgingly, I think — "It wouldn't be the worst thing in the world for you to join us for the Seder. You're also a Jew, after all."

Oh, no, she doesn't! I was not going to let her get away with that. "Mrs. Landau, I must tell you right now that I will be there only in the capacity of Murray's medical supervisor. Under no circumstances will I be pressured to participate in your antiquated religious rituals."

And then she had the gall to laugh. "It sounds like you're reading from one of those anti-Semitism pamphlets. Don't worry, Dr. Cohen. We won't force you to drink wine and eat matzah. Now, can we get back to Mordy? Can you tell me exactly what we'll need to get for him, and from where? I want to get started."

I tried to mentally lower my blood pressure as I rattled off a list of the things we would need. I could bring most of the stuff from the hospital; many of the patients used to go out on furloughs and Dr. Boyer allowed them to take the equipment they needed as long as they returned it. He also took a deposit, which I knew the Landaus would not mind putting down.

Mrs. Landau asked a lot of questions, and by the time the conversation ended we had more or less called a truce between us. But I had a feeling that the battle was far from over.

CHAPTER 34

E phraim Baruch was so thrilled with the plan to bring his brother home for Pesach that he threw himself into the preparations wholeheartedly. Besides helping with the regular cleaning and scouring for Yom Tov, he had volunteered to give up his room for Mordy and Dr. Cohen. He worked tirelessly cleaning it, dousing every comer with bleach to make sure "there were no germs that could hurt Mordy!"

He gave the entire room plus the ceiling a fresh coat of paint, wobbling cheerfully at the top of the stepladder, then left the windows open for two days to dispel the fumes quickly.

He accompanied his father to buy the special bed, and then to the medical supply store for the antipressure mattress and pillows "to prevent bedsores," Ephraim read off from the list. He'd made his own copy and carried it around with him everywhere.

His excitement was contagious, even the two little girls, Maya, nine, and Rena, five, wanted to help — although they weren't quite sure what it was all about. They followed Ephraim Baruch's orders like trained soldiers. Dr. Cohen came to the house a few times to make sure everything was up to his standards. It was ironic because on the ward the patients sometimes lacked even the basics. He had even added a few items to the list he gave Devorah, things that Murray could easily do without, but he reasoned that if Murray could have the best, why shouldn't he? He didn't require a book with maps of the world and another on aquatic sea life, both in full color, but if the Landaus were happy to supply them, according to Jeremy's calculation, they should. He didn't want Murray to be too pampered, especially if the arrangement did not work out, so he held back on the idea of a motorized wheelchair and settled for a top-of-the-line manual one.

After he'd spoken to Mrs. Landau, Jeremy started dropping hints to Murray about the "trial run." Jeremy couldn't help but think of it in quotes, but he couldn't think of a better term for it either. To Murray he only referred to it as a visit.

"If we could arrange it, what would you think about a short visit?" He couldn't bring himself to say "home," even though he supposed that's what it was. What made something a home? Was it the house itself, the people in it, the feeling of warmth or the opposite? If Murray didn't even know his own family, could it be called his home? But the hospital wasn't "home" either. Jeremy groaned. He had to stop ruminating and start preparing Murray in earnest.

"Did you like the Landaus? Would you want to spend more time with them? Uh...there's a holiday called Passover... Have you ever heard of it? It's like a Jewish Thanksgiving!"

It didn't take long for Murray to catch on that Jeremy was up to something. "What's going on, Doc? What are you trying to tell me?" Jeremy knew Murray would catch on eventually, but he had still felt it important to pave the way. Now he spoke frankly to his patient, sitting down facing Murray in his wheelchair. He picked up the Rubik's cube Murray used to strengthen his hands and fingers. He'd solved the puzzle long before, while Jeremy had yet to succeed even once.

"Uh...the Landaus called me," he began.

"My parents?" Murray's eyes lit up.

"Yes," said Jeremy. "Your parents!" He outlined the plan and watched Murray's excitement gain strength and take off like a tornado.

"Really?" he interjected after every sentence. "Really?"

Finally, Jeremy burst out laughing. "Yes! Really! Is that all you can say?"

"And you'll be coming with me?" asked Mordy.

"I will," said Jeremy.

"And it's Passover? I'm going to read up on it. I'm going to be a Passover expert!"

"There's no need to get carried away," Jeremy said quickly. He didn't want to put too much emphasis on that part of the plan. "I think they'll just be happy to have you there!"

When Yitta heard the news of the impending visit, she realized that she was fighting a losing battle. Observing her beloved grandson's enthusiasm and genuine excitement was the only thing that could soften her heart toward Mordechai, if only not to disappoint Ephraim. How could she object to such a pure act of love on Ephraim's part?

She could still invoke the image of that Chinese child Aharon had taken her to see, totally oblivious, consciously, at least, but who knows what happens beneath the level of consciousness of the great love bestowed on him, riding on his father's back like any healthy toddler might. She had stayed furious with Aharon until she couldn't bear it any longer, but they never spoke of it. Aharon had made his point and she was indeed pierced by it.

So, she worked along with Ephraim, doing whatever her grandson asked and marveling at his maturity, hoping and, yes, praying that everything would go smoothly. She would never forgive Mordy if Ephraim's heart was broken along the way.

Before they knew it, the day arrived. There had been much discussion of when exactly to bring Mordy home. If he arrived at the last minute before sundown of *Leil Pesach*, the trial run could dissolve into pandemonium, and they didn't want to frighten Mordy. But to bring him home a day or two before so that he could get acclimated might create too much pressure on everyone. They decided to bring Mordy home the day before Erev Pesach. By then, the cleaning would be finished, the house would start to absorb the wonderful aromas of chicken cooking in wine, tzimmes, and flanken, and vats of compote. Mordy could join them for *bedikas chametz, biur chametz,* and all the last-minute preparations. They would just have to make sure they were fully organized so that all would proceed calmly and peacefully when Mordy and Dr. Cohen arrived.

The whole family, even Yitta, now waited quietly in the living room. Up until an hour before, the house had rumbled as though in an earthquake, with feet pounding up and down the stairs, two vacuums running at full blast, last-minute hammering and voices calling to each other like a flock of seagulls hovering over the sea.

But then, as if by prior agreement, the din diminished. They each retired to their rooms, even the younger ones — again picking up on the atmosphere without knowing why — where they combed their hair, washed their faces, changed into their nicest clothes. The hush was palpable: something incredible was about to happen.

CHAPTER 35

Bringing Mordy home, even for a short visit — or trial run, as they all now called it — was no simple task, and while Jeremy didn't quite regret agreeing to it, he felt that he hadn't been given enough time to prepare Murray and himself, to tell the truth. He felt guilty when he realized that, with the exception of the time Murray had spent in the hospital when the surgeon operated on his cleft lip and palate, Murray had never left Ravensfield for longer than a few hours at a time.

He'd seen very little of the outside world on the extremely rare day trips the hospital or Jeremy himself had arranged.

Jeremy had convinced Dr. Boyer occasionally to allow him the use of the hospital's minibus. He would pack it with as many children and staff as could safely fit and bring them to a park or other wheelchair-accessible place like the Staten Island Ferry.

The wind was sometimes an issue, and some of the kids required medical attention on their return. But the lift to their spirits, he'd found, was always beneficial.

Jeremy had done so much for those kids, much more than any other staff member, he thought. But then again, what did he know? He hadn't broadcast his activities; perhaps there were others who'd also extended themselves beyond the regular work hours.

He mentally reviewed the roster of colleagues, examining their faces as though viewing them through a two-way mirror in a police lineup. The irony of that unfortunate comparison was not lost on him. Did he blame them for merely doing their jobs but no more? No, he couldn't, but there was not one person he would consider as dedicated as he was, and no one knew better than he the price he had paid for it. He would see his colleagues go home to their families, he would hear them complain good-naturedly (most of the time) about their spouses, brag about their children. These kids were all Jeremy had.

Even though the Landaus would be supplying just about everything Murray would need physically, preparing him emotionally to leave the hospital for an entire week had resulted in an unexpected physical response to the excitement. A short time before the "big day," a 103-degree fever overtook him, and if not for Big Mike's quick reaction, he would have been one step away from having a febrile seizure. Then he developed skin sores on his legs, and his neck began to wobble uncontrollably, despite them having worked for a long time on strengthening it. After each onslaught, Jeremy was on the verge of canceling the visit. He could not in good conscience expose Murray to more foreign germs when he had insufficient antibodies to protect himself. Jeremy had no choice but to start him on prophylactic antibiotics, and that too took its toll. He asked himself over and over again if it was worth it, obsessively weighing the pros and cons.

The cons were way ahead in his view, but one pro argument held him back from postponing the trial run so powerfully that he could not bring himself to do it: Murray's face. His enthusiasm, his shining eyes, his nonstop chatter, and his insistence on meeting everyone in the family beforehand.

In the end Murray had been too ill, so he'd called Aharon and Devorah from the nurses' station and asked them to bring pictures of everyone so he'd know who everyone was. Murray had "hitchhiked" in his wheelchair to the hospital library to search for books on Passover but returned to his room woefully empty-handed, with the exception of a few books for children. They provided Murray with a general idea of the holiday but not enough to reveal its deeply religious nature.

Murray was usually fairly quick on the uptake, but a person doesn't know what he doesn't know, and his utter lack of exposure to Judaism blocked his full understanding. Jeremy left it that way, wondering how the actual experience would affect Murray.

Meanwhile Jeremy and the medical team, well aware of the importance of the trial run, worked valiantly to put out the fires Murray's body was igniting one after the other and to strengthen him physically. They seriously considered tranquilizing him to calm his excitement and let his body heal, but they couldn't bear the thought of watching Murray act like a zombie when he so deserved every ounce of joy just the mere expectation was giving him.

The first Seder was to be on Wednesday night, and they were scheduled to arrive on Monday. Jeremy decided that if Murray's health wasn't completely back to normal by the Thursday before, he would call it off. He didn't voice his decision, but super-sensitive Murray intuited it, and by Wednesday, a day early, he was back to his baseline and even a little above and, therefore, fit to travel.

Jeremy was ashamed enough to admit to himself that he had been hoping Murray would have a relapse and they wouldn't have to go, but it seemed just the opposite was happening. Murray was eating more, sleeping better and able to sit upright for slightly longer periods in his wheelchair. In the same unusual way his body had broken down, it was now building itself up as if by an unseen force, and by the time Monday rolled around, Jeremy wouldn't have been totally surprised if Murray had stood up and walked out the door by himself — so to speak.

Murray was strangely silent as Jeremy bundled him up — it was still chilly for this time of year — and secured him and his wheelchair in the van. He had already loaded everything else, including all kinds of treats and gifts from the staff. He didn't know how the Landaus were going to react to the non-kosher candies and wine, but decided that it was their problem. He briefly debated leaving everything in the car, but Murray had already scrutinized each package for "leaven" and would be disappointed if he couldn't give the gifts to his family. Murray didn't know, of course, that the food also had to be kosher.

Both he and the Landaus will be embarrassed, Jeremy thought to himself. *And I'm being such a hypocrite. Embarrassment is much worse than disappointment. I'd better do this all the way or turn around and go back to the hospital.*

Self-chastened, he explained to Murray that they would stop off at the kosher store and get real kosher-for-Passover treats. He could still remember the sugared orange peels at his grandparents' house, their strange yet pleasant taste, so sweet it made his teeth ache; perhaps the Landaus would enjoy them as well.

CHAPTER 36

T he collective hush held as the assembled Landaus watched through the large picture window as the van pulled into the driveway. The spell was broken as a debate broke out whether they should all go outside to greet them or wait inside.

It was Yitta's opinion, which was accepted unanimously, that it would be better to wait inside because he might feel embarrassed to have them all watching him being lifted out of the van and getting settled in his wheelchair, as he might want them to see him at his best.

Another discussion immediately ensued about whether to open the door before they rang the bell or wait...until Ephraim's patience snapped. He flung open the door and ran over to the van, nearly knocking Jeremy over. Flushed with adrenaline and momentum, Ephraim didn't quite know what to do with himself, so he clapped Dr. Cohen on the shoulder and was about to do the same to Mordy, but Jeremy stopped him just in time.

"Easy does it, cowboy," said Jeremy.

"Cowboy?" Ephraim said. "Like Purim?"

"Purim?" said Jeremy. "I thought it was Passover."

Their verbal dance was interrupted by a smiling Mordy. "You must be Ephraim! My brother! Hello!" One of the many things the two boys had in common was the decibels to which their speech climbed when they were excited. "I am!" he cried. "I am Ephraim! Ephraim Baruch Landau!" He still didn't know what to do with his hands, so he put them on his hips. But Mordy put out both of his hands and grabbed Ephraim's wrists and shook them. His grip took Ephraim by surprise, but only for a second and he bent down so that his face was on a level with Mordy's, and as he smiled, an identical smile reflected back at him.

If it wasn't such a shock he would have thought it weird. He had a cousin who looked a little bit like him, but his sisters were girls and looked nothing like him. But this was like looking in a mirror at something exactly the same yet something very different, and it was a little scary, also, because Mordy looked like what Ephraim might look like if he wasn't *frum*. Jeremy took hold of the handles of the wheelchair, making sure all the necessary bags and tubes were tucked under the blanket wrapped around Mordy's legs. He maneuvered him up the newly installed ramp with smug satisfaction.

On one of the many inspection visits to the Landaus', Jeremy had spent a lot of time measuring the doorways throughout the house, and then visited the few places he knew of that had ramps installed. He'd come back then and supervised the construction of the outside ramp leading to the front door.

The Landaus had sought advice on making their entire home, inside and out, wheelchair accessible, and had spared no expense to make it happen, and for this Jeremy could not help but have a grudging respect.

The rest of the family soon followed Ephraim and streamed out the door and gathered around the wheelchair. If Jeremy thought Murray would be on "overload" from all the attention, he was deeply mistaken.

It was as if Murray were a human sponge, soaking it up, grabbing at it joyfully with both hands. Jeremy noticed they were reluctant to touch him, but that didn't stop Murray from reaching out to each one and grasping their hands with his exercise-strengthened grip.

The family crowded around the wheelchair, ushering Mordy and Jeremy inside and directly over to the fully extended dining room table, which was filled with delicious-looking platters of food and bowls of snacks and treats.

Mordy had eaten institutional food all his life, with the exception of an occasional snack from a vending machine and food that Jeremy's mother had brought him. So his diet had usually consisted of a variety of brown- and beige-colored food with an occasional grayish-green vegetable thrown in. The only fruit served was apples in the fall, spring and summer, and oranges and tangerines in the winter. He'd seen pictures of gourmet food in books and magazines, but he had not yet tasted any of it.

The Landaus wished to shower Mordy with the best of everything. When Mordy saw this mouthwatering feast spread before him, his smile wavered for the first time. Jeremy couldn't be certain, but was Murray crying? Jeremy pressed lightly on his shoulders, which, surrounded by such specimens of health and vigor, suddenly seemed unbearably frail.

"You're all right," he whispered, speaking to both Murray and himself, for Jeremy, too, was almost moved to tears. His life was in some ways no less circumscribed than Murray's: He too ate most of his meals at the hospital, with the exception of vending machine snacks and his mother's cooking; he too rarely ventured into the outside world; he too rarely socialized and spent time with family, neither his nor anyone else's.

He could feel Murray rally, the thin muscles tightening beneath his grasp, the smile returning to his face. "What is all this?" he asked shakily. Jeremy winced. "It's all so...so colorful!" The adults — even Yitta — all smiled indulgently, and Ephraim too, even if he did not quite understand why.

Suddenly nine-year-old Maya couldn't hold back any longer and walked up to Mordy's wheelchair and pulled on his sleeve.

"Who are you? Why can't you walk? And," she said, pointing to the table, "why are you asking what this is? It's food. Don't you know what food looks like?" Then she burst out crying and ran over to hide her face in Devorah's lap. Maya was young, she'd recover and get used to Mordy, Devorah supposed, but it seemed that they hadn't quite prepared the little girls sufficiently. All their explanations beforehand did not convey the reality to them. When she looked at the big picture through their eyes, she could imagine their fright and confusion, and it felt very familiar. Devorah gazed at the scene as though someone had turned down the volume all the way. Aharon was sitting on one side of Mordy, Ephraim on the other. Jeremy was still standing behind the wheelchair, no one having yet invited him to sit.

Yitta was slowly filling Mordy's plate. Jeremy was remonstrating with her to not give Murray so much to eat all at once.

Maya was crying, and little Rena was curled up on the couch. Devorah's eyes were so dry she could hardly blink as she panned her imaginary viewfinder around the room. She took a deep, deep breath and held it as long as she could.

So this was it, then. It had started. The trial run.

CHAPTER 37

Mordy woke up with a start the morning after his arrival, not sure where he was, until he looked around him. He smiled.

The room they had prepared for him and the doctor was about three times bigger than his room at the hospital. Large windows let the light in, and he enjoyed the feeling of warmth on his face.

The hospital bed was brand-new, the pillows were soft, and the sheets and blankets felt like silk to his touch and were strikingly patterned in different shades of violet. Next to the bed was a long, low bookshelf, filled with all the books he knew Dr. Cohen had asked them to buy for him.

But a quick look the night before had revealed another whole shelf of books with strange, intriguing titles written by authors he'd never heard of: *Akiba* by Marcus Lehmann, *Once Upon a Soul* and *Soul Survivors* by Hanoch Teller, *Avraham ben Avraham* by Selig Schachnowitz.

He'd pointed that one out to Dr. Cohen and asked him how to pronounce the name, but the doctor had turned around quickly, walked over to the bookcase, and scrutinized every book. Then he'd angrily started plucking out some of the books, one after another, but Mordy stopped him. If there was one thing Mordy would not let anyone do, it was take away his books. He so rarely got hold of any new ones that he was not about to let any of these out of his sight until he'd devoured them all.

"These aren't for you," Jeremy had said when Mordy protested.

"I believe they are," Mordy had answered. "I mean, they're here, next to my bed, with all the other books. So they must be for me. Why are you taking them away?"

"I'm not *taking* them. I'm..." Jeremy had taken a deep breath and ostentatiously looked at his watch.

"Listen, buddy, it's been a looong day. Let's get some sleep and we'll talk tomorrow." He had been about to walk out of the room with the books he'd already grabbed, but Murray was watching him. He turned around, smiled, and put them back on the shelves, but he had a feeling the matter was far from over.

Jeremy had watched them the night before — the Landau family in action — and, though he didn't want to admit it, it was a powerful pull. During his preparatory visits he'd seen bits and pieces of their family life but never all of them interacting together as they had done last night.

They'd treated Murray as if he were one of the New Seven Wonders of the World, and while Jeremy was happy for his young patient, he had to keep reminding himself that Murray was not a patient, not a son, but in reality an abandoned child, left on his own in the world before he had any say in the matter.

It burned a little to see them all now, acting like it was the most natural thing in the world for the long-lost son to return home.

Who had been there through all of Murray's many illnesses? Who had taught him, painstakingly, to talk, to read, and even to think? Who had been the one to discover the unique, intelligent individual inside, struggling to get out?

After Jeremy had put out the lights, Murray crooned suddenly, "Are we okay? Are you mad at me?"

"No!" Jeremy had said. "Of course I'm not mad at you."

But was that the truth?

When Jeremy woke up he was greeted by the sight of Murray holding his face up to catch the full rays of the sun.

"You're acting like you've never seen the sun before," said Jeremy.

"This sun must be different from the one we have in Ravensfield," Mordy said. "It feels so nice and warm."

Jeremy chuckled. "It feels that way because *you* feel that way. The Landaus are taking very good care of you."

Murray looked at him oddly. "*You* take care of me. Right?"

"Of course! Always, buddy. I just meant that they were spoiling you rotten. How am I ever going to get you to eat chicken and mashed potatoes after you've had all that gourmet food they're pampering you with? And the presents! Whew! You are one lucky kid."

Mordy blushed. "It feels like it's happening to someone else, you know?"

"I can imagine." While they were talking, Jeremy was going through Murray's morning routine, which he'd rehearsed with Michael — even though he was the one who had devised it, he wanted to make sure Murray would be completely safe while they were away from the hospital. He knew that the Landaus had even taken out insurance to cover Murray in all eventualities.

"Left leg," he ordered. "They seem very nice, though. Do you like them?"

Mordy winced as Jeremy pulled slightly on his ankles to stretch the limbs. "I like all of them. There was even a grandmother there. My...uh...father's mother. Can you believe I have a grandmother?"

"I'm happy for you. Come, let's get you in your chair and we'll go out and face your 'adoring audience.'"

"Hardy har-har."

Jeremy maneuvered the chair out of the room and down the short hallway into the kitchen. They hadn't seen it the night before. They now looked around in astonishment. It looked more like a spaceship than a kitchen. Every surface was covered either in sheets of tin foil, PVC, or plastic wrap. There were white socks on the faucets and most of the cabinets were sealed with tape. On the far side of the kitchen there were two huge closets on wheels, with all the doors ajar.

Mordy's mouth was a full "o" and Jeremy's wasn't much different. But Jeremy began to feel afraid. He knew this was just Passover stuff, but this kind of thing was extreme — even fanatic. Passover in his own house had been hardly any different from the rest of the year. His mother would eat buttered matzah for breakfast, but the rest of the family had eaten bread.

His grandparents' house had been kosher, but nothing like this. There were a few cloths spread around and some large boards covering the counters. In other words, normal.

He was just about to spin Murray around and get them both out of there when he spotted Aharon coming up a flight of stairs from the basement.

"Good morning!" Aharon sang. He came up to Mordy and placed a hand on his shoulder. "I hope you both slept well." He threw his arm out and gestured to the surrounding kitchen. "Pretty crazy, huh? We were up all night getting it ready." He looked over at Mordy then and laughed. "I'm sure you're wondering what this is all about."

"You bet I am," said Mordy.

"Well, I'm going to tell you all about it. But not before some breakfast."

What would you like?"

"Just some toast for me, and coffee," said Jeremy. "It's not Passover yet, right?"

"Me too!" said Murray.

Aharon frowned to himself. That was the last thing he needed right now. But what could he offer them?

He spotted a box of egg matzah they'd been giving the

younger kids. They didn't eat *matzah ashirah* on Pesach and usually put it away with the kitnios. But in this case, it would be just the thing.

"How about some delicious *matzah brei?*"

"What's that?" he and Jeremy asked in unison.

Aharon spread out his arms to encompass them both, but when Jeremy pulled away Aharon pulled him back. "My poor *Yiddishe kinder,* who don't know what *matzah brei* is, you are in for a wonderful treat!"

CHAPTER 38

Jeremy and Mordy watched as Aharon made his way around the kitchen, pulling eggs and milk out of the refrigerator, which was lined with what looked like window screens. In the few times he'd met him, Aharon had seemed reserved. Jeremy had no idea he could be so expansive.

He sat them down, explaining what he was doing as he broke the egg matzah into pieces and soaked it in the milk. Jeremy and Mordy were mesmerized, not so much by what he was doing but by the way he was doing it. Jeremy had never seen anyone so...so...happy? Was that the word he was looking for? The Landau children drifted in one by one, and

Aharon broke into a little dance with each one of them as they entered. Mordy and Jeremy were shocked, however, when Ephraim came in and jumped onto his father, climbing up onto his shoulders like a monkey in a tree.

"What are you doing?" Mordy shouted with glee.

"Don't worry," said Ephraim from his perch. "My father would never let me fall — right, Tatty?" As Devorah entered the kitchen, Ephraim's comment brought them all to a standstill. The moment was so poignant that an observer would have found his eyes filling with tears. For, of course, Ephraim was right: His father would never let him fall. A boy with such a father was both very lucky and blissfully oblivious to his great good fortune. A boy with such a father was strong, he walked straight, held his head high, talked and laughed and sang with utter confidence, because he knew that no matter what happened, his father would be standing right behind him, supporting him.

Comparing the exuberant Ephraim at that moment with the pale, nearly translucent Mordy could have been heartbreaking, for this same father had let Mordy "fall." The one that had been standing behind Mordy all these years was a dedicated and often exhausted doctor. It wasn't anyone's fault, but the difference between the two boys was staggering, and so, they all froze, the truth hanging over them like a mountain.

It could have been heartbreaking, but it wasn't, because Mordy's pure soul came shining through with such force that it was hard to feel sorry for him. All eyes turned to him as he said with shining eyes, "I want to try!"

Jeremy intervened immediately. "Sorry, buddy," he said. "No way!" But the lines were beginning to blur. Who was in charge of Mordy now? The Landaus had signed their rights away when they admitted Mordy to the hospital, so technically, the hospital was in charge, and Jeremy represented the hospital.

Now that the hospital was closing, giving up their custodial rights, who was responsible for Mordy? If the Landaus were, what was to prevent Aharon from bending down, picking up Mordy and letting him try, somehow, to work his way up to Aharon's shoulders?

The two men faced each other, not for the first time and not for the last.

"It's dangerous," Jeremy said quietly.

"I'll hold him tightly. He won't get hurt."

"You're willing to take such a chance?"

That gave Aharon pause. He had to be careful. He knew nothing of Mordy's capabilities, and in his zeal to give him a "normal" life, he could easily end up hurting him. He realized that this was a trial run for him and Devorah as well. He wondered if Jeremy had the power to prevent Mordy from living with them permanently and if he had to submit to whatever the doctor said, even if it had nothing to do with Mordy's health.

He owed Jeremy a debt of gratitude, but where did it end? If he was going to bring Mordy home forever, he was going to be his father in every sense of the word. He looked down at Mordy with a pained smile. "Next time, tzaddik, okay?"

Mordy nodded. "Okay. It just looked like fun. Maybe one day... What's a tzaddik?"

They all watched carefully, and it was clear that the moment had passed without much of an impact. Devorah answered then. "A tzaddik is a person who works hard on himself to do good things and be a good person."

"I don't do that," said Mordy.

"A tzaddik is a person who wants to be close to Hashem, and do His will," added Maya, who had been sitting at the table, quietly observing.

Mordy turned to her and smiled. "I did not understand even one word of what you just said."

"That's because you're not religious," said Maya. "So how would you know?"

Devorah aimed a firm "not-now" look at her daughter, but Maya shrugged. "I'm just saying the truth. He's not like us. How is he going to live here with us?" Devorah walked over to where Maya was sitting. She tapped her on the shoulder and pointed to the hallway. "Why should I go out?" Maya complained. "Why can't I say what I think? You always tell us to 'express ourselves,' so I'm expressing myself. You just don't like what I'm saying."

Ephraim chose that moment to jump off his father's shoulders and land perfectly balanced on the balls of his feet. He held his arms out like an acrobat taking a bow. He was doing it to impress and entertain Mordy, but Mordy's eyes and his attention were focused on his sister.

"Why do you think that? Is there something wrong with me?" he asked. "Do you not want me to be here?"

Maya was nine, clearly precocious, and not always aware that her sharp words didn't just disappear into thin air after she spoke them. Today, they'd landed deep inside Mordy's heart.

"I...no. No. It's not that. I...you..."

Her mother glared at her balefully.

But Mordy smiled. "Cat got your tongue?"

"That's a gruesome image, but yeah, I guess so," said Maya, ashamed of her outburst but unwilling to concede her point.

"Maya, be quiet. You have such a big mouth. Mordy, don't listen to her," Ephraim said. "She doesn't know what she's talking about."

"Ephraim, don't talk to your sister that way," said Devorah, even though deep down she felt the same.

"I think she does," said Mordy. "I think she knows exactly what she's talking about. The only problem is that I don't understand the problem. Can somebody please explain it to me?"

CHAPTER 39

Mordy's question hovered like a cloud of smoke. Devorah, furious with Maya, began speaking to deflect the issue.

"First of all, Mordy, you are not a problem. There is *nothing* wrong with you."

Mordy smiled. "Um, I beg to differ. Have you noticed that I can't walk?"

Devorah was so surprised at his response that she burst out laughing. That broke the tension better than any explanation, and Aharon moved to resume making *matzah brei* for everyone.

"Mommy, these poor people never ate *matzah brei*," Aharon said, indicating Mordy and Jeremy.

"Oh, you are so lucky. Tatty makes the best *matzah brei*," Devorah broke in.

"Are you trying to change the subject?" asked Mordy earnestly. Devorah checked to see if he was kidding and when she saw that he wasn't, she sat herself down across from him and looked him in the eye.

"I wouldn't say that," she replied. "I think that if Maya is upset about something, or if anyone else is upset — and that includes you, my boy — in this family, we let them give their opinion and we listen *respectfully* to what they have to say.

"But I also think that there is a time and a place for everything, and the middle of breakfast on *Erev Bedikas Chametz* is neither the time nor the place for that kind of discussion. The subject deserves better."

Mordy listened, nodding. He looked around and, realizing that Jeremy had left the room, he smiled at his mother more broadly than he might have had Jeremy been hovering nearby. "I really want to thank you for all of this, Mrs. Landau. I feel like it's a dream and I'm gonna wake up soon."

"I'm so glad. Oh, looks like the *matzah brei* is ready. You can eat it with sugar or with salt and pepper. Both ways are good. And by the way," she said, handing him a plate of the steaming *brei*, "I hope that one day you will feel comfortable enough to call me Mom, but until then we need to come up with something besides Mrs. Landau."

Mordy laughed. "I'd start calling you Mom right now, but I don't want to upset Dr. Cohen."

"Oh?" said Devorah.

"He's sensitive about these things. I think he's going to miss me when I come here to live with you. Once the hospital closes he's not going to have anywhere to go. I don't want him to feel bad that I have somewhere to go and he doesn't."

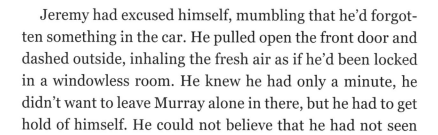

Jeremy had excused himself, mumbling that he'd forgotten something in the car. He pulled open the front door and dashed outside, inhaling the fresh air as if he'd been locked in a windowless room. He knew he had only a minute, he didn't want to leave Murray alone in there, but he had to get hold of himself. He could not believe that he had not seen this coming.

He knew that Murray would be in for some culture shock, that was only to be expected considering the Landaus' extreme lifestyle. There were definitely going to be differences and misunderstandings, but he'd thought... He stopped himself right there. What had he thought? That the issue of Murray not being religious wasn't going to come up? That they were all going to ignore the elephant in the room and pretend that the fact that he wasn't religious made no difference at all?

He had willingly and knowingly brought Murray into a hornet's nest, but then, what choice had he had?

Several months earlier Jeremy had briefly considered adopting Murray. He'd known that the hospital was going to close, and that most of the children would either be returning to their homes or moving on to other state-run institutions. Since Murray's parents had never initiated contact, Jeremy had been afraid that Murray would get sucked into the system with no one to protect him from its harder edges.

He'd started doing some research and might have continued if he hadn't run into his friend Tim Kelly roaming the halls of the hospital. They'd gone down to the cafeteria and grabbed some sandwiches and coffee.

Jeremy was just about to ask Tim what he was doing at the hospital when Tim broke into his thoughts. "How's that kid you were working with? The cleft palate?"

"Murray. Murray Landau. He's doing okay, I think. He's made a lot of progress."

Tim had gazed around the room with an expression that Jeremy could only describe as fond, which he found perplexing.

"You can't get too attached to the patients, you know," Tim had said. "It's not good, not for them and not for you."

"I'm not attached," Jeremy had replied.

"Don't get defensive," Tim had cautioned.

"I'm not defensive," Jeremy had snapped, and they'd both laughed.

"It's funny that you're bringing up his case, though," Jeremy had commented, "because I was actually thinking of adopting the kid."

Tim had stood up as if Jeremy had punched him, and started pacing around the table. "I would *not* do that if I were you. That is *not* a good idea."

"Why not?" Jeremy had asked. Although he knew very well why not, he was finding it difficult to rid himself of the idea. "They're closing the hospital. Where's he going to go? Who's going to take care of him?"

"I hate to point this out to you, pal, but I doubt any court will let you adopt a kid without you being married. That's the first thing," Tim had said. "Besides that, it's a bad, bad, *bad* idea."

That's when Jeremy had realized that there was a lot Tim wasn't saying, that his interest was not theoretical. He'd sat quietly and waited to see if Tim was going to explain himself.

"I guess nobody told you," Tim had said finally.

"Told me what?"

"Didn't you ever wonder why I come around here all the time, how I was able to get you your job, how you got away with sneaking the kid out for the operation?" Tim had asked.

"I wondered," Jeremy had admitted.

Tim had looked at him sadly. "I was brought here as a newborn. I grew up here. My mother died in childbirth and my father just left me in the hospital after I was born. I stayed there for a while and then they sent me here to Ravensfield and put me in a crib. That was about the last time anyone really looked at me."

He paused a moment. "Things were different back then. There were no Jeremy Cohens around, looking to save the world." He smiled tightly, drawing his lips together like a bow, shooting out words like arrows.

"When I was about five, I think, I noticed that this lady started coming around, looking at all the kids, talking to them, giving out candy. I was all for candy, so every time she came, I made it my business to talk to her so she'd give me some. I already knew a little bit about the way the world worked, even at that age.

"After a while I noticed that she wasn't looking at the other kids anymore. She was looking only at me. I didn't mind, what did I know? More candy, right? But you're never going to guess who she was."

CHAPTER 40

J eremy was standing outside the Landaus' house, but his mind was elsewhere.

Dr. Kelly had told Jeremy that he'd been a young, orphaned patient at Ravensfield himself and someone there had become attached to him. Tim had asked Jeremy to guess who she was, but Jeremy hadn't had any idea.

"I know you're wondering who in Ravensfield would do that, right?" Tim had laughed. "No guess? Then I'll tell you. It was Mrs. Boyer, Dr. Boyer's wife."

Jeremy's coffee cup had clattered down onto its saucer. He'd looked up at Tim, whose expression was dead serious.

"Hard to believe, huh?" Tim had continued. "Hard to believe I fell for it. But she and Dr. Boyer didn't have any children of their own, and even though I was pretty much a wild animal at that age, they knew enough about these things to know I could be educated."

Jeremy had tried to smile at Tim's dry humor but couldn't do it. Finally he asked, "So what happened?"

"Before I tell you, I need to say that in spite of the outcome it was still the best thing that ever happened to me. They taught me how to eat properly, how to read, how to keep myself clean, and speak well. I'm grateful to them. Dr. Boyer acted a bit differently as a father. Tough but not quite as cold."

"Okaaay," Jeremy had said, already getting a bad feeling. "And what happened then?"

Tim had sighed and shaken his head. "Well, it turned out the Missus was temperamental, to put it nicely. She wanted a toy child, not a real live messy little boy. The doc didn't mind me so much and he actually handled me pretty well, but after almost four years, Dr. Boyer packed me up and brought me back here to the hospital."

"Wow," Jeremy had responded. "But hadn't they adopted you? Aren't there laws about this?"

"I'm sure there are," Tim had replied. "But they never actually adopted me. It was more like they borrowed me. So for them, returning me was no big deal. No one was the wiser anyway. But it was so hard, for me, after tasting the sweet life in a real home."

"So why do you keep returning here to Ravensfield?" Jeremy had asked. "I would think you'd want to get as far away from here as possible."

"This is my home," Tim had said simply. "My only home."

"And Dr. Boyer..."

"The only father I ever had. Like I said, he doesn't mind me hanging around, even now."

"But I wouldn't do that to Murray. Never!"

Tim had looked at him pityingly, then stood up to go. "Trust me, Cohen. It's a bad idea."

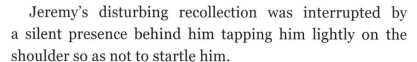

Jeremy's disturbing recollection was interrupted by a silent presence behind him tapping him lightly on the shoulder so as not to startle him.

"Everything okay?" said Aharon. Jeremy's mouth twisted, ready to shoot off a sarcastic reply, but he stopped himself. "Not really," he said instead.

As they stood side by side, the contrast between the two men was stark; even though Aharon was older, he was tall, broad, and pulsating with life. His face was flushed from the warm kitchen and he cut a dignified figure. Jeremy was shorter, slightly hunched over, and his face was worn and far older-looking than his years. If it hadn't been for his mother's attention to his clothes and shoes, he would have appeared slovenly.

Jeremy wasn't entirely depressed, though; the preparations for his planned children's home were falling into place. He'd found two large apartments that the work crew had joined together in a city housing project.

Although it wasn't a prime residential neighborhood it had one major advantage: The neighbors voiced no protest over an influx of residents with special needs. He had attended a residents' meeting and when he presented his proposal, he'd expected opposition and was prepared to counter it. Instead, reactions ranged from total indifference to mild interest.

"They steal?" one man had asked. "We got enough criminals around here. We don't need no more."

Jeremy couldn't picture even one of the children from the ward, with the possible exception of Murray, figuring out any of the steps involved in committing a robbery, but he kept that to himself. "No, sir," he replied. "They are very well behaved."

"Okay, then," the man had said.

So he shouldn't have felt as bad as he did.

"Mordy is worried about you," said Aharon.

Jeremy raised his eyebrows. He'd always felt that their relationship was one-sided, so this came as a surprise.

"Why?"

"He's afraid you'll miss him when he comes to live with us."

"Who says that's going to happen?" Jeremy shot back. "We've been here only one day."

Aharon stroked his beard, a gesture that had begun to annoy Jeremy. "This should be about Mordy," he said. "It shouldn't be a power struggle between you and me. Every decision we make has to be about what's best for him."

Jeremy turned on him fiercely. "How dare you?" he snarled.

Aharon held his hands up. "Hey, hey. This cannot continue. I did not make the decision to admit Mordy to the hospital entirely on my own. We were advised by a wise and knowledgeable rabbi that it would be the best thing for our family."

"As I suspected. You don't think for yourself. How can you be trusted to take care of Murray?" A burst of noise broke out behind them: Maya and Rena had come to drag their father back inside.

"This is not a conversation for now." Or ever, Aharon wished. "Let's just try to get through the next week peacefully. I'll hear you out, I promise, just not now. Let's enjoy the holiday and see where it takes us."

Aharon knew that everything would be different after Pesach; it always was. Things that were unclear before gleamed with clarity after, like a window washed clean of dust and grime. Aharon knew it would be okay. He didn't know how, as Jeremy was so bitter, but he too was a Jew and not immune to the power of Pesach.

As Aharon turned to go, he smiled at the back of Jeremy's head, excited about the miracles he was sure were about to unfold.

"Don't think it's going to be so simple," said Jeremy, not turning around.

"What do you mean?" asked Aharon. He sent the two little girls on ahead of him, and he turned again to Jeremy.

"The only way you'll get to keep Murray is if I sign the release form."

CHAPTER 41

When Aharon returned to the house he was so angry he could hardly speak. Devorah was, fortuitously, standing right by the door. She'd been about to call him in and was able to intercept him. She gestured for him to follow her into her shop — immediately.

"What's going on?" she asked. "What happened?"

"Devorah, if I wasn't so grateful to that guy for taking such good care of Mordy, I don't know what I would do to him right now."

Devorah sat down on one of the soft chairs in the salon

and looked up at Aharon expectantly.

"Cohen just told me that he has the final say on whether we get to bring Mordy home or not!"

"That's ridiculous," said Devorah. "He can't tell us what to do with our son. And anyway, the hospital is closing! What is Dr. Cohen going to do, leave him there all alone?"

Aharon blotted the perspiration from his face with one of the fancy tissues Devorah kept in the salon for her customers.

"He says that for us to take Mordy out, he has to sign the papers in order to make sure that Mordy is going to an 'appropriate venue'! Mordy's own family is not an *appropriate venue*? And as for what he would do with him, he would happily cart Mordy off to that children's group home he's opening after the hospital closes for good. He thinks we're religious fanatics."

Devorah smiled. "Well, he got that right."

"Devorah!"

"Sorry, couldn't resist. Seriously, Aharon, I hear you. I know you're very upset. But we're not bringing Mordy home this minute. Tomorrow is Erev Pesach. Let's just hang out and try to relax. The worst thing we could do right now is make an issue of this. You have got to chill out, Aharon. Do you hear what I'm saying?"

She tried to keep her voice light and a small smile on her face so it didn't sound as if she were scolding him.

"Let's just pull *ourselves* together," she said kindly, "and put on a happy face. Hashem doesn't need us to sell the Torah or *Yiddishkeit*. We're buyers, not sellers. The Torah speaks for itself, okay? This is not a test, Aharon. This is real life." She stood up and looked him in the eye.

He stared back at her as if mesmerized by her words.

"Yes," said Aharon. "You're right, as usual."

The excitement in the house was palpable as Aharon prepared to perform *bedikas chametz*. He stood in the middle of the living room and made the *berachah* while Maya stood at his side armed with a flashlight, a bag filled with ten pieces of bread, each wrapped in aluminum foil, and a pencil and paper to write down where they were hidden. She handed some to Ephraim and Rena, then placed one or two in Mordy's lap.

"We hide these so Tatty will have something to find," she explained. They'd already instructed him on *bedikas chametz*. Maya got behind Mordy's wheelchair and said, "Tell me where to go!"

Mordy, thinking quickly, directed her to the couch and placed one wrapped piece behind a large pillow, and then they moved to the stairs, where he placed one inside Rena's shoe that was lying there.

"Will he look there?" asked Mordy.

"Don't worry, I'll make sure he does!" said Maya.

Aharon came up from the basement where he'd gone to make sure his workroom was closed and locked. He often sold all his products before Pesach — not only because he didn't always know exactly what was in them, but also because he wanted to make sure he would not be tempted to work. He always missed out on a few big sales over Pesach, but somehow, he made up for it later in the year.

Everyone, including Mordy, was shouting excitedly and directing Aharon this way and that way to make sure he found all ten pieces, and of course he did. There'd been one year, though, when the tenth piece had not turned up, so now they were extra careful. Mordy shouted with glee when Aharon found his piece in Rena's shoe with some helpful prodding from Maya. And the more Mordy's face glowed, the more Jeremy glowered, threatening to put a damper on everything.

Help arrived from the most unexpected corner.

"Such a tumult!" Yitta said, sitting down across from Jeremy at the kitchen table and smiling. "I think they're putting on an extra bit of a show for Mordy," she said. "Aharon is such a wonderful father."

Jeremy suddenly saw the image of his grandfather standing in the kitchen holding a short, wide candle, opening every drawer and cabinet, running the candle along each side and corner and looking sharply at Nana after each one. She would nod nervously and Papa would move on to the next cabinet.

Luckily, he'd only search the kitchen, at least while Jeremy was there. His mother would be in the other room, looking through a magazine, and it was his father who'd put one hand on his shoulder and the other on his brother, Alex's, and held them firmly in place until Papa had finished.

Jeremy recalled, sitting there with Yitta, a feeling of holding his breath and letting it out only once Papa had finished. Why did he have to check every nook and cranny when he knew very well that Nana kept the house spotless even when it wasn't Pesach, and that Mommy had been over a few times to help Nana clean even though there wasn't one crumb anywhere? Didn't Papa realize that?

Jeremy looked around at the "spaceship" kitchen and compared it to the grim, dingy walls of his grandparents' house, gazed at all the happy faces and compared them with Papa's accusing glare. He had loved his father, but he and Alex had never clung to him as the Landau kids did to Aharon. Why hadn't they?

"Dr. Cohen?" said Yitta. "You look as if you could use a drink."

She stood up and filled a paper cup with water. As he reached out to take it from her, it was only after he exhaled deeply that Jeremy realized he'd been holding his breath. Again.

"It will be all right," said Yitta.

"I can't do this," said Jeremy, gritting his teeth.

"You can, and you will. Do it for Mordy."

"Murray."

"Whichever. Just do it."

CHAPTER 42

I t was rare indeed to share the event with a child who was hearing the story of *Yetzias Mitzrayim* for the first time, with no preconceived notions or prejudices. Although Aharon included all the children as he conducted the Seder, it was clear that it was essentially taking place between Aharon and Mordy. Never had Aharon felt a mitzvah fill his heart and soul with such fierce emotion. He had to hold himself back, afraid he would scare Mordy off, but even so his soul was on fire. The others held back in silence, aware that something miraculous was going on even if they could not define it. Maya had been prepared to fight Mordy for center stage, unwilling to share her father's attention. However, before long the matter was taken out of Aharon's hands when Maya fell asleep on the couch, followed shortly by Rena. Ephraim was only too happy to join his father in retelling the story of the Haggadah, taking turns as they recounted the plagues and the miracles with relish, finding themselves speaking to a captive audience. Mordy was enthralled. Devorah, Yitta, and Jeremy sat quietly and observed, each laden with their own thoughts. Devorah was bursting with pride, Yitta was missing her late husband deeply, still feeling uncertain at someone else's Seder table even if it was her own son's. Jeremy, trying to take Yitta's advice, leafed through the pages of the Haggadah and cooperated when instructed to wash and dip, and drink wine from his cup.

If he had known that Passover would burn so hot inside him, that he would be plagued with painful memories and his own unanswered questions, he'd have thought twice about accompanying Murray. He could still call a nurse to take his place, but was afraid that wouldn't go over very well with the Landaus.

He could tell Murray was tiring, he needed to eat something and get to bed. He had no energy reserves to draw on and no way to catch up if he overdid it. Making up for it the next day wouldn't work for him. Jeremy started to fidget, debating whether to interrupt or let Murray grab in a few minutes more of whatever it was that was making him so happy. But when Murray's head began to wobble, so slightly that only he noticed it, Jeremy knew it was time to intervene.

Jeremy moved over to the empty seat next to Murray and started taking his pulse, signaling to him that this charmed evening was about to end.

"Ready to go, buddy? I'm going to get you something to eat and then it's lights out."

Ephraim looked upset. "We...uh, we have a Shabbos clock. You don't need to turn the lights off, they'll go off by themselves."

"Ephraim," Aharon said with a smile, "it's just an expression people use when they mean it's time to go to bed."

"Can I get some food for him?" said Jeremy.

"We're not done yet!" exclaimed Ephraim. "Pesach, matzah, *maror* — that's the whole point! He won't be *yotzei!*"

"Ephraim, calm down. It's okay."

"He didn't eat the matzah."

"It's okay," said Aharon. "He doesn't have to."

"He does have to. Who knows when he'll be at a Seder again?" His face was wet with tears.

"What do you mean? He'll be here with us!" said Aharon, noticing Devorah gesturing frantically only a moment too late. The elevated atmosphere of the Seder was snuffed out like a blanket had been thrown over it, and everyone got quiet.

"What?" Aharon turned to Devorah. "What did I say? Mordy is part of this family!"

"Mr. Landau," said Jeremy, "I'm going to have to ask you to stop acting like this is a done deal. It's not. You're going to give him false hope, and if it doesn't work out—"

"Why wouldn't it work out?" Aharon had drunk two cups out of four, and his cup held a very large *shiur* of wine. "Why? Tell me. Why do you keep threatening me? He's my son." A huge sob threatened to spill out and submerge the entire room.

"Tatty, I'm sorry," said Ephraim, starting to bawl, going over to his father and hugging him. "I didn't mean to make you upset. You have me. I'm also your son."

The Seder was about to shatter into a thousand pieces until Yitta looked over at Mordy and smiled. His face was lit up and he was watching the proceedings avidly. He caught Yitta's eye and started laughing. "This is so great! So much drama! I don't really understand what's going on, but it's great!"

"Murray!" Jeremy was mortified at his insensitivity, but everyone else burst out laughing.

"What?" said Mordy. "What did I say?"

Everyone laughed again, but Jeremy was lost. He went quickly into doctor mode to keep any and all feelings at a distance.

"Mrs. Landau, Murray needs to eat right away. Please bring some soup and cut up the chicken and vegetables into small pieces."

Devorah stood up to get the food. "You are so sweet, you know that?" She pinched Mordy's cheek on her way out of the room. "Tzaddik!" she exclaimed over her shoulder.

Aharon went to sit on the couch, and Ephraim took refuge next to his grandmother.

"Dr. Cohen, are you all right?" Mordy asked. "You seem really upset."

"I'm not upset," said Jeremy. "I'm just...confused."

"You? Confused?" Mordy hooted. "That's a first!"

Jeremy looked at Murray to see if he was joking, but he saw that despite his jocular tone the boy was serious. And even though he was so frustrated at this whole situation a tiny bright spot suddenly appeared: Murray trusted him.

Many times over the years Jeremy had been hesitant and unsure what to do when it came to Murray's care, but he'd somehow managed to put up a strong front for his gentle patient, and this, now, was his reward.

"Hey, you," he said, in the wise-guy imitation they both enjoyed, "watch your mouth!"

Devorah came in and set down a plate in front of Mordy. She sat down next to him and waited for him to start eating, but he simply sat and stared at the food.

At Ravensfield, he'd never had to exert himself either physically or emotionally; he spent most of his time in bed or in his wheelchair, reading or doing crosswords or staring out the window, and his limits had never been tested. These past few days had pushed him way past any border he'd ever come to before, and he was about to pay the price.

Mordy turned his chair around so his mother wouldn't see and showed Jeremy his hands.

CHAPTER 43

Mordy pulled his hands out from beneath the blanket covering his legs. The right hand, closest to his mother, formed a tent over his left, which had contracted into a claw.

"What is this? How long has it been this way?" said Jeremy.

"Shh," Mordy whispered. "Don't tell them..."

Jeremy looked around. Aharon and Ephraim were speaking softly to each other, waiting for Mordy to eat something so the Seder could resume. Yitta watched from her seat at the foot of the table. Devorah was intent on cutting Mordy's food into small pieces.

"Enough is enough, Murray," said Jeremy sternly. "You've been overdoing it, and this is what happens."

"Can't you just give me some medicine for it? It's happened before. I just don't want it to happen now."

"What do you mean, it's happened before?" Jeremy stopped whispering. His suddenly raised voice drew everyone's attention, and Mordy quickly said to Ephraim, "So, what were you saying, Ephraim? Pesach, matzah, and what...?"

The table was starting to get the rumpled look that Devorah loved. The tablecloth was a bit wrinkled and already wine-stained. She had been trying to hear what Mordy and Jeremy were whispering about. She wished that Jeremy would either participate in the Seder or go to his room and wait there until it was over. His sour face and negative attitude were ruining the atmosphere that Devorah had worked so hard to create, and she knew were it not for him, Mordy would be theirs, no strings attached.

But there was no way she was going to turn away a fellow Jew from her Seder table. That was out of the question, and she knew Aharon agreed with her. She almost wished they had arranged for the non-Jewish nurse to come with Mordy, because dealing with a not-yet-observant-Jew, especially one as recalcitrant as Jeremy, was not only a headache, it was also a heartache.

She and Aharon had been trying to figure out a way to get through to Jeremy, especially when he raised the stakes by claiming his was the final signature on Mordy's release. She wondered if that was absolutely true, but she couldn't

— wouldn't — allow her own ulterior motives to get in the way of trying to bring him closer.

"Murray," said Jeremy, standing up, "it's time to call it a night. You need an anti-inflammatory before you get into more trouble. How long has your hand been that way?" he asked again, insisting on an answer this time.

Mordy ignored him. His eyes fixed on Aharon and Ephraim, he was anxious to continue the Seder.

"What's the problem?" asked Devorah.

Jeremy sighed in frustration, grabbed Mordy's hand and lifted it up. "Do you see this? It's not supposed to look like this. He's been hiding it from me because, I'm sure, he wanted everything to go smoothly this week. You know, we almost didn't come — he was ill. Is this what you want?" He glared at Devorah, almost shoving Mordy's hand in her face.

Mordy turned a deep red.

"Mom?" said Mordy.

"Yes, tzaddik?" she replied.

"Don't call her that, Murray," said Jeremy. "You're just going to get hurt."

The room went quiet. Yitta clucked her tongue while Aharon and Ephraim hoped that the Seder was not now beyond repair.

"Doc," said Mordy, hastily covering his hand once again, "look at me. I am already hurt. I am here because I am looking for the opposite of hurt."

"Murray," Jeremy said tightly, "let's just go."

"No, let's just wait a minute," said Mordy. "I am loved here. I am wanted. What is so wrong with that?" His voice choked up, and even Jeremy was surprised — he had rarely seen Murray cry, even as a baby.

"Why are you so against it? So what if my body is messed up? I'm still a person." His tears overflowed then, setting off a relay of waterworks. First Devorah, then Aharon, and finally, even Yitta covered her eyes. It was just too painful to watch.

"Okay, buddy," said Jeremy. "Okay. I'm sorry."

After some moments Mordy's tears dried. "So I can stay?"

"Yes, you can stay, but you have to eat right now, and take an anti-inflammatory. Are we clear?"

"You bet," said Mordy with a smile, "we're clear." It lightened the moment, and once again everyone was smiling. Jeremy continued to hover over Mordy, but he was determined to remain uninvolved in the Seder. If this was going to be all about Mordy, so be it.

But the Landaus were not prepared to exclude him. "Dr. Cohen," said Aharon, turning a page in his Haggadah, "This is a very important part of the Seder. This is when we invite Elijah the Prophet to join us."

"A real prophet?" asked Mordy. "Coming here? Now?"

"Well, it's a bit difficult to explain. We can't see him, but we know that he comes to every Passover Seder, of every Jewish family, all over the world."

"Aw, so he's not really coming."

Jeremy whispered, "I told you so."

"Oh, but he is," said Aharon. "And when he comes and drinks from this large cup of wine here in the middle of the table, you can pray for anything you want. He will take your prayers straight up to Hashem."

Aharon was so serious and sincere that Jeremy did not find it in his heart to mock him. Aharon stood up and beckoned to Jeremy, hooked his arm through his, and walked with him to the front door.

He held up his Haggadah before the two of them. As Jeremy looked at the English translation, he paled. "Are you crazy?"

Aharon looked down at him, his face aflame with belief. "I will take my chances," he said, and flung the door open wide.

———————◦◦———————

The next time Jeremy tried to extricate Mordy from the Seder was easier because not only was the Seder over, but the boy had fallen asleep in his wheelchair.

"It's been a long night for him," said Jeremy, releasing the safety pedal on the wheelchair, "but I think he enjoyed it."

Ephraim was nodding off as well, and Yitta excused herself too.

Aharon and Devorah were exhausted, physically and emotionally, and they had no energy left to play word games with Jeremy. "We know you mean well, and that this is hard for you," Devorah began, but Jeremy cut her off.

"I'm fine, and as you said, this is not about me. It's about the kid."

"What happened to his hand?" asked Devorah.

"My best guess is that he's developed arthritis, especially if he says it's been spasming like that for a while. I'll have to run some tests when we get back home..." Aharon's sharp intake of breath was loud in the quiet room. "...back to the hospital, whatever." He shook his head and started wheeling Murray out of the room. "You people. You just don't give up, do you."

Devorah got up and leaned over Mordy. "Good night, tzaddik," she whispered in his ear. "Gut Yom Tov. I love you."

CHAPTER 44

Jeremy tossed and turned in his bed for quite a while after the Seder. Even though Murray had been exhausted and sleepy, they still had to take care of his nightly routine. Jeremy had spent some time massaging and manipulating Murray's hand to assess the problem, but it was hard to diagnose so quickly. Of course, Jeremy understood why Murray had been hiding it from him — there was so much at stake for him. He would have done the same. Jeremy was afraid that the time had come for him to let go. His group home was almost in operation. The apartment had been renovated to accommodate six teenagers at present, with room to expand. The hospital was nearly empty. Dr. Boyer had already jumped ship and opened a medical supply company, making only a token appearance at the hospital once a week. Jeremy had to leave.

But he was not prepared to do that, and not just because of Murray, although that had a lot to do with it. Jeremy had come to Ravensfield right after completing his residency. The urgency of a round-the-clock job combined with being able to live on the premises had made Ravensfield more than just a place to work. For him as for Murray, Ravensfield was home.

Of course he had been free to come and go as he wished, but he hadn't done so. The overwhelming needs and demands of his patients, the woefully understaffed facility, the indifferent administration had, tornado-like, simply sucked him in. Many staff members had come and gone during his tenure — he was the only doctor left from those who had been there when he arrived.

His mother had never given up her gentle prodding for him to meet a nice girl and settle down. It was hard for her to understand his thinking — she and Jeremy's father had married relatively young and were already parents at his age. He had always assumed he would marry and start a family, but here he was, thirty-seven-years old and no closer to building a real life than he'd been fifteen years earlier.

He had been trying to convince himself that Murray needed him, that he could not leave until Murray was settled. But now that there was a real chance for him to reunite with his family, Jeremy was resisting. It made no sense.

Yet Jeremy, for all his faults, was an honest person, and deep down he knew the truth even if he didn't care to acknowledge it: It was the religious thing that was driving him up a wall. These people — the Landaus and all the others like them — why were they doing this to themselves? Why were they cutting themselves off from the rest of the world?

But wasn't he doing almost the same thing? He too had cut himself off from everything outside Ravensfield. He couldn't remember the last time he had eaten in a restaurant or seen a movie. The only friend he had, and he could hardly be called that, was Dr. Tim Kelly.

But still, he told himself, *I have a choice. And I do not engage in such bizarre, outlandish behavior.* Who in this day and age observes ancient religious rituals? How could they actually tell Murray a prophet was coming to the door! And the poor kid — he really believed them. They believed it themselves!

"Come on, Jerry, your grandfather wants you to go to the door with him," his mother was saying.

"I don't wanna go with him. I wanna stay here with you."

"It'll be fine. I'll hold your hand, okay?" Diane Cohen remembered her father making the same request of her when she was Jeremy's age, and how she too had resisted. Her mother had merely pushed her forward, and she had approached her father with trepidation. She'd been scared too. "No! I don't want to go!"

"It's okay, Dinah," he said, using the Hebrew name she'd long left behind. "I'll handle it." Jeremy's father arose from his seat at the far end of the table. His mint-green satin yarmulke with stamped gold lettering on it came to a peak at the top of his head, making him look to Jeremy like a pistachio ice cream cone. Jeremy wanted to laugh out loud. But Papa got very upset when Jeremy laughed.

"Yirmiyaaaah!" Papa boomed out again. Papa never called him Jerry or Jeremy. And the way Papa said it so loud made Jeremy think of an earthquake even though he'd never been in one.

"This is a veeerry important part of the Seder. This is when we open the door for Eliyahu Hanavi."

"Who?"

"Eliyahu Hanavi. Elijah the Prophet. Dinah, aren't you sending him to Talmud Torah as I asked? I gave you money." His mother had looked down, avoiding both her father's and her husband's gaze. Her husband had been all for sending Jeremy and Alex to Hebrew school, but she had wanted to wallpaper the kitchen and dining room. While normally Diane was amenable to her father's wishes, this time she'd dug in her heels and resisted.

"He's starting soon, Papa," his mother had said in a small voice. Rob Cohen stood up and took his wife's place next to Jeremy, holding his hand. "Go ahead, Papa," he'd said respectfully. "We're listening."

"Ha! Of all of them, you're the one that's interested."

Rob smiled. "I love you, Papa. You and your daughter are the best thing to ever happen to me."

"*Ah shande*," Papa muttered. He turned again to the small boy at his side.

"Eliyahu — Elijah — was a very important person. G-d would talk to him directly and give him messages."

"G-d talks?" said Jeremy. He had a very vague idea about G-d — his mother sometimes said it when she was surprised or worried. His father never said it. But this was different.

He didn't know G-d talked. "Would He talk to me?" he asked.

His grandfather looked annoyed. "No. It's a special language, and only special people can hear it."

"Mommy says I'm special."

"Jerry, c'mon, let Papa talk." Rob's voice was calm and soothing.

But Papa was out of patience. He opened the door and, leaving it open, took a few steps out into the hallway. The building was very clean and well maintained, but it was hardly the Jewish enclave it had been when they'd moved in. All sorts of "miserable elements," as his grandmother called them, had started moving in, and the only time Jeremy had ever seen Papa open the door was if he had to go out, and then he pulled it closed fast behind him and locked it in one quick movement.

"Papa, close the door!" Jeremy cried.

But Papa ignored him and held the Haggadah up close to his eyes. "Pour forth Your wrath..."

"Papa, nooo!"

"Jerry, quiet down now."

"Daddy, I'm scared. Take me home."

Papa's face curdled with disgust. "What kind of Jewish child is afraid of Eliyahu Hanavi?"

"I was," said Diane.

Papa threw a withering look at her and then at Rob. "And look where that got you."

"Papa, please, don't start."

"Don't start?" The large vein on Papa's forehead bulged and throbbed. "You don't start! We gave you everything, Dinah. Everything. What were you missing? Nothing. And look what you do to us. You're killing your mother."

"No, Jonah. Please. Let's just finish the Seder. It's going so beautifully." Nana had twisted her hands together in her lap.

Papa had looked at his wife and blew out his breath. "Fine. Come, Yirmiyah. Sit with Papa. Follow along with me."

CHAPTER 45

Jeremy lay thinking, listening to Murray breathe. He'd often stayed nights at his patient's bedside when the boy had been sick, and sometimes just to watch over him when he felt it was necessary to monitor his condition. So it wasn't so unusual for him to be awake while Murray slept.

What was unusual was the direction of his thoughts. He rarely pondered the past — why should he? There was nothing he could change, and even if he could, the past was not his enemy. He'd grown up in a normal, happy family, become a doctor and helped people. He hadn't built a family, but he still considered that as part of his future.

The only blip through all of that had been the death of his father, and even that had been quick and trauma-free. His father had kept himself fit and healthy, habits he'd developed in the army — except for one. He'd become addicted to cigarette smoking while stationed in Japan, and not only had he never tried to quit, he'd never wanted to. It hadn't affected his normal functioning...until it did.

X-rays taken just before his death revealed a pair of lungs riddled with holes and flaming with infection. His mother had rushed his father to the ER and called both her sons. Jeremy had rushed to meet them there, but he arrived only in time to look into his father's eyes one last time before he passed away.

Jeremy had been twenty-six then, totally immersed in his work at the hospital, and he realized now that it had never fully hit him. He'd been out on his own for so long that, even though he'd visited regularly, they were no longer as close as they had once been.

His father was kind and warm but reticent. Actions spoke much louder than words for Rob Cohen. And when his mother told him that his father had left instructions to be cremated, Jeremy remembered being taken aback, though he couldn't say exactly why, like seeing something odd from the corner of his eye but moving on regardless. Now, on Passover night at the Landaus, with their matzah and *maror* and all the rest of it, the past was rising up before him unbidden. Now a picture of his grandfather's death gathered clarity in his mind like a developing Polaroid: He saw his mother, dry-eyed, then the funeral home, which he recalled thinking was a weird name for a place where no one lived, many people, most of them old, Papa's friends from shul, a big, plain coffin in the front of the room. Jeremy remembered being relieved that it was closed.

Then the drive in a big, black car back to his parents' house. Surprised to see so much food prepared and wondering who had done it, Jeremy saw a low wooden stool in the living room. His mother sat down on the stool and nodded to all the people who came by and said a few words to her.

Jeremy also remembered that as soon as everyone had gone, she told his father to get rid of the stool. He had hesitated at that, questioning her, and then she'd cried and his father went out with the stool, and the stool was gone for good.

He automatically compared the tumult of his grandfather's death to the utter silence surrounding his father's. He held up the two pictures in his mind, one next to the other, and something wasn't right. He couldn't put his finger on it, but he knew then, suddenly, that there were parts of the picture he was not seeing, or had never been shown. Why did Papa always seem so angry when they came to visit? Why did he say such unpleasant things to his father, and why did his father always respond with respect and equanimity? He would yell at Jeremy and his brother from time to time, get frustrated or tense, and he was perfectly capable of standing up for himself, so why did he let Papa act so unkindly toward him? Why didn't he ask him to stop?

Jeremy could hardly distinguish between the voices playing out in his head: Young Jerry...Dr. Jeremy Cohen... Jeremy at the Landaus' Passover Seder. He was seized with an urge to talk to his mother and ask the questions burning on his tongue. He looked at his watch and saw that it was

1 a.m. His mother would most likely be up, but it would be unconscionably rude to wake up the Landaus.

Instead, knowing that Murray slept like a stone and wouldn't be disturbed, he turned on the light and pulled out the medical journal he'd thrown in his knapsack at the last minute. But as soon as the light flashed on Mordy woke up, as if with second sight. "No lights!" he cried out in a whisper.

"What do you mean, no lights? I want to read. Go back to sleep." He looked into Murray's eyes and saw real concern there. "What is it?" he asked.

"Ephraim told us we're not supposed to turn on the lights on Passover. Remember when you said, 'lights out' and he got all upset? He told me we're not supposed to turn the lights on and off on the holiday."

Jeremy nodded. "*They're* not supposed to turn the lights on and off. But we are allowed."

"How can that be?" said Mordy. "Aren't we also Jewish?" Jeremy held his head between his hands and said with simulated exasperation, "Yes, we are Jewish, but no, we are not Jewish like the Landaus."

"What's the difference?" Mordy struggled to sit up.

"Murray, please, go back to sleep, okay? We'll talk about it in the morning."

"No, we won't, you know we won't. You'll keep finding excuses not to." His hair was messed up and, Jeremy realized, kind of long. At the hospital they were careful to keep the children's hair very short for hygienic reasons, but he'd been lax, and so had the nurses. He should have had Murray's hair cut before they came. He considered his own uncombed curls and Aharon and Ephraim's short hair and long *peyos*, which shouldn't have made them look like angels to him but did.

"Why are you so upset?" Mordy asked, turning to face him. "Why do you keep getting so mad at the Landaus?"

Jeremy gazed fondly at Murray. It was a given that a doctor did not ever confide personal things to a patient. He and Murray had had many conversations on many different topics, but rarely if ever had he made a personal comment. When the person inside Murray had finally "awakened," for want of a better word, his mind had been a clean slate, and it was no trouble at all to find ways to fill it up without bringing himself into the picture. So, no, he wouldn't answer Murray's question — to Murray. But if he was ever going to be able to let Murray go, he would have to answer that question to himself. Why was he so angry with the Landaus?

CHAPTER 46

Jeremy didn't get to sleep until it was light outside, and he would have continued sleeping if he hadn't been awakened by a strange, drumming noise. His mind ran at lightning speed through various possibilities as to the source of the sound and where he was and that it must be coming from Murray's bed.

All of which took less than a second. The next moment he was up and out of bed and over at Murray's bed, indeed the source of the noise. Murray was having a seizure. The bed was shaking, and it was the repeated, uncontrollable thrashing of his body in the bed that had awakened Jeremy.

It had happened before, but usually not on Jeremy's watch, and for the first time in his medical life, he froze. He knew the drill: Bring the patient to the floor to avoid injury, place him on his left side, and so on, but he was trapped in this room. Where was the phone? How was he going to remove Murray from the bed to avoid further injury without another pair of hands? Where was the bag with all of Murray's medications? And, most importantly, what exactly was wrong?

As he was deciding whether to attend to Murray first, alert the Landaus, or find a phone, there was a furious banging on the door and Aharon and Devorah burst in.

"What's happening? What's wrong with Mordy?"

Jeremy struggled to speak calmly. "He appears to be having a seizure." It was Devorah who ran to her son's bedside and placed her cool hand on his forehead.

"He's burning up. Aharon, call Hatzolah!"

It was Yom Tov morning but Aharon did not hesitate for a moment. He ran to the phone in the kitchen, startling Ephraim and Rena who, without their cornflakes, were at a loss what to eat for breakfast.

"Tatty, what are you doing?" Rena screamed. "It's Yom Tov!"

"Sha," said Ephraim.

"Aharon Landau speaking. I live at fifty-two Gordon Lane. My son is having a seizure and he is burning with fever...I don't know exactly, I didn't take his temperature... Yes, he has cerebral palsy. Please, hurry!"

He ran to unlock the front door, pulled it open, and ran back to Mordy's room, where Devorah was sitting at his bedside holding his hand, and Jeremy was hovering. The convulsion was slowly tapering off, and Mordy fell back asleep.

"You called?" Devorah asked.

"Yes, they'll be here soon."

She turned to Jeremy. "Hatzolah is our own volunteer ambulance service."

"What do you mean, your own? Didn't you call 911?" He ran his hand roughly through his hair. He could not for the life of him understand what they were saying.

"No, we called the—" Aharon's explanation was interrupted by three men bursting into the house. Aharon ran out to bring them quickly to Mordy's room.

"What happened?" It was the neighbor from down the block, Moshe Werner. He and Aharon davened at the same minyan.

Aharon turned to Jeremy, who quickly filled in the blanks. "I was in a deep sleep and I heard a loud, banging noise. I woke up and saw that Murray was seizing. I'm his doctor. But before I could do anything," he paused and looked over at Aharon, "they barged into the room and took over. Who are you people? What are your qualifications?"

"I was just about to ask you the same, but let's take care of the patient first." The other two paramedics had already inserted an IV into Mordy's arm and administered ibuprofen. "Temp is 102.6, BP 160/90, pulse 150," the paramedic reported.

"Okay, let's lift him from the bed, easy does it, and put him on the stretcher."

"He can't move his legs," said Rena, who was peeping in at the door with Ephraim. "He's paralyzed."

"No, he's not," Ephraim cried. "He only has CP," repeating what he'd overheard without really knowing what it was.

"We're taking him to Booth Memorial," Moshe said.

"I'm going with him," said Jeremy, as Aharon moved to follow the stretcher out the door.

"Sorry, only one in the ambulance," said Werner to Jeremy. "If you think he'll need you, you can follow by car."

Aharon froze, but his brain was processing *hilchos Shabbos* faster than he knew was possible. He came to a conclusion and said to Devorah, "You go."

She nodded. "Yes, that's the right thing to do."

Devorah didn't take time to change out of her housecoat. She grabbed her raincoat as she passed by the hall closet and emptied the pockets as she ran toward the door. The medics had strapped Mordy to a stretcher and were ready to move.

"Okay, I'll follow you in my car," Jeremy said quickly.

"One second," said Moshe Werner." He turned to Aharon. "Are these your Yom Tov guests?"

Aharon took a deep breath and looked toward Mordy's bed, where he'd been only moments before. "This fellow here," pointing at Jeremy, "the doctor, is my guest."

"And who's the kid?"

Ephraim and Aharon spoke together:

"He's our brother!"

"He's my son!"

Jeremy looked at Ephraim angrily. "Can't you tell this kid to be quiet?" he said to Aharon.

Aharon was about to retort when Moshe put a hand on his arm. "Hey, both of you, cool it!" he said.

"What's going on here, Aharon?" Moshe asked. "Since when do you have a teenage son with CP?" He knew of plenty of cases where kids were hidden away, for all kinds of reasons, but didn't connect that with his neighbor. Being a paramedic made him privy to a lot of information he wished he didn't have.

"I should be with Murray," Jeremy said anxiously, "instead of standing around trying to explain myself to some amateur ambulance driver."

"His mother is with him," said Aharon gently. "A mother's tears — and prayers — shouldn't be taken lightly. And, despite your opinion, these guys are certified EMTs."

"But I'm the one who knows his history. That's it. Enough talk. I'm leaving." Jeremy turned to Moshe Werner. "Get in your bus," he barked, "and let's go! I'll follow you."

He grabbed his jacket and stormed out the door. Almost immediately they could hear his car revving up loudly.

Moshe raised an eyebrow at Aharon. "We'll speak after Yom Tov." Aharon nodded wearily. He'd sent Devorah because he wanted to give her the chance to mother Mordy, but Jeremy really did know Mordy's case history better than either of them. Aharon rarely doubted himself, but whenever there was a decision to be made about Mordy, his brain just didn't function right; it was a machine whose wires popped and flung out cogs and screws in every direction where Mordy was concerned.

CHAPTER 47

Moshe Werner and his partner, Bergman, the two Hatzolah EMTs, rushed Mordy into the emergency room of Booth Memorial Hospital, with Devorah at their heels. Although they had stabilized Mordy, he was given priority due to his extenuating circumstances. Werner and Bergman lifted him carefully off the stretcher and onto the hospital gurney. They hurried along and burst through the swinging doors into the ER; the nurses were working on him so quickly that their movements were almost blurred. A few minutes later Jeremy came huffing in. "What's happening? Where is he? What did I miss?" he asked Devorah without stopping to breathe.

"Not much," said Devorah. "They're just settling him in."

"Did they take a case history yet?" he demanded.

"No, not yet. They said the doctor will be down in a few minutes."

"Good. But we have to make sure the attending physician sees him. No interns. No residents. No students." This was not the first time Jeremy had accompanied Murray in a rush to an emergency room. Even though Ravensfield was technically a hospital, it was not at all equipped to handle real medical emergencies. Jeremy was very familiar with emergency room routines: recording blood pressure, temperature, inserting the patient's IV before anything else. But as he watched Devorah with Murray he had to admit that she was much better on the emotional level than he was. Even though Murray was sedated and not responsive, she kept speaking softly to him, patting his hand gently, and adjusting his blanket.

Jeremy tried to wrap his mind around the fact that although he knew Devorah was Murray's mother, this was the first time he actually felt sure of it. He didn't understand the mechanism, really. True, she'd given birth to him, but she hadn't seen him in fourteen years. How was she able to pick up where she'd left off, loving and caring for him as though she had been doing it all his life? He considered the many times he had sat at Murray's bedside. Although attentive to Murray's responses and progress, he'd never kept up a patter of soothing, one-sided conversation with him, or patted him gently, or connected with him in any way except through some difficult examinations and treatments, a few jokes and punches on the shoulder. Nothing Jeremy had ever done or had to offer compared to the scene unfolding before him now.

As they waited for the doctor, Jeremy paced back and forth, then stopped suddenly and faced Devorah. "How come Aharon sent you instead of him? He seemed pretty anxious to come along." Devorah took a deep breath. Should she just dodge the question and avoid confrontation, snide comments and sarcasm, or tell the truth and let the chips fall where they may?

The answer was clear to her, of course — if Jeremy were ever to become religious (*It could happen*, she thought. *One can never give up hope...*) he would remember the conversation that was about to ensue here, she was sure of it.

"There is a Jewish law—" she began.

"I knew it!" said Jeremy. "Another crazy law! Don't you see how these laws could have harmed Murray? What if something happened to Murray on the way, or here, and someone strong enough to lift him or carry him was needed, or something like that?"

"Well, Dr. Cohen, we were in an ambulance with two experienced paramedics, and then we came right into the ER with plenty of help available. There didn't seem to be much danger involved."

"That's just my point," he shouted. When Devorah winced he lowered his voice. "That's just my point. You don't know what you don't know. Anything could happen."

"I have raised three other children," she said. "I do have some experience."

"Three healthy children. Big difference."

"Are you guys still fighting? Why are you always fighting?"

Mordy's eyes were half open and his voice emerged hoarsely as if he were opening it with a can opener.

"Hey, buddy," said Jeremy. "You're awake!"

But Mordy only had eyes for his mother. "What happened? Where am I?" he said groggily.

"Everything's okay, tzaddik. You're fine. You're in the hospital but we're here with you, so there's nothing to worry about."

"I'm not worried. I just want to know what's wrong."

Before she could answer, the attending physician bustled in, picked up Mordy's clipboard chart, and scanned it quickly. Devorah's heart sank as she eyed the doctor's name tag pinned to the pocket of his white coat. Dr. Shimon Goldberg. She didn't know for sure, but she assumed he was allowed to do *melachos* on Yom Tov. Nevertheless, she wished Aharon was here to guide them if any halachic problems came up. "Gut Yom Tov," she said warmly. The doctor looked puzzled. "I'm sorry?"

"It's Passover today," she tried again, pointing to the name tag. "A Jewish holiday."

He touched the name tag and looked down at it. "Oh, I get it. My name's not Goldberg, I just grabbed Goldberg's coat as I rushed down here because I had to throw mine in the laundry bin a few minutes ago. My name is Tommy Lucero. Dr. Tommy Lucero."

Jeremy rolled his eyes and interrupted them heatedly. "Can we move along here, please? You know, examine the patient and all that?"

CHAPTER 48

Between them, Devorah and Jeremy were able to give the attending physician the short version of Mordy's case history. When it became obvious that Jeremy knew a lot more about the patient than his own mother, both Dr. Lucero and the Hatzolah paramedic Moshe Werner, who knew the Landaus as neighbors, looked at her with pity.

After examining Mordy and giving him a barbiturate to inhibit further seizures, Dr. Lucero told them he was going to admit Mordy for a day or two just to keep an eye on him. Again, their mismatched reactions raised eyebrows: Devorah asked if it was absolutely necessary and Jeremy said, "Very good."

"Don't worry, Mrs. Landau," Jeremy said magnanimously. "You go back to your holiday. I don't mind staying here with Murray and keeping him company. We're used to it, right, buddy?"

If there was a way to smile and not smile at the same time, Mordy was trying to perfect it. A smile to one of them hurt the other, but if it was a choice between smiling or not, he'd choose smiling every time.

"I just think that if we can care for him at home — especially with you there as a doctor — we can avoid admitting him. It would be so much nicer if we were all together at home, especially on the holiday, and also because we haven't seen him for such a long time. We want to make the most of every day we have to spend together."

Jeremy turned to her and asked slyly, "Even at the risk of Murray's health?"

And Devorah took the bait. "That's not what I meant, and you know it!" She heard Aharon's voice in her head: *Easy does it, don't let him get to you,* but she was not able to stop herself. "Why do you keep implying that we are trying to hurt him or do things that will be bad for him? I know you said what you said just now because you think we don't know how to care for him, but who wins when you do that? Anyway, you know we wouldn't risk his well-being."

Jeremy had the grace to look chagrined. "What I've been trying to tell you — in a very clumsy way, I admit — is that you don't know what you're dealing with. You think Murray is a perfectly normal boy with a problem with his legs, but it isn't like that. Sometimes with CP you think the body will react one way, but it does something completely different. You are so anxious to get your hands on him and convert him to your crazy lifestyle that you are not really thinking about him and what he needs. Right now, his body has just undergone a trauma. He needs fluids, rest, and quiet."

"We can give that to him at home!" Silence settled over them all, Devorah's raw emotion chasing everyone's words back into their mouths. Dr. Lucero seemed at a loss. He wasn't about to become emotionally involved with the patient or his family. He knew the kid needed a night or two of observation, but he didn't know if he had the nerve to pull him out of his mother's arms. Jeremy realized he had said enough. It was Moshe Werner who stepped in then.

"Mrs. Landau," he said, using his calm but firm paramedic's voice, "I can't imagine how you are feeling right now. None of us can, especially your son over there, who's looking very worried."

They all turned to look at Mordy, whose face had gone blank. "I'm okay," he said softly. "Dr. Cohen, will you stay here with me? The kids are probably missing, uh, their mom. It's okay, Mom," he said, turning to Devorah. "You can go. I'll be fine here."

Mordy's words pierced her heart. "We have to stay anyway until after the holiday is over, tzaddik. It's too far to walk home. We'll talk about it again later."

"Well, that's settled," said Dr. Lucero, anxious to get on with his work. "I'll be back in to check on you, young man, then we'll move you to a room."

He stepped out of the curtained cubicle quickly and they heard his footsteps hurrying away.

———————◦———————

Mordy had drifted back to sleep. Devorah was exhausted. Jeremy sat rigidly with his arms folded tightly across his chest. Moshe Werner sat down between them, perplexed. He'd seen a lot, but this was something new.

"Ravensfield?" he said, turning to Jeremy. "I thought it closed a couple of years ago." In Werner's other life he sold health insurance and was familiar with the various healthcare institutions around the city.

"It did." Jeremy sighed. "But it's taking a while to clear everybody out. Most of the patients there either didn't have family or weren't wanted by them. The ones who did want their kids back," he said, turning his eyes toward Devorah, "well, it takes time to get everything organized."

Werner nodded his head as if he understood and asked the unspoken question with his eyes: Two years to get organized?

"Murray was different."

Werner's eyebrows rose.

"He was there since he was an infant. And it took the Landaus a while to decide what they wanted to do. And there were a lot of other cases to deal with, so I didn't take care of his first."

Werner nodded sympathetically. So you got attached to him, the nod said. Perfectly understandable.

"We took very good care of him, as you can see." Jeremy pointed to Murray, who was sleeping with a serene smile on his face.

"He looks like a special kid," said Werner.

"He is," Jeremy replied. Werner stood up and put a thickly gloved hand on Jeremy's back. Be that as it may, it said.

"He's staying with us for Yom Tov as a trial run," said Devorah. "We want to bring him home permanently."

Jeremy started to reply, then felt that hand pressing heavily on his shoulder.

"I'm sure I can help you get set up with all the special coverage you need," said Werner. "Although you've done a pretty good job already."

"Dr. Cohen helped us a lot," said Devorah, trying to follow Aharon's advice to cool it.

Werner patted Jeremy on the back with his big hand.

"And I'm sure he will continue to help you. You were lucky to have such a fine doctor caring for your son all these years. Have you ever told him that?"

Devorah sat back. "I'm sure my husband said something like that to him, but what difference does it make? He was just doing his job." She looked directly at Jeremy. "You were just doing your job. If it wasn't you it would have been somebody else. The point is that he's home now."

Jeremy pushed Werner's hand off, stepped quietly out of the curtained space, and walked out into the hallway. Devorah resumed her place at Mordy's bedside.

"Mrs. Landau," said Werner, "if you don't mind my saying so, I think you are making a terrible mistake."

"What do you mean?" she said, hovering over Mordy as though Werner was going to whisk him away. "We want him home with us."

"And you should have him home, by all means. But I was referring to your attitude toward his doctor."

"What do mean?" she repeated.

Werner gave her a stern look. "Don't you see that his heart is breaking?"

CHAPTER 49

Devorah nearly laughed out loud. "You think Dr. Cohen is upset about losing Mordy? No, it's us he doesn't like."

"What makes you say that?" asked Werner.

"Don't you see how hostile he is? He doesn't want us to make Mordy *frum*. He thinks it's dangerous! Have you ever heard of anything so ridiculous?"

They heard footsteps coming down the hallway and after a moment the curtain opened to readmit Jeremy, accompanied by an older woman in a polyester pantsuit and eyeglasses suspended from a long, beaded necklace.

"Good morning," she said. "My name is Frances Murphy. I'm the social worker for the hospital." Werner's hands were safely clasped behind his back in case she decided to shake hands, but it was Devorah she was interested in.

"The patient's doctor has been giving me some background information, and he thought I might be able to be of help. I understand you don't want to admit your son to the hospital for treatment."

"*Oy, G-ttenyu,*" said Werner under his breath. "This is going from bad to worse."

Devorah took a deep breath and stood up, looking down at the petite Frances Murphy, as her name tag read.

"That is not what I said," she replied evenly. "If he needs treatment, then of course he should be admitted. My question was whether he could receive at home the treatment he needs just as well."

"Oh, I see," said Murphy, nodding. "We spoke to Dr. Lucero and he seems to think hospitalization is indicated."

Devorah knew when she was defeated and accepted it gracefully. "Very well, then. If it is what is best for my son, then that is what we shall do."

"So we're all agreed, then?" she said.

Devorah nodded sadly. "Thank you for your help."

"All part of the job," she replied. She took another look at Devorah. "Are you all right, ma'am?"

Devorah looked down at the older woman. "No," she said. "I am not all right. I am angry and frustrated. Wouldn't you be if you were in my place? This man," she pointed at Jeremy, "is trying to keep my son away from me."

Werner startled. Just when he thought she'd fended off the lion, she'd thrown it a steak. "Mrs. Landau, I'm sure we can settle this among ourselves. We don't need to involve anyone else." He looked at her meaningfully.

She took his words as meaning that she should not air their "dirty laundry" in public, but she did not see Mordy as dirty laundry.

Murphy, now keenly focused, took a chair and sat down next to Devorah. "What do you mean, hon? Is there a problem here? Dr. Cohen seemed very concerned."

"Yes, he is very concerned about making sure we do not get to take our son home. He is holding him hostage."

"What?! Hey, wait a minute!" Werner and Jeremy both protested, but Frances Murphy only had eyes for Devorah.

"Would you like to explain why you feel that way?"

"It's not just the way I feel. It's the truth." She told Frances Murphy the story from the beginning, starting with the traumatic birth, all the way up to the present. Despite his anger, Jeremy found it interesting clinically to hear the story from her point of view.

"So he told us that in order for us to bring our son home permanently, he was the one who was going to have to sign the release papers, and he was going to do it only if he was satisfied that we would take proper care of him. And that is what we are doing!"

Frances Murphy's smile hardened as she turned to Jeremy. "Dr. Boyer is in charge there, isn't he?" she asked.

"He was. He found other work, but he still comes in a few times a week for administrative things."

"And he was the one who empowered you to discharge the patients?" she continued.

"More or less," said Jeremy.

"More or less?"

"He said I should use my discretion."

Murphy nodded. She knew that the state institutions had discharged all their patients when the government closed them down. As long as there was someone to claim them, or a private institution willing to accept them, the patients were free to go.

"Why don't you come with me back to my office?" she said neutrally, "and we can discuss this further."

"No," Jeremy said, "I want to stay with my patient."

Her lips curled in a sad smile. "You opened this Pandora's box, Dr. Cohen. I'm afraid we must see it through to a solution."

———————⊃◦⊂———————

Frances Murphy took out a binder containing the rulings on Ravensfield and other places like them. "We keep up with these things," she said. "Many of our patients come from Ravensfield, Creedmoor State Hospital, and a few others like them. So you know that you can let him go anytime they want to take him home. What's holding you back? Do you feel the child will truly be in danger? If so, you must tell me, and I will make arrangements to keep him here until the matter is resolved."

To speciously implicate the Landaus as criminals was further than Jeremy was willing to go. "No, no. The family is fine. They're very loving and caring. But just between you and me, I am afraid that if I allow them to take him home, they will force him to become religious. You saw the guy with the black beanie on his head in the ER? The religious Jews have their own private ambulance service, did you know that?"

She nodded. "They're wonderful. Sometimes they are better and more professional, certainly faster responders than the regular ambulance service."

The fluorescent light in the office was making Jeremy's eyes hurt, and he suddenly realized how tired he was. He'd barely slept, and the morning's events were taking a toll. All he wanted to do right then was lay his head down somewhere and sleep.

"Dr. Cohen..." Murphy's voice sounded like it was coming down a long tunnel. "As long as the child is safe and his medical needs cared for, I'm not sure you can refuse to send him back to his own family just because of their religious beliefs. He is their natural child, isn't he?"

"Yes, but they gave him away. I've been taking care of him since he was a baby. Me and nobody else. I was the only one who cared about him."

"I'm sorry, Dr. Cohen," said Murphy.

"Yeah, me too."

"Do you need me to help you with this?" she asked kindly.

"If you could, I would appreciate it. I think it'll make things easier for everyone."

She nodded. "Why don't you get something to eat at the cafeteria? I'll call you after I've finished some paperwork."

"Yeah, okay. Thanks." If someone had seen Jeremy an hour earlier, they might not recognize him now. The candle that had lit his face from within had gone out.

CHAPTER 50

MORDY

I ended up spending thirteen days in the hospital as the doctors tried to bring my arthritis attack under control. My mother and father took turns staying with me in the hospital, and it was interesting to spend time with them, both together and alone with each. They seemed very nice and treated each other respectfully.

I wasn't used to seeing other people, really, let alone parents, and I was surprised and delighted the more I got to know them. They brought me games, things I could play by myself, even though I mostly liked to play Solitaire, and games we could play together.

Dr. Cohen had taught me how to play checkers and tried to teach me chess, but I think I was too young when we started. I knew the pieces and where they go and what they can do, so when my father set up the board and taught me a few opening moves, I was ready. We played a lot and I got better at it every day. They also got me Battleship, which I loved, and Scrabble, not so much. I tried not to be too obvious, but I kept waiting for Dr. Cohen to show up. I was afraid to ask, but finally the suspense got too much for me and I asked my mother when he was coming. She didn't answer me right away, and I realized that she didn't want him to visit me. I don't know how I knew this, but I was sure that if I didn't tell her right away how I felt she wouldn't let me see him. So I told her, and I could tell she was a little upset, but two days later Dr. Cohen came to see me when she wasn't there. I think it was planned, but I was too happy to care. He stayed for a few hours and brought me take-out — a hot dog with mustard and French fries. He'd done that twice before, and it was so delicious I wished he had brought more.

But when my parents came by later, after Dr. Cohen had left, they immediately noticed the wrappers we had forgotten to clear off the folding table. My parents looked at each other in a way I hadn't seen before and it scared me. My mother was just about to say something when my father made a weird sound, like a click and a shhh and a tsk all together, and she closed her mouth. My mother quickly gathered the wrappers and threw them away, and then rinsed her hands in the sink. When I was finally discharged, part of me wanted to stay right where I was. I didn't want to go back to Ravensfield — that was for sure! I had had it with that place, especially now that I knew there was something different — but at the same time I was afraid to go forward, especially without Dr. Cohen.

My parents came, and after bundling me up carefully in new clothes, wheeled me down in the hospital wheelchair to their van, which had an elevator and a special seat to hold me in tightly. They locked it in place and brought me "home."

I don't think they realized what was happening inside me. My! Own! Coat! The only coat I'd ever worn was one out of a pile of old, used coats they kept in the hospital for outings. It was about a thousand years old and did not keep me warm. The coat the Landaus bought me was brand-new and so warm I almost began to sweat with it on. It was dark blue with a really soft lining and it felt so good I didn't want to take it off.

Everything was so new! So exciting! I was so ecstatic over the coat I could tell they didn't understand why — what's the big deal about a coat? My father said, "We're glad you like it," but he didn't really get it, and I was too excited to say any more.

Leaving without Dr. Cohen was harder than I thought it would be. I'd been in hospitals before, and he had always taken me there and brought me back. So this was going to be something different. Everyone was waiting for me at "home," like when we'd first come for Passover, but I think they had been warned to stand back a little, which was fine with me.

I said hello to everyone, and I could tell Ephraim Barook was waiting to talk to me, but I was so tired — the short car ride and all the excitement must have knocked me out — so I told everyone I was going to rest and they all said, "Okay, have a nice rest, Mordy." I don't know why anyone would wish someone that, but it was nice to hear.

I didn't know what to do about being called Mordy.

I didn't really understand what it meant or why they called me that and not my real name, Murray. I'd been afraid to talk it over with Dr. Cohen because I knew he'd blow his top, so I had decided on my own to let them call me that name, but truthfully, it was making me cringe.

I didn't understand a lot of words they were using, but some of them had the same sound they made when they said my whole name. I tried but I couldn't make the sound. I guess it's something you have to be born with. My father carried me into my bedroom, which really embarrassed me. I'm used to being tossed around here and there — my nurse Michael was a little rough at times — but my father carried me like I was a newborn baby. He looked at my face with so much — I can't really describe it, but maybe it was "love"?

It wasn't something bad, but I could feel my face and my neck getting hot. I hid my face against his shoulder until we were in the room, and when he set me down on the bed I gasped with surprise, because sitting at the end of the bed was a really spiffy, new, mechanized wheelchair. The room looked the same yet different — a lot of stuff had been added, but my father took off my shoes and helped me lie down, and before I knew it I was asleep. Believe it or not, I slept until the following morning! More embarrassment. When I woke up everything looked and smelled different, and it took a second to remember where I was. My room at Ravensfield usually smelled like ammonia and medicine and stale food, but when I woke up at home, the sun was coming in through the window and I didn't recognize the smell, but it was good.

I was nervous when I woke up about what they would think of me, sleeping so much, but it was about 11:00 in the morning and actually nobody else was there except my grandmother.

CHAPTER 51

MORDY/MURRAY

My grandmother was sitting in a chair right next to the door of my room — outside, not inside — knitting. All I could see were her hands moving. At first I thought it was my mother, because who else would it be? But somehow I sensed they were not my mother's hands.

I didn't know what to do. Was I supposed to say something, or call out, or start moving around so she'd know I was awake? I needed an instruction manual to tell me what to do in these situations. Maybe I should write one. I didn't have to worry, though, because she knew right away I was awake and came in to look at me.

"Hi," I said. I smiled at her but she didn't smile back.

"You finally woke up," was what she said.

I was going to explain that I'd been so tired and that's why I had slept so long, but the way she was looking at me was so intimidating that I couldn't open my mouth. Families can be scary sometimes, I realized. So I just nodded.

Then she said, "Put your hands out." Again, too scared not to comply, I put my hands out in front of me wondering what she was going to do.

"Put them over the side of the bed. I don't want the sheets to get wet."

Was she planning to give me a "bird bath"? That's what we called it at Ravensfield when Mike would wash my face, hands, neck, and feet with a sponge. No way was that happening! I was prepared to put up a big fight, scared or not.

Instead she picked up an oversized plastic mug with two handles and a matching basin, both white and obviously new. What now? I didn't say it out loud but I wanted to. What new weird thing was going to happen to me? I closed my eyes but all she did was pour water over my hands from the cup, right-left-right-left-right-left. Okay. She handed me a towel and I obediently dried my hands.

"They couldn't find a nurse for you. They must have interviewed fifteen people, but none of them was good enough for the prince."

"S...so you...?" I stuttered.

"Is something else wrong with you? Why don't you talk normally? I heard you talk at the Seder so I know you can."

Before I could answer she went on. "They hired someone

temporarily to come in for a few hours, but he won't be here until the afternoon. My son had to work and my daughter-in-law had to go to Rena's school for some reason. She called in a panic and asked me to stay with you until she comes home.

"What could I do? I couldn't say no. I missed my ride to the supermarket so I told her that if Aharon takes me later, then I'll come. But I've been sitting here since 8:00 this morning. What do you want to eat? My daughter-in-law..."

"You mean my mother?" I whispered.

My grandmother raised her eyebrows and pursed her lips but she said only, "She was puttering around with your breakfast for half an hour because she didn't know what you like to eat. I told her to make you oatmeal — everyone eats oatmeal, for heaven's sake.

"She wouldn't make it, she said it was too plain, and if I hadn't stopped her she'd have written out a restaurant menu for you to order from. I told her if she spoils you too much there's going to be trouble down the line, but does she listen to me? No.

"I'm going to make you oatmeal, and if you want something else after that I'll bring it to you. You are nothing but skin and bones. I'm not going to take you out of bed because I'm afraid something will break. I'll be back."

Without waiting for me to answer, she turned around and left the room, and she closed the door. I had some strange things happen to me at Ravensfield, but this was supposed to be family! I hate oatmeal, but that was hospital oatmeal. Maybe this kind would be different.

She came back a few minutes later with a small glass of orange juice and the bowl of oatmeal. The orange juice was cold and fresh and absolutely delicious, with little pieces of orange floating around inside, and it was just right for my sleepy throat. I finished it in one gulp.

Then I took a look at the oatmeal and I learned a lot about my grandmother.

Until now, including the time I was here for the Seder, she hadn't struck me as such a nice person. In most of the books I've read, and I've read a lot, the grandmother is a sweet old lady. And I knew that they smelled of cinnamon and vanilla because that's the way Dr. Cohen's mother smelled when she brought him home-cooked meals that he shared with me. She was my idea of a real grandmother.

This grandmother smelled like the soap they used in the hospital and it made me feel a little nauseous. Now I learned that books are not always right.

But I also learned that things could look one way on the surface and another way underneath. I hadn't read about that. First of all, it was a perfectly sized bowl, not too big and not too small. It was hot — but not too hot. Yes, really! It looked like it came from one of the recipes in the ladies' magazines I sometimes found at the nurses' station. A ring of raisins was arranged in a circle around the edges. Some slices of banana were arranged to look like a flower, with cinnamon sprinkled on to look like the stem and some leaves. I could see the little crystals of brown sugar shining through.

One of the things it always said in the recipes was "made with love." My grandmother terrified me, but this bowl of oatmeal made me feel warm all over. I wasn't used to having conflicting feelings like that, but there were two things I did know for sure: The first was that my grandmother was a mystery I was going to have to solve, and the second was that there was no way I was not going to eat that oatmeal.

MORDY/MURRAY

We fell into a little schedule those first few weeks at home. At the hospital, everything was done mostly on time — wake-up, meals, doctors' rounds, bed-time, all that stuff — so I was used to a routine. Too used to it, I think, because whenever anything wasn't on time at the Landaus' when I expected it — and I kept track — I started to get anxious. They didn't find a twenty-four-hour nurse for me like they were planning to. My father took care of me in the morning and at night before I went to bed, and made sure

I did the exercises Dr. Cohen had prescribed. I loved when he came in and everything was quiet and still in the house and he talked softly to me about all kinds of things. An aide came in for a few hours in the afternoons. My mother and everyone came and went, but they were all super nice to me.

My mother tried to spend as much time with me as she could, and I hoped she was not neglecting the other kids. She was very busy planning Ephraim's bar mitzvah. They tried to explain to me a hundred times what a bar mitzvah is, and I got the general idea, but I don't really understand how a thirteen-year-old boy is suddenly considered a man. Ephraim looked like a kid dressing up in his father's clothes — I mean, my father's...our father's.

But the best part, surprise of all surprises, was my Grandma Landau. Her oatmeal told the true story. She came in every single day, most of the time by taxi. My mother picked her up sometimes but not all the time, and didn't drive her home.

My grandmother is just a prickly pear, thorny on the outside but very nice and sweet inside. I was so surprised. She seemed so mean at first. She was slowly helping me out of what she called my "institutional mentality." She trimmed my fingernails and toenails and scrubbed them really well. I didn't know I was supposed to do that — I just waited until they broke off by themselves. I can't always feel my feet or even see them easily, so I was surprised when she showed me how long my nails were. I wondered why they didn't take care of these things in the hospital, but you just don't know what you don't know.

She also told me some amazing stories. She would take this thick book, with English on one page and Hebrew on the facing page (I knew what it was because I asked, and she said she'd teach me to read it one day) and she would read me stories about Abraham, Isaac, Jacob, and some others. I'd seen the names mentioned in some books, but I had never known who they were really or where they came from.

"I'm reading from the Torah," she'd say, gazing with pride at the book. My father had a little stand that she brought in and lowered so she could rest the book on it at a comfortable height when she was sitting down. I listened and asked questions, and every time she answered one she'd either say, "Slowly, slowly," or "One step at a time."

But then came the big happening with my hair. I had no idea that how you wore your hair was such a big deal for them. I knew of course that my father and Ephraim have long curls in front of their ears while the rest of their hair is cut almost down to their scalp. My mother came in one day with an electric razor, which I thought she was going to use to give me a shave. I could feel I was starting to get a beard and I was happy to start shaving. The beard was scratchy. But then she turned the thing on and pointed it at my head!

"What are you going to do?" I screamed.

And I found that I had an ally. "Devorah," my grandmother "scolded" my mother — I think that's the word? I was learning how hard my grandmother tried to keep the peace, so I was shocked. She asked my mother to step out of the room with her, but I could hear them talking.

"What are you doing?" my grandmother said.

"I'm cutting his hair. I'm making him *peyos*," my mother said. There was a silence then, and I had a feeling they were staring at each other. I'd seen them do that before.

"You can't just go and cut his hair without explaining to him what you're doing. And he is nowhere near ready for *peyos*. Nowhere near."

"Why not?" said my mother. "He can see Aharon's and Ephraim's. Why wouldn't he understand that we'd make him *peyos* too? If he wasn't so big I'd make him a regular *upsherin*..."

"I'm sure you would," said my grandmother dryly. "But if you don't mind my saying so—"

"I do mind. He's our child. We'll make the decisions for him."

"Have you spoken to Aharon about this?"

My mother didn't answer and the silence made me nervous.

"Aren't you even going to ask the rebbe?" I thought that was what she said, whatever that was.

"Aharon is asking on the important things," said my mother.

My grandmother sighed. "You are so level-headed most of the time, Devorah. Don't look so surprised. I see you, I understand you, I appreciate you. But ever since Mordechai came home, your brain has turned to scrambled eggs. Pull yourself together! You can't treat him like a ventriloquist's dummy you brought home from Toys 'R' Us!" After that I heard crying. My mother was crying! There was silence again for a while and then I heard my grandmother sigh and she came back into the room.

"I'm going to explain to you what your mother wants to do, and then you can decide whether you agree or not," she said.

"Grandma," I said. I knew she wanted me to call her by the other name, the Jewish one, but I could not get my teeth around it. "Grandma," I said again, "will everyone be mad at me if I don't want to?"

Underneath her stiff expression I saw her eyes soften and her face kind of melted a little. "No one is going to be mad at you," she said firmly. "But you do need a haircut. Your hair looks like a shaggy mop." We both laughed, and I was so relieved when she went out of the room and came back with an ordinary pair of scissors and a spray bottle of water.

"Thank you, Grandma," I said as she sprayed water on my hair. When she was done she showed me how I looked in the mirror and I almost didn't recognize myself. With my hair shorter I looked a lot like Ephraim, and I could tell my grandmother noticed it too. We looked at each other, understanding each other without having to say anything. I could feel her understanding me. Was this love?

CHAPTER 53

MORDY / MURRAY

One day my mother came flying into the living room and pulled up a chair right next to me. I usually sat in my wheelchair, so if I needed anything I could wheel myself around and get it myself. My parents were strict about letting me do that, and I really appreciated it. I enjoyed the independence I was slowly getting used to. But that day I was sitting on the couch and she had a captive audience.

"Mordy!" she said. Sometimes in my mind I put exclamation points or question marks next to the things people say to me. "I have a big surprise for you!"

I tried to match her excitement but I was too nervous. "Really?" I said as brightly as I could. I really wanted them to like me and I tried to agree to almost everything. The haircut was the first time I balked, and I still felt bad about it.

"Well, you know that we're planning for Ephraim's bar mitzvah, right? I had an idea, and I talked to Tatty about it a little. He wasn't so sure, but I think it would be great if you become a bar mitzvah like Ephraim at the same time! Wouldn't that be wonderful? Ephraim can read the *parashah* and you can say the *berachos* for something called *maftir* afterward. We were never able to make one for you..."

Her voice broke a little when she said that and I saw she was getting teary-eyed... "and you are already 14. We usually do it on the boy's birthday, but yours is months from now, and it's so long to wait." I felt a tiny prick of pride that somebody knew when my birthday was.

My mother might as well have been speaking Chinese, though. The only part I sort of understood was, "you become a bar mitzvah like Ephraim," and how could I refuse when she looked so happy?

I had let them put a *kippah* on me, and I'm getting used to wearing it, and when I'm about to eat something my mother or Rena will hand me one of those little books and point out which blessing I'm supposed to say. The words are Hebrew and the letters are English but I have no idea what I'm saying.

I wonder what it would have been like if my family wasn't Jewish like this. Would it be easier or harder? I like what they do. It's interesting to watch and everybody seems happy, but from where I'm sitting, the mountain just seems too high to climb.

I said yes to my mother and the smile on her face was worth it. I had no idea what I was letting myself in for, but it didn't matter. My mother was happy.

The best part about it was that it meant spending more time with my father, who began to teach me what to do and say. He wrote everything out for me with English letters, on small white cards, and numbered them so I wouldn't read them out of order. He told me he'd be standing right next to me and would show me everything. "I won't let you fall," he said one day, looking me straight in the eye. "You can count on me," he said. I looked back at him and I believed him with all my heart. Both my mother and my father took me to buy a suit. Ephraim begged to come too, but they thought he would be a distraction. My parents had a whole discussion about the suit, and this time my father put his foot down. "A regular suit, Devorah. Navy blue, not black." He lowered his voice and said, "You have to stop rushing him."

"I'm not rushing him. He's missed out on so much already. I want him to have everything."

I was listening — I couldn't help it. I was right there and they were acting as though I was invisible. My father looked over at me and gestured to my mother to move out of hearing distance. But I was fine.

The store was nice, and although people looked at me like they'd never seen a person in a wheelchair before, Dr. Cohen had told me what to do when that happened, to just smile and nod and be polite. That was easy for me, I really like smiling, and every now and then, when someone didn't turn the other way, I'd get one back.

"Devorah," my father said, "you are such a wonderful mother..." — he said that a lot, and I could tell it made my mother very happy — "and I know you want what's best for him, but it's not about what you want, it's about what he needs."

"Let's just see," she said to my father, before turning away.

She began to push my chair quickly through the crowd and people were annoyed, but there was nothing I could do about it. I felt as if I was losing control.

She pushed me over to a rack of suits and started pulling them out one by one, asking if I liked this or that one. I looked at them hard, trying to figure out why they looked odd to me, and then I realized, when she held the hanger up in front of her, that they must have been raincoats. Tatty wore a short coat but with a belt around it, and a long coat on the weekend.

"Do people wear raincoats to a bar mitzvah?" I asked. I knew that Ephraim's new coat was pretty long, but I thought maybe they'd bought it long so he could grow into it.

My mother started to laugh and everyone turned to look at us again, but now I could feel my face turning red. I noticed that my father's face turned red too.

"It's not a raincoat?" I said. When she heard me say that and realized I was serious, she stopped laughing. She put her hand over her mouth, but it was too late.

I looked up at her and she looked down at me and miles of ocean washed between us. There was no quiet voice like Grandma's, no gentle encouragement like my father. Was it normal to feel this way about your own mother? I didn't understand why she was laughing at me, and it hurt. I'd been sure she liked me, but if she liked me why would she try to hurt me? Was she trying to hurt me, or was it just a mistake? I'd thought she would never try to hurt me, but she had. I didn't understand. I felt like I was drowning. Why was this happening?

I tried to get the words out, but they wouldn't come, so I did the only thing that would release the pressure building up inside me.

I screamed.

CHAPTER 54

AHARON

All the customers in the store stared at us as poor Mordy screamed aloud. The scream couldn't have lasted more than five seconds, but to paraphrase the old saying, it was the shout heard around the world. I rushed over to Mordy immediately and, after making sure that he was physically okay, I wheeled him out of the store and started walking with him in his wheelchair around the parking lot. Devorah tried to follow us, but I signaled to her to wait a little until Mordy calmed down.

He wasn't shouting anymore, but neither was he really alright. His whole body was shaking and he was sweating hard. I thought of taking him to the emergency room, or at least calling Dr. Cohen, but decided to wait a few minutes to see if his body could regulate itself. Cohen's words came back to me as I circled the parking lot, that Mordy's condition was more complicated than it seemed and we shouldn't be deluded into thinking that just because he was so bright and articulate his condition was not serious.

After about ten minutes, when we had both calmed down, I wheeled us over to a bench and I sat down with Mordy facing me. I took both his hands in mine. They were clammy and cold, and I held them tightly to infuse my warmth into him. His face was paler than usual, but he had stopped trembling and seemed to be getting back to normal.

"Hi," I said softly.

"Hi," he answered. We had fallen into the habit of repeating this, back and forth, three or four times until we both smiled. It was silly, but that's what we did.

"Everything okay?" I asked.

"Better now."

"I didn't realize you had such strong lungs," I joked.

He rolled his eyes. "I'm sorry. I'm so sorry. I just..."

"There is no need to apologize," I said.

"I don't know what happened. I felt like a pot filled to the brim with water, boiling and boiling until finally—"

"The lid blew off." I was no stranger to this somewhat unusual but effective reaction to stress. "You think you are the first Landau to have a meltdown in public?"

I remember the first time it happened to me — I must have been about eight. When I started screaming in the middle of the supermarket because my mother hadn't realized how hungry I was, and I'd been pestering her to buy something to eat and she thought I was just being a brat, my father put me in a shopping cart and wheeled me out of the store and into the parking lot. That's how I knew what to do with Mordy. As we walked around and around, my father told me about a few of the times it had happened to him as well.

I was glad I had this story to tell Mordy — it would make him feel less alone, and part of a chain, a family, a lineage. I wish my father could have known Mordy. I wonder if my decisions would have been different if my father had been alive.

"What happened back there?" I finally asked. "Did something frighten you?"

"Yes. Mommy." As soon as the words were out of his mouth he seemed to be mortified. He apologized over and over again, saying he didn't mean to say anything against her, but I told him I understood what he meant, that it was okay this time, but he should be more careful in the future about the way he talks about his mother.

"I just didn't understand why she started laughing, and I knew she was laughing at me. It was like a car was speeding toward me and I couldn't move out of the way. That's one of my nightmares, by the way."

I nodded, not wanting to tell him that I spent a good deal of my time conjuring up potential accidents he might face and what I could do to prevent them. I also didn't want to tell him that I felt that way sometimes too, with Devorah.

"Is Mommy mad at me?" he asked.

"Mad at you? No. Why would you think that?" I asked.

"She was laughing at something I said, but I wasn't trying to be funny. I didn't understand why she was laughing. It was so confusing, like little needles jabbing at me from different directions and they all hurt!"

I listened to what he was saying and again thought of Jeremy Cohen. He had been talking about Mordy's physical condition, but I realized it also applied emotionally. We were treating Mordy like he was a normal kid who'd been living a normal life before coming to us. But aside from very few staff members, the only person he'd had an actual relationship with was Dr. Cohen, who was not exactly a sterling role model. The fact that Mordy is able to do as well as he does is even more amazing than we give him credit for. His intellectual age is much older than his emotional age, and Devorah and I keep forgetting that.

"Yes, it must have been frightening," I said, squeezing his hand in empathy, "especially when it's your own mother."

He nodded his head vigorously. "Right! Right! I didn't understand how someone who loves me could make me feel that way."

I didn't smile, but I wanted to, and say to him, "That isn't even a fraction of how complicated love can be!"

He was finding it out on his own.

"Let's get some facts straight," I said. "Number one, Mommy loves you. No matter what it seems or sounds like to you, whatever it is comes from love. And even if you don't exactly understand what I'm saying now, remember it, because soon it will make sense to you. Got that?"

Mordy nodded.

"Secondly, even when somebody loves you, it takes time

for them to get to know and understand you, and sometimes they make mistakes."

Mordy looked at me strangely.

"What?" I asked.

"How come it's the opposite with Grandma? She acts like she doesn't love me, but the feeling I get is completely different. Her words are saying one thing but I...uh, hear something else. It's not a voice. It's a—"

"A feeling?" I said.

"I guess so. It warms me up."

I had a hard time picturing someone feeling warmed by my mother, she's had a hard life. Devorah mentioned this miraculous relationship between Mordy and my mother but I had yet to witness it.

"People have different ways of expressing themselves. What about me? How do I seem to you?"

"Daddy..." I winced as he said that. I was not going to force him to call me Tatty or Abba, but it was unsettling to be called anything else. "You take such good care of me. You are all one piece. What you say, what you do, and the way I feel when I am with you or thinking about you, all match. You make the most sense to me."

CHAPTER 55

AHARON

was just processing Mordy's glorious assessment of me when Devorah walked over and sat down. She looked — for lack of a better word — abashed.

"Hi, there," she said gamely. "Everything all right here?" Mordy looked down, embarrassed, and didn't reply.

"Everything is fine," I said reassuringly. Devorah is nobody's fool. She is an amazing wife and mother, a powerhouse, and smart, but no matter how confident one is, everyone needs a good word now and then. If I had confronted her about what happened with Mordy, it would have broken her even more, so I tried to keep it light.

Since Mordy had come to live with us, everyone, even the children, noticed that Devorah was behaving oddly. While I ordinarily wouldn't go so far as to call her laid-back, she is usually calm and almost always level-headed. She gives good, clear advice and can analyze a situation and work out a game plan very easily.

Before bringing Mordy home, we had spoken a good deal about taking it slow, giving him time, letting him get used to us and our *frum* life. We considered all the factors in Mordy's former life and how much he was going to have to get used to, both moving from a hospital setting to a home setting and adjusting physically to a new environment. He would first have to get used to the idea of living with family before even considering actually building relationships. We would have to make sure he was getting the care he needed — the list was endless, and when we spoke, Devorah was logical and clear-eyed about what we were taking on.

But as soon as Mordy moved in, everything we'd spoken about went out the window and she became a small but very intense bulldozer. If she hadn't verified the story my concerned mother told me about her trying to force *peyos* on Mordy, I would not have believed it. When I asked her about it, all she could say was that he had already missed out on so much, his life had been so hard, and we had missed out on having *nachas* from him, and wasn't it about time?

I had to keep trying to restrain her zealousness, for hadn't we decided together that we were going to take it very slow with Mordy and give him plenty of time to adjust? She would say, yes, theoretically that was the plan, but she couldn't bear each day that went by that Mordy was not keeping mitzvos.

"What does it matter to him?" she said. "He's been in a hospital all his life. What difference does it make to him if he lives a *frum* life or not?" It was hard to reconcile that this was my brilliant wife talking. When I questioned her attitude, she would turn away or change the subject.

"He is a person," I said at one point, pulling her back onto the subject. "It's a miracle that Hashem allowed Mordy's mind and his *sechel* to develop at all, let alone so nicely and normally. Let's stop and think about that for a minute. The likelihood of that happening naturally is about zero percent. Hashem has given Mordy the *keilim* to build a *kesher* with Him, but it's up to us to help him. Forcing him is going to have the opposite effect. You know it! It could take a very long time, and we need to accept that."

Devorah nodded, seeming to agree with me, and then she had started the whole business of the bar mitzvah. All of which led us here, to this parking lot, with a very sad and frightened boy on one side of me and his apparently remorseful mother on the other.

"Mordy," she said, "I'm so sorry. I didn't mean to hurt your feelings." He still couldn't look up. Devorah was about to get up and hug him, but I stopped her with my eyes. "Give him a minute," I mouthed.

I put my finger under his chin, lifted his head up and waited until he looked me in the eye. If we were ever going to get anywhere, it looked like I was going to have to be the one to take the first step.

"I know that you're upset, but when your mother talks to you, you must do your best to be respectful. You don't have to say anything, but you can look at her and nod your head."

Then, smiling, I put my hands on either side of his head and nodded it gently. He smiled back at me.

"Be patient with us," I said. "We are working very hard to be good parents to you!"

"I know," he said quietly. "And I am trying hard to be a good son, but I am not doing so well."

"Mordy," said Devorah. "Please don't talk that way. You are doing very well. You're a wonderful son."

Then his eyes welled up with tears. "But you keep getting upset with me and I don't know what I'm doing wrong!"

My eyes started tearing as well. I tried to imagine a similar conversation with Ephraim Baruch, and that's when I really understood how fragile Mordy was.

Ephraim would have come back at us with a hundred reasons and rationalizations, displaying his brilliant mind and winning his arguments by a landslide. We were able to give him a proper *chinuch* only because the two of us working together were able to outsmart him, but not by much. He had the advantage of youth, and a mind that was as agile as an acrobat's body.

I thought about the many interactions he'd already had with so many different types of people, with family, friends, teachers, and the many others who populate a boy's life, and the subtle lessons and messages learned from each one of these encounters. Each one built upon the other and created a huge archive of experiences that he grew from.

We took a lot of things for granted with Ephraim that we could not afford to with Mordy. The boys were equally bright and sensitive, but parenting Ephraim was like driving a car with an automatic transmission while Mordy was a stick shift. Even a small deviation in the road required switching gears, otherwise the car would stall. The enormity of what we were trying to do rose up like a wave coming up behind me suddenly and breaking over my head. I was terrified of the responsibility. While Devorah was metaphorically biting her nails, I was staring at my shoes, overwhelmed and furious with myself for thinking that we could actually do this on our own. Then I heard Mordy. "Um, Dad? Mom? I'm sorry I shouted. Can we go get the suit now?"

The three of us looked at each other and burst out laughing. I don't know what we would have done if Mordy hadn't laughed as well, but fortunately he did. As we rose and Devorah started wheeling him back into the store, I allowed myself to believe that we would be able to do this. If I'd known then how badly I was deluding myself, perhaps our story would have turned out differently.

CHAPTER 56

AHARON

I t was with great trepidation that I kept an appointment I had made months earlier to visit a faux caviar production plant in northern Norway. It was owned by an elderly Yid, Leo Axelrod, whose father had seen the "handwriting on the wall" just ahead of the Nazi incursion into Czechoslovakia.

The family had boarded a ship in Prague, sailed down the Vltava River, and kept on going until it docked in Narvik, a port in Norway. They continued by fishing boat to Bodø, with some other refugees and remained there until 1940, when that city was bombed by the German Luftwaffe. They rowed to one of the Lofoten Islands and stayed until the end of the war, remaining there to this day.

The family eventually had expanded enough to form a minyan of their own, and somewhere along the way they'd fished some salmon from the sea and concocted a delicious, insanely expensive fish paste, an imitation caviar, for which they received kosher certification. I included this item in my product list along with my truffles and other exotic foods, and it sold like hotcakes.

The kashrus certification I worked for knew I was already familiar with their production facilities, but they wanted me to visit again.

I called our *rav* and explained the precarious situation with Mordy — hence my trepidation — but he *paskened* that I couldn't stop my life and my work indefinitely, and that I should go.

I left on a rainy Monday, aware that I'd be traveling for quite a while. I packed plenty of food and some *sefarim*, both to learn on the way and some new ones to leave with Leo. *Sefarim* were hard to come by there, and I was happy to add to his meager collection.

Only Mordy was awake to see me off, as I'd woken him early to take care of his needs. He was sad to see me go, but wished me well and said to please hurry back. I told him I'd be home before Shabbos, and I could tell he was relieved. We'd hired a male nurse to care for him until I returned.

The trip door to door took more than twenty-four hours. I flew to Oslo, then transferred to a ferry that steamed through the Norwegian fjords in the North Sea. This was my favorite part of the trip — the air was so cold and clean and fresh I wished I could bottle it along with the fish paste and bring it home. I'd make a fortune.

"My friend," Leo greeted me. His English was surprisingly good, despite his Hungarian accent, which had hung on like a barnacle, but he helped it along with quite a few Yiddish expressions inherited from his father.

The table was already set with at least five fish dishes and an assortment of root vegetables: potatoes, carrots, beets, and onions. The setting was plain but beautiful, with a bouquet of local wildflowers gracing the center of the finely crafted table, hand-carved by Leo's father and uncles, as were other pieces of furniture in the house. Leo's wife and children came out to greet me, then discreetly absented themselves, allowing us to catch up.

Learning came first for Leo, even before eating, although I managed to nibble something as we learned. Leo's enthusiasm and brilliance made the learning *geshmak*.

After we ate, he drove us up the mountain road to fish and watch the midnight sun do its midsummer's nightly magic, descending to the horizon, taking a bow, then climbing back up to its perch in the sky. Huge mountains rose out of the water surrounding the spot like stone geysers, and it was mesmerizing, *nifla'os haBorei* that would stay with me for months after I returned home.

Leo set up a small brazier, two chairs, two fishing poles, and a cooler of kosher beer.

"So, Aharon. Something's changed, no? I see you from year to year, and this time you seem to me like a different person."

I nodded. Unburdening myself to Leo was perhaps another reason I'd dared to leave my family at such a crucial time and trek to this remote northern outpost. I told him the entire story, starting with the trauma of Mordy's birth, up to the present. Leo listened intently, rarely interrupting to clarify certain details. I ended, with tears in my eyes, telling him about my wife's strange and unsettling behavior. We sat silently for a while, staring out at the horizon and watching the sun. Leo's fishing pole started wobbling with a bite, but when he reeled it in the fish had escaped. He recast, placed his pole in the pole holder, and clucked his tongue a few times.

"Do you know what it means, the word '*avreich*'?" he asked me. "It's not just a man who learns all day long. It's from *Parashas Mikeitz*, and Rashi says it means to bend a knee, describing Yosef Hatzaddik and his total selflessness."

I had no idea where he was going with this, but I listened carefully, knowing that he usually ended somewhere I'd never imagine.

"Your wife, Aharon. Oy, she is suffering." He tsked-tsked a few times in sympathy. "Can you imagine, waiting for a child not just for nine months but for fourteen years? Can you imagine her pain and suffering? No, you can't." I tried to interrupt, to explain, but he hushed me with a raised hand. "Nor can I. No one else can."

"And therefore?" I was genuinely puzzled.

"It's all coming back up now. If you'll pardon the expression in relation to your holy wife, she is emotionally regurgitating. She has been waiting all this time to mother this child, certain she'd never get him back, and suddenly, there he is. She is turning, she is falling..." His English faltered for a moment.

"When she didn't know what she was missing it didn't hurt as much. Now she sees what has become of him, ignorant of Torah, emotionally deprived, and she wants to give him everything all at once."

That made sense to me — in fact, I knew it on a certain level, but I hadn't thought of it the way he described it.

"So, *nu*, what's the *eitzah*?" I asked. "What can I do?"

He sank into a long silence, but I didn't mind. I enjoyed silence and wasn't afraid of it. Nor did I fear what he would say, because I knew it would be the *emes*.

"Two things," he said finally. "First, you must be an *avreich*, selfless. You must submit yourself to your wife as you would to a person who has been suffering a terrible ailment for years and years. No arguments, no fights." I nodded. I didn't love the idea, but I understood it.

"Secondly, you must get her help. Right away. The way she is acting may be annoying or frustrating to you, but it is ingrained so deeply she doesn't even realize what she is doing. Help her, Aharon. Help your wife."

CHAPTER 57

AHARON

Leo and I parted two days later, better friends than ever. We didn't speak much more about my situation — mostly we learned, ate a great deal, hiked, and fished. I inspected his factory and found everything in perfect order.

By the time I returned home, I was in a different frame of mind. Instead of focusing exclusively on Mordy, I was determined to give most of my attention to Devorah. She was my top priority.

Once I stopped judging her, I could see much more clearly. I knew she was happy to have Mordy home, but it was happiness tinged with anxiety. I could see now the tightness in her jaw and limbs. I could see that she'd lost weight too, that she was neglecting her business, that she was obsessing about the bar mitzvah. I could see that the other children were no longer sidling up to her for a hug or a squeeze or a taste of whatever she was cooking, as they usually did.

I could see that Mordy too had grown quieter, his exuberance tamed, his smile halfhearted and apologetic. Although we didn't allow him to hibernate in his room, he spent most of his time with his head in a book, looking up only when someone spoke to him. The kids had kind of given up on him, they had so little common ground, and I sensed they were wary of him.

It was like having a statue in the house.

What saved the situation was my mother, who arrived faithfully each morning and spent three hours reading to Mordy, playing cards or checkers with him, and keeping up a running commentary the entire time. When I was home to help her in and out with his wheelchair, she'd take him for long walks, which I know was difficult for her. She seemed to have received a new, self-replenishing source of energy when it came to Mordy.

Neither Devorah nor I dared to mention her former virulent resistance to his return home, and we were just gratified that someone was getting through to him.

I thought very hard about how I could help Devorah — Leo's words were as clear in my mind as when he said them — but it was hard to catch her alone and unoccupied.

She'd developed a frenetic energy, and it was hard to pin her down.

Then I remembered date night. We hadn't gone out alone since well before Pesach and the trial run with Mordy. It was the perfect place to start, to at least re-establish communication and rapport. I admit I'd been at odds with her for the way she was acting toward Mordy, but it was time to change tactics. Devorah came first.

The first few times I suggested going out, just the two of us, she turned me down, saying she couldn't leave Mordy home untended, she was too busy, she had too much to do, a client was coming. I didn't want to ask my mother to return in the evening to babysit, so it occurred to me we could just as well go out in the morning. I didn't have a desk job, and although I appeared at the office regularly, technically I didn't have to. So that's how Devorah and I ended up at the Flushing Meadow Park Zoo on a beautiful spring morning.

It was as if we were on a *shidduch* date, just getting to know each other, keeping it light and breezy. Although I was very anxious to have a deep discussion with her, I knew that if I jumped in too fast she'd retreat. So, as hard as it was, I acted as though it was our first meeting. We walked around and admired the animals, especially the enormous walruses at the far end, and we even took a ride on the merry-go-round. We were the only ones there. It was so much fun that Devorah was laughing out loud, and I realized how long it had been since I'd heard that sound.

Afterward we bought ices and settled ourselves on a bench. Devorah was glowing, and I was glad to be making a start. We made light conversation, with a lot of "remember whens" that made us laugh. Eventually, though, and inevitably, the talk turned to Mordy. "He's doing amazingly well, don't you think?" Devorah said.

Here was my opening. I could have said, "Actually, I'm not so sure," and we could have taken it from there. I wanted to get to the bottom of this, to solve it as soon as possible, but I forced myself to hold back.

"He's doing very well in his bar mitzvah lessons," I offered, dodging her question. "We had to start from *aleph-beis*, but there's time."

"Ephraim is going to *lein* the *parashah*. Do you think Mordy can do a few lines, or maybe the *haftorah*?" Devorah asked, her eyes pleading with me to make this miracle happen.

I could feel my frustration rising. Didn't she realize the only reason Mordy was doing the whole bar mitzvah thing was to make her happy? I hadn't even started teaching him the *berachos*. He was always agreeable and willing, but I could tell his heart wasn't in it.

Of all the things I had thought about as we considered bringing Mordy home, although I knew that his adaption to *Yiddishkeit* would require an adjustment, I, like Devorah, had assumed that he would take to it automatically. I never thought it would become a sticking point, but he was withering from the pressure, both overt and covert, we were putting on him.

"Devorale," I said gently, "let's just stick to the basics, okay?"

She shook her head. "There isn't time."

"What's the rush?" I replied, although her answer unsettled me.

"I told you already, he's missed so much. We've missed so much. I can't take it that he's not *frum*."

"He does whatever we tell him," I said. "He wears a yarmulke. He says *berachos* when we remind him."

"But we're not getting through to his *neshamah*. Not at all."

And there it was. A light turned on in my mind as if it was a darkened room, suddenly illuminated.

We'd been working from the outside in, hoping that instructing him would somehow translate into understanding and then to belief. *Reishis chochmah yiras Hashem.* Talk about sticking to the basics... We'd dived into the pool before filling it with water, and expected Mordy to jump in after us.

I had no idea how to teach him about *emunah* and *bitachon* in a way that made sense to him. The other children had simply absorbed it from early childhood, and everywhere they went — school, camp, family — it was reinforced.

The thought of starting from scratch reminded me of those mountainous cliffs jutting out of the water that I'd seen in Norway with Leo, beautiful to look at but impossible to climb.

CHAPTER 58

AHARON

T atty, what's going on here?"

Ephraim Baruch, attuned to everything, as usual, even the sighing of the trees. He was our "canary in the coal mine" — whenever things went slightly awry, if by chance we weren't aware of it he would let us know.

I could have held him off with a short reply, like, "Nothing at all, business as usual," but we were long past that. There were so many things going on that I asked him what he was referring to.

"I don't know, exactly," he replied, wrinkling his nose as he did when trying to figure something out. "That's why I'm asking. Ever since you all went suit shopping for Mordy, things feel upside-down. Is he feeling okay?"

I looked down at my sweet son, hovering on the cusp of adulthood but still very much a child. "He's feeling fine in his body, but I think he's a little sad."

"Right! That's what I mean. He doesn't smile so much anymore. He used to smile all the time, right? Like me." He flashed me one of his dazzlers and I pretended to be blinded by the light.

I smiled back. "You got used to us quickly because you grew up with us. It's taking Mordy some time, that's all. It's a big change from where he grew up."

Ephraim nodded gravely. "It sounds like it was scary there."

I raised an eyebrow. "How would you know?"

"I asked Mordy about it."

I looked at him in surprise. I should have known he'd interrogate Mordy at some point — I just didn't realize he'd already done it. "When?" I asked.

"I don't know. A couple of weeks ago."

"What did he say?" I asked.

Ephraim shrugged. "I don't know. I asked him questions and he answered. Like did he go to *cheder* and what was it like to spend Shabbos there and who his friends were. That type of stuff."

"And he answered you?"

Ephraim thought for a second. "Not really. He let me ask the questions and I just kept talking." He smiled again. "You know me."

I did know him, and I wondered if his questions had set Mordy off.

"But also Mommy," he appended.

I nodded. "Also Mommy. I think she's just thinking about the bar mitzvah, and you and me, and Maya and Rena..."

But Ephraim was shaking his head. "No, it's something else."

"I'll look into it, okay? Are you worried?"

"No," he said. "I just want things to be good for everyone. The way it used to be."

"Got it," I said.

And I did get it. The atmosphere in the house was different, but how could it not be? We had thought, when we reconnected with Mordy and started to spend time with him, that because he was so charming and personable, he would figure out a way to fit right in.

At some point Mordy was going to have to go to school. We hadn't thought that far ahead yet, but we couldn't just leave him sitting in the living room for the rest of his life. We needed help.

There was a choice of two directions in which I could proceed: via Mrs. Mirsky or via Dr. Cohen, or both.

I considered very carefully whether I would be betraying Devorah by calling Mrs. Mirsky and asking her to come and speak with us, and then I realized that it was not a contradiction. I would just ask Devorah what she thought, and when I suggested it to her she agreed. Mrs. Mirsky was thrilled to hear from us and invited us to her home that evening. Part of me wanted to bring Mordy with us so she could get a feeling for who he is and what he's about. But I felt it would be too awkward, so we brought a picture of him and a tape recording of him speaking.

I saw her face change as she looked at the picture and listened. "Mmm," she murmured, then looked up at us. "Someone did a very good job with him."

Devorah and I looked at each other and nodded.

"Someone did," I said, and Devorah went on to tell her about Dr. Cohen and all he had done for Mordy.

"You were very lucky," she said. "This story could have had a very different outcome."

"We know," I said. "But he isn't thriving with us at all. He needs activity and stimulation."

"Well, of course he does," said Mrs. Mirsky.

"What are the options?" Devorah asked.

Alerted by something in her voice, Mrs. Mirsky paused and caught Devorah's eye. "I have a different question," she said. "How are you doing with all of this? It must be a tremendous adjustment for you."

"Me?" said Devorah, surprised at the turn in the conversation. "I'm perfectly fine."

Mrs. Mirsky started laughing, and we joined her. "Sure you are, Devorah. Tell us about it."

Devorah smiled and hung her head a little. "It's complicated," she said softly.

"You bet it is. This can't be easy for you." Mrs. Mirsky's compassion just overflowed.

"It doesn't matter if it's easy or not. Nothing matters except Mordy."

"Do you really believe that?"

"What's the question? You're a Jewish mother. You know what it's like. What won't we do for our children?"

"We won't be able to do much for them if we don't take

care of ourselves as well. You know the story of the mother with twelve children and one egg."

Devorah laughed. "Don't tell me you go in for that hocus-pocus stuff! Who has time for that? I just want Mordy to have everything he needs, and I'm willing to do anything to make that happen. I thought you would agree with me on that point."

"Of course I do, but that doesn't blind me to certain things. I find it hard to believe that everything fell into place smoothly when your precious child reappeared after fourteen years, after he was practically pried from your arms as a baby, and you are perfectly okay with that! Your insides have to catch up with your 'outside,' you know. You're only human. We're all only human."

Devorah stood up abruptly. "Mrs. Mirsky, I really appreciate you giving us so freely of your time. Aharon, you ready?"

We were saying goodbye and out the door practically before we'd said hello. I looked back at Mrs. Mirsky and was glad to see she wasn't insulted. Her face was a picture of sympathy and understanding. "Give it time," she whispered, and I nodded.

"Well, that was a bust," said Devorah as we settled into the car. "Why do people think we have all the time in the world to 'get ourselves together'? I'm afraid we're almost out of time. What kind of mother waits around to feel good when her child — when all her children — need her?"

"I hear you." I nodded. After hearing her say it so many times, I was starting to believe her. I always knew she was strong — why would now be any different? We had rarely mentioned Mordy over the years, mainly on his birthdays, so it was very possible she had dealt with the pain a long time ago, and now that he was back she was simply in full "*tachlis*" mode, primed to get things moving.

If I had learned anything in all the years of married life, it was to never, ever underestimate my wife.

CHAPTER 59

JEREMY

I can't say I was surprised when Aharon Landau called me. I understood that the Landaus were trying to do things on their own, in their own way, and I'd made my peace with it, even though I knew they'd need me eventually. And they did.

I don't know why they thought it was a good idea to cut Murray off from the only person he felt close to, but if I learned anything at all at Ravensfield, it was that there was no telling people what to do. They had to figure it out on their own, and it was always much better that way. I missed that kid, but I knew that we were both in the right place, doing the right things. Still, I wondered what they were up to. How could I not?

The previous few weeks had been extremely busy for me. After Murray left Ravensfield, it took no time at all for me to formally resign, pack up my stuff, and move in with my mother until I could get myself set up in a place of my own nearer to the residence I was building. A salary for my work at the group home was stipulated in Mrs. Genzel's grant, but it would still take a while to get it up and running.

My mother was happy to have me, and truth be told, I could do with a little mothering myself. Only after I left Ravensfield did I realize what a heavy toll I had paid working in such an intense environment. For a while I did little but sleep and eat, until I slowly recovered and turned my mind to the group home.

Even before I'd left Ravensfield I'd had a good idea of which patients I would be bringing with me into the home. Some had nowhere else to go and others would be coming with the full input, support, and cooperation of their parents.

We were aiming to accommodate teenagers with a middle range of function who had the potential to grow. The home had space for twelve residents but I took in only eleven, leaving one bed open as what I called a respite bed. But deep in my heart, even though I wouldn't say it out loud, I was leaving the bed available for Murray.

Mrs. Genzel was extremely generous and spared no expense to make the residence comfortable and accessible. There was nothing she didn't think of, and with me adding my two cents, I have to admit the home was going to be a jewel.

The planning and programming was of course my responsibility, and it was a pleasure to be allowed to create protocols and practices that would allow the clients to reach their maximum potential. This included everything from teaching the kids to ride public transportation independently to wrangling meaningful work opportunities from all kinds of employers. From my experience at Ravensfield, I knew exactly what they were missing. I was thrilled to be able to fill in the gaps in their education, and there suddenly seemed no end to my creativity and my resourcefulness.

I consulted with colleagues and could sense some jealousy on their part that I was involved in such a positive, constructive program. We all knew that the time had come for such a home, and I was grateful to be at the forefront of these exciting developments.

My mother was my "right-hand man" as I tackled each hurdle. I had clearly inherited my resourcefulness from her, and she far surpassed me in locating funding and services for my little group. True, it was an experiment, but no matter which way it went, the clients would still come out ahead. And even if we failed, someone else would come along and pick up where we would leave off. I could tell from my colleagues' responses that they would give anything to be involved.

There were certain licenses and permits I needed to apply for, which required some official documents, so I asked my mother where she kept all that kind of stuff. She was distracted when I asked, and I wonder if she would have agreed so readily to direct me to it if she'd had time to think about it. She pointed to a cardboard box at the back of a large, deep closet.

I pulled out the box and wasn't too surprised to find a mess of papers piled haphazardly inside. I found what I was looking for easily. However, I couldn't resist poking around a bit among my mother's papers, and I didn't think she'd mind.

There were lots of pictures, of course, gorgeous black-and-white candids, and Polaroids, segueing into color as the years passed and the faces aged. My baby shoes, an envelope of hair, a tiny, unraveling baby sweater with little elephant buttons.

A pair of U.S. Army dog tags clinked against each other as I moved the stuff around in the box, and I picked them up, assuming they were my father's. But even though the punched-out lettering was worn and faded, I realized they couldn't have been his, because the name on them was not Cohen but Carolan, and instead of the J for Jewish, which should have been there, there was a C.

I don't know why I cared, or why it bothered me that my mother had some stranger's dog tags in her possession, there were a million and one reasons why those dog tags *might* have been in there, but only one reason why they *should* have been: the first name was the same as my father's. Were it not for that, I'd have tossed them back to spend eternity unacknowledged in a cardboard box at the back of a closet.

I held on to them and, after making sure I had all the papers I needed, I taped the box back up and left it where I'd found it. I moved too quickly — I know that now. I should have taken at least a minute to consider the ramifications, but I was already in motion, and a man in motion remains in motion until he crashes into a wall.

"Hey, Mom?" She'd finished what she was doing and was sitting at the kitchen table, a cup of coffee in front of her, skimming through a homemaking magazine.

"Yes?" She looked up at me, slightly startled. She'd lived alone for so long she wasn't used to having someone else around.

I held up the dog tags and dangled them between my fingers. "Whose are these?"

I could feel the energy of an avalanche building, but I couldn't figure out where it was coming from. I just knew that something big was about to happen.

CHAPTER 60

JEREMY

My mother turned a page in the magazine she was looking at and replied, "They're your father's. Why? Whose did you think they were?"

"I don't think so," I said slowly. "Take a look."

She looked for a second and handed them back. "What's the problem?"

I was still in motion. "Look at the last name," I prodded. "Look at the letter signifying 'religion.' Last I checked, our last name was not Carolan and our religion was not 'C.'"

My mother put down the newspaper, unperturbed, and that's when I learned how tough she really was.

"Well, Jeremy…" she said slowly, her nerves of steel sending out sparks in my brain. Her voice was perfectly even. "I'd hoped you would have figured it out by now without my having to explain it to you. Your brother has known for years."

"Known what?" I asked, still not getting it. My voice was quivering, my hands were shaking.

She looked me right in the eye. "Your father wasn't Jewish."

If she'd shot an arrow through my heart I doubt if I'd have felt more deeply wounded. The news fell on me like that avalanche I'd sensed was on the way, but this was an avalanche that threatened to bury my heart.

"Explain," I demanded. Now, I'm a generally good guy, a good son, but this was almost too much for me.

"It's not that hard to understand," she said. "We met when your father was stationed in Fort Hamilton before he shipped out, and we decided to get married. We didn't tell Papa and Nana at first, because we didn't know what would happen during the war, but your father—"

"Don't call him that!"

"Oh, Jeremy, stop being so dramatic. He's still your father. As you know, he came through just fine. We couldn't tell my parents the truth, though, so we legally changed our name to Cohen."

"Don't tell me Papa fell for that." My father's features formed in my head, and I wondered how I could have been so blind.

"Whether your grandfather knew or didn't know, we stuck to our story. It was actually your father's idea. I was willing to come clean, but your father couldn't bring himself to hurt them. It came out later, after you and Alex were born, but by then Papa adored you two so much it was moot. After Nana died, your father took care of Papa with all his heart. He loved and respected him even though Papa could never accept him."

I remembered my father taking care of my grandfather with tender care, even as Papa kept up a steady stream of slights and insults. My father just smiled and let the insults bounce off him.

I didn't know which was worse, my mother marrying a non-Jew, the lie, the betrayal or, to my surprise, the loss of my identity. Despite my lifelong objection to organized religion, I'd always considered myself a Jew and felt that gave me the right to express my criticism and disgust with all the rituals.

I was in shock. My mother looked at me strangely, almost mockingly.

"Jeremy," she chided, "what do you care? You never showed one bit of interest in anything Jewish. Look how you behaved with Murray's parents. You gave them such a hard time."

"That's not the point," I sputtered, at a loss for words. Because my mother was right. Why should I care?

"Then what *is* the point?"

I sat down, suddenly exhausted. "I don't know yet, but there is a point, Mom. How could you let me live a lie for so long?"

"To tell you the truth," she said, and I could not believe this was my own mother speaking, "to tell you the truth, Jeremy, it was none of your business. It was a decision your father and I made, and we knew it wouldn't really affect you. You and Alex are still Jewish — we asked a rabbi — so no harm was done to anyone."

Except me! I wanted to cry. And what about Papa and Nana? It must have destroyed them. There's no way they could not have known, right from the beginning. Suddenly some of Papa's remarks over the years now made sense to me. I also realized how much they'd loved and cherished their daughter, my mother, that they were unwilling to disown her, preferring to bear the disgrace.

And to my shame, because I had loved my father with all my heart, the thought of non-Jewish blood running through my veins totally unnerved me. I had always tried to live my life honestly, to behave with integrity when what I saw around me was so dishonest. And all this time deception had been embedded within me like a seed waiting to germinate, coloring my every action and interaction without my knowledge or consent.

"Is that why—" I couldn't bring myself to say "Dad," not right then. "Is that why he didn't have a funeral?"

"He was cremated," my mother said. "It was what he wanted."

That's when I lost it. I ran into my room and slammed the door. My mother came knocking after a while, but I didn't answer her. A wall had sprung up between us and I didn't know if it could ever be breached.

I stayed in her apartment for a few more days. I went out and rented an apartment near the group home, packed my belongings, and left when my mother was not at home.

So when Aharon Landau called a couple of weeks later, I was still in quite a state. I knew he needed to talk about

Murray, and I would let him, but first I needed to tell him what had happened to me. I'm sure it wasn't what he bargained for when he finally picked up the phone to call; it must have taken a lot of effort and humility on his part to admit that he needed help.

But for once in my life I put myself first. I poured out the story so fast he could barely keep up. After I finished he was absolutely silent. I was sure he'd have no sympathy and tell me that it was coming to me, and it would have been one hundred percent true.

Then I heard his voice answering me. It was so different from what I expected, as though it was coming from a place deep inside of him, and after all we had been through — no, after all I had put him and his family through — my respect for him grew by leaps and bounds.

"Dr. Cohen," he said, and his voice caught in a sob, "I am so, so sorry to hear this. You must be absolutely devastated."

CHAPTER 61

JEREMY

Aharon Landau spoke so kindly to me, so compassionately, that remorse washed over me in another landslide. I wondered how long it would take to be completely buried. But was I really so devastated? It felt like I was, but I wasn't sure why.

We spoke for a long time, or I spoke, repeating myself over and over again, analyzing each word my mother had said. Landau didn't respond to any of that, all he did was murmur words of consolation and hope.

"You are still completely Jewish, you know," he said a few times. "Judaism is passed down through the mother. You are still Jewish."

I finally wound down, spent, but realized he still needed to talk about Murray and I hadn't given him a chance. "I'm afraid I'm in no shape to talk about Murray right now," I apologized. "Is it urgent? Can it wait?"

His silence, which I'd learned was as eloquent as his speech, let me know that he was deeply distressed. "Is he in danger?" I asked, suddenly worried about someone besides myself. "Is he in pain?"

"No, it's nothing like that." While listening to my troubles his voice had sounded so warm and close, as though he were in the room with me, but now his voice seemed to come from far away.

"He's fine, I guess, but we're in trouble. My wife and I."

I had no strength, but I knew I needed to find some, fast. "I can be at your house in two hours," I offered. "I just need to pull myself together."

He sighed. "It'll be Shabbos by then." A pause. "Would you like to join us? If you stay a while you can really assess Mordy's situation."

My heart sank. I'd had enough of religion — or lack of it — these past couple of weeks to last me a lifetime. To throw myself into the fire seemed foolhardy and dangerous, but what could I do?

"Uh...sure. I can do that," I said, trying to keep my voice level. A scream was boiling up inside, a shout of anger and frustration that I hoped I would be able to control.

"Mordy will be thrilled to see you," said Aharon. "I know he's missed you."

"Whose fault is that?" I snapped. I could hear Landau suck in his breath and my shame knew no bounds. This man had just spent an inordinate amount of time listening to a virtual antagonist moan about his own problems and I had the nerve to shoot barbed words at him. "I'm sorry," I said lamely. "That was uncalled for."

"Indeed," he said, chuckling. "I don't expect you to change overnight."

This guy was unreal. Nothing rattled him.

"I'll be there soon," I said. Aharon chuckled again and hung up.

By the time I arrived, it looked like everything was ready for Shabbos, and I realized I'd cut it very close — it was only minutes to sundown, as Aharon informed me. He was calm, sitting at his weird book-desk with a big volume spread open on top of it, barely containing its bulk.

Mrs. Landau came in holding a tray with small plates of chicken, potato kugel, and a slice of apple cake. It looked and smelled delicious, and my stomach rumbled. "You have six minutes to finish it all," she said, and poured me a drink of ginger ale.

The Landaus never asked you what you wanted — they just served you, assuming you'd partake. I liked it.

I'd been in such a rush that it took me a second or two to notice that Murray had pulled up his fancy wheelchair at my side and he tugged at my elbow. I turned to look at him and I had trouble hiding my shock. He looked like a different kid, and not in a good way.

"We'll be sharing a room again," he said, and only then could I detect the sparkle in his eyes that had defined Murray in my mind since that first moment I'd noticed it, when it had called out to me from his crib.

"Great to see you, pal," I said, almost whispering in the hope of conveying to Murray that his secrets were safe with me. "Are you okay?"

"I'm fine!" he said. "I love it here." I knew immediately that he wasn't telling me the truth — did he think I didn't know him anymore? Whenever he said, "I'm fine," with the stress on the "fine," I knew the opposite was more likely.

I didn't doubt that he liked being with the Landaus, but whatever the case may have been, fine he was not.

"You should eat," he said.

"It's almost *sheh-ki-yah*," he pronounced carefully.

"N-i-i-ice," I said, smiling. "What does it mean?"

"Sundown," he said proudly.

"Cool. We'll talk later. Let me eat. I'm starving." We were back into our rhythm. Murray knew how much I liked home-cooked food, and he left me to it, sitting quietly beside me while I shoveled down the food. It seemed like hours passed until Aharon and his son came home from shul and we got through the main meal, and it was all much more pleasant than I'd expected. By the time we finished I was stuffed and drowsy, so I poured myself two cups of black coffee, downed them, and followed Murray into his room.

I saw he had his own room and wished he'd been able to room with his brother, but his apparatus simply took up too much space.

Murray seemed comfortable there, though. Most of his things were stationed at arm's reach from his bed, which was good and bad. It was good because why not make his life easier, and it wasn't good because even small stretches of mobility were very important.

This was one of the small things the Landaus had no way of knowing.

"So," I said, turning the wheelchair to face me. "Speak." He turned his face down and I turned it right back up. "I can't help you if you don't tell me what's wrong."

"How can anything be wrong?" he wailed. "I'm living a dream come true! What's wrong with me?" He was an inch away from tears, and while there was emotionally nothing wrong with that, crying tended to make his blood pressure rise.

"There's nothing wrong with you, Murray," I said softly.

"Who's Murray?" he said. "And who's Mordy? Which one am I?"

CHAPTER 62

JEREMY

froze for a moment, fearing a hot geyser in my chest. Was Murray declining neurologically?

"What do you mean?" I asked carefully.

"You know what I mean!" *Ah, okay, he was back on track now.* "You call me Murray. They call me Mordy. I feel like I'm being pulled into two pieces."

I can relate, I thought.

"What would you like to do?" I asked him.

"I don't know," he said.

"I think you do know."

Murray shook his head vehemently. "I can't leave, Dr. Cohen. There's no way! After all they've done for me…"

I waited a minute before speaking. I wasn't surprised, I'd been half-expecting something like this to happen. When I had started out planning his return to his family with a trial run, this was one of the things I'd been worried about. Totally immersing him in this religious rigmarole was like suddenly dunking him into a freezing cold pool.

"Nobody said anything about leaving," I replied.

"Then what?" I could see a spark of hope in his eyes, I knew what I had to do but I had no idea how I was going to do it. I wished, for once in my life, that someone had some faith that I knew what I was doing. My mother obviously hadn't, and neither have the Landaus.

There was no reason why this could not have been a completely successful integration if it had been done the right way. The whole process should have taken not less than a *year*, and it ended up being a week. The way it had been done was guaranteed to fail, but I honestly believed that all was not lost.

When I went out of the bedroom later on to get a hot drink, Aharon Landau was sitting at his desk again poring over a large tome. "Don't you ever get tired of it?" I asked, but not in my usual confrontational way, and he could tell that I meant it sincerely.

"No," he said. "There's always something new to learn and think about. Would you like me to show you?"

"No, thanks," I said, taking a step back, and we both laughed.

"You're a hard sell, Dr. Cohen," said Aharon. "So, what's with Mordy? Any insights?"

"A few," I said.

Aharon cleared a pile of books off a chair and motioned for me to sit down. "This is not going to be good, right?" he said, after getting a look at my face in the light. "I'm not going to like this."

I had thought a little about how to bring up what I was thinking, trying to twist and turn it and make it more palatable, but I knew the only way to go was head-on.

"Listen, first of all, you guys have done an amazing job."

Aharon smiled. "Coming from you that's high praise."

"Look, I know I owe you an apology. A big one. My behavior was inexcusable."

"That's between you and the One Above," he said, whatever that meant. I could never get a normal answer out of this man.

"Right. Okay. So. What I think is that we need to take a look at the big picture. Back when we first met, we spent a long time discussing a trial run. Do you remember that?" I asked. I wasn't trying to be adversarial — I was just trying to paint a full picture we could both look at.

"Of course I remember. It didn't work out so well, but what difference does that make? This is his home. Where else was he supposed to go, even if we are religious?"

"I'm not sure that's the only issue." I *was* sure, actually. Murray had nearly everything he could possibly need or want here, except for that.

Aharon stared me down and I caved immediately. "I think adjusting to family life would have been hard for him in any family," I said, which was true. "I think the religious part added an extra layer of difficulty that we weren't prepared for."

"Who do you mean when you say 'we'?" he asked.

"Well, Murray for sure, and maybe also you and your wife. And myself, of course. If I had had more time, we could have made it easier on all of us. But there's no going back. Let's go forward."

"What do you have in mind?" Aharon asked.

"I haven't spoken to Murray about it yet, and it's not something that needs to happen overnight. But I think we need to rewind the tape and start from the beginning."

I saw Aharon's face fall and I knew he could see where I was headed. He looked, suddenly, so young and innocent. I thought about the differences between the two of us, the parallel paths our lives had taken, destined never to meet — until Murray joined us together. We both carried a lot of responsibility each in our own way, but I was not a father, and that was crucial.

"I think," I continued, with Murray's dejected face etched in my mind and Aharon's so-similar dejected features in front of me, "I think I have a solution that might work."

"I know what you're going to say," said Aharon, a rare note of bitterness flattening his tone. "You want to put Mordy in your group home. It's what you've wanted all along."

"Hold-it-hold-it-hold-it-hold-it," I said, raising my hands like a police officer trying valiantly to control traffic in rush hour. "In order for this to work, and to work out best for Murray, who, let's not forget, *is our primary concern*, we're going to have to call a trust truce."

Aharon rolled his eyes. "What are you saying now? Sometimes I feel like you're speaking Chinese."

Right back at you, I thought.

"I only mean that we can't keep accusing each other of ulterior motives. Just *listen*, okay?"

Aharon took a deep breath. "Okay," he said. "I'm listening."

"So, yes, you're right, I was going to suggest that we put him in my group home as a *temporary* measure. Let's start from the beginning and do it right this time. He'll stay in the home, where he will have the full-time care he really needs…"

"Wait a minute! He is getting everything he needs right here!"

"Aharon, please. You've got to pull yourself together and hear me out."

"I can't," he admitted. "I just can't. We did *everything* you told us to do. We followed *every* single direction you gave us and then some. Why isn't it good enough? Why? Did Mordy tell you he wants to leave, or are you putting words in his mouth?"

His voice broke, and I almost broke along with him. He was crying now.

Suddenly I heard a door slam and footsteps coming down the stairs, and I knew I was in trouble.

"Good Shabbos," said Mrs. Landau sleepily. "What's going on? I heard loud voices and…" Her head was turning as she spoke, inclined naturally toward her husband, and I watched her stop in her tracks.

"Aharon! What's wrong? Why are you crying?"

She turned to glare at me. "What happened? Is Mordy okay? What kind of trouble are you stirring up now? Haven't you done enough?"

CHAPTER 63

DEVORAH

Good Shabbos, Devorah," Aharon said to me, drying his tears as I rushed in to find out what exactly was going on. I could count on one finger the number of times I'd seen him cry.

"You came down just in time," he added.

"I can see that," I said. "What brought this on?"

It was true that I did not trust Dr. Cohen, but I didn't really dislike him either. So I didn't understand why, whenever I spoke to him, my words sliced the air like sharp knives.

Aharon says it's the mama bear syndrome, that undeniable instinct a mother has to protect her young.

"Have a seat," Aharon said. "Dr. Cohen and I were just talking...about Mordy."

I sat down next to Aharon, the two of us facing Dr. Cohen. I hoped we looked at least a little bit threatening, but a Shabbos robe and an old snood were not exactly intimidating.

"What does the good doctor have to say?" I asked, as if I didn't know. I'd been listening to the conversation from upstairs, waiting for the right moment to come down. The last thing I expected was for Aharon to start crying, and then I flew down to rescue him. I knew how closely he's attached to Mordy — maybe even more than I am? — and the thought of losing Mordy would be especially painful to him.

"You won't be *losing* him," said Dr. Cohen, reading my mind. Sometimes the more I try to look neutral and stoic the more I betray my feelings. "You'll be *gaining* your son, but the right way this time."

I nodded instinctively, because part of me agreed with him, but I didn't want Aharon to think I was betraying him, nor did I want to admit that I knew what they had been talking about.

"As you said, Aharon," Dr. Cohen continued, "you've done nothing wrong and everything right. The only thing off was our timing, and that turned out to be more important than we thought it would be."

I appreciated that he was not rubbing it in our faces. He *had* warned us repeatedly how crucial it was to take the adjustment period slowly, regardless of the fact that we were religious. I had assumed the matter had been taken out of our hands when Mordy was hospitalized and that social worker got involved, that it was *min haShamayim* that we skip over the trial run and jump right in, and that everything would work out. It was only when I started to get obsessive that I realized something was not right, and that it was I myself who needed help.

Were I even to *attempt* to forgive myself for letting them take Mordy away from me at birth and then ignoring him all those years, the one thing I will *never* forgive myself for is letting Mordy grow up without *Yiddishkeit*. Deep down I knew I was rushing and pressuring my son because I couldn't tolerate my own guilt and I wanted to rectify it as soon as possible. But I couldn't stop myself. I was out of control. I thought of him missing out on so many important things in a Jewish boy's life. Even though, *b'chasdei Hashem*, he did have a bris, what about all the other things he had missed? While I'd had such joy and *nachas* from watching Ephraim Baruch pass through all stages of growth, I hadn't thought about Mordy much at all. I'd locked him away in the back of my mind. But during those times of *simchah* I would dream about him. Or when whatever we were doing coincided with his birthday, he would somehow come and find me. But I never put two and two together until I laid eyes on him at Ravensfield. Then the door I'd slammed in his face came flying open with such force that I thought the guilt would bring me to my knees.

Every time I looked at him it was a fresh wound, a cruel reminder of all that I — and he — had missed. Instead of doing *teshuvah* like a normal person, forgiving myself and forgiving others, I passed the burden on to Mordy himself, making him feel worse than he already did. The more he tried to please me, the more demanding I became.

And indeed, here I was, ready to capitulate to Dr. Cohen's suggestion, not knowing how to do it without hurting Aharon. How could I explain that Mordy's *neshamah* was more important to me than anything else and that I simply could not handle the conflict? I wanted to spin the wheels of his life in reverse and start all over again. But of course that was impossible.

I suddenly felt — spurred on, perhaps, by Aharon's tears or the resolute but surprisingly compassionate expression on Dr. Cohen's face — that what I had to do now was let Dr. Cohen care for Mordy's physical needs while I tended exclusively to his *neshamah*, slowly, step by step. I knew the logistics would be complicated — no way was I going to let Mordy eat *treif* again — but there had to be some compromise we could reach. We wouldn't do anything without *da'as Torah*, but still...

"I'm assuming you're talking about putting Mordy in your group home," I said flatly with my heart pounding a mile a minute.

"Yes, Mrs. Landau, I'm sure you would agree—"

I could, but not at that moment. I had to at least put up a decent fight. "You've been planning this all along, haven't you?" I accused. "You *knew* we weren't going to succeed with him."

"*Kas bashalom!*" said Dr. Cohen, meaning to say, "*chas v'shalom.*" For a moment we all went silent and then Aharon started laughing. That broke the tension and Dr. Cohen and I joined in the laughter, briefly.

It was only when I felt a sweet presence, my firstborn leaning against my arm, that my laughter turned to sobs.

Mordy looked around, trying to gauge the dynamics of the situation but succumbing to hopeless confusion. "Can I ask what's so funny?" he said, looking between Aharon and Dr. Cohen. "Or what's so sad?" he continued, looking at me. "Or both?"

CHAPTER 64

DEVORAH

T he rest of the night became what I had only dreamed of. The four of us — including Mordy — spoke for hours, sharing our real thoughts and feelings for the first time. It was like group therapies but better because we were all working toward the same goal.

We agreed — also including Mordy — to think about what would be best for him, and let him be our guide. It took some time to convince him that his opinion was not only valid but essential.

"Why can't you just make the decisions for me?" he asked. "I'll be happy anywhere."

Aharon looked at him so lovingly it almost broke my heart. "That's exactly the problem, tzaddik. Part of living in the 'real world' is figuring out where you belong. Spi-ri-tu-al-ly and e-mo-tion-al-ly." He said the words slowly to make sure Mordy understood, but Mordy was way ahead of him.

"I belong here," said Mordy.

"That's correct," said Aharon. "But there are other things you need that you might not get here. Dr. Cohen is a medical professional and he can help you in ways that we can't."

"But you're my parents," said Mordy. "Why can't you do everything for me?"

We all sat quietly for a moment, pondering the depth of Mordy's question, wondering which one of us would come up with a good enough answer.

It was, surprisingly, Dr. Cohen. He turned to Mordy and looked him in the eye. I could tell by the way they were facing each other that they had had many heart-to-heart talks, and I felt a little jealous. My heart softened a bit toward this cranky doctor who, in our absence, had stepped up and cared for our son. I realized that I really should be nicer to him and show some gratitude.

"Hey, buddy," he said, and I winced. "I tried not to talk to you too much about families because I didn't want to get your hopes up. But here's the big secret: Parents are only human, like everyone else. They make mistakes, they say things they don't mean, they keep secrets. You with me?" I wondered if Dr. Cohen was thinking of his own mother and father when he said that.

Mordy nodded solemnly. I wished I could hold his attention the way Dr. Cohen did. I decided that I should stop pushing the good doctor away and take some lessons from him instead.

"Most parents," he went on, "have a kid and grow along with him. In your case, your parents would both have been busy all day long every day making sure you had what you needed."

"I do have what I need. Look at all this." Mordy threw his arm out and gestured to his surroundings.

"Right, you have all this because I explained how they had to fix up their house to accommodate you. But your parents don't know about a lot of the other things that will make you strong. It's going to be hard for you to get around in your wheelchair without them, because they don't know how to teach you that. In the group home, there will be a whole team of smart people who know exactly how."

I was looking at Mordy and I saw the moment the penny dropped. He looked at me and then at Aharon like he was seeing us for the first time: two kind people who loved him very much but were essentially clueless amateurs. He looked at us sadly. "Won't it be hard for you?" he whispered, his long lashes falling like curtains over his eyes as if to hide how sad he was for us.

"Yes, it will," Aharon and I answered at the same time as we often do — or used to do. We'd been through a lot this year. "It will be very hard for us," said Aharon, starting to choke up again.

"But what most parents are really good at," I said, "is doing what's best for their kids. So if that means sending you to the group home for a while so you can learn things we can't teach you—"

"And you'll be able to come home anytime you want!" Dr. Cohen interrupted.

Mordy nodded at him gratefully.

I continued, "Then that's what we'll do. We'll be sad, it will hurt, but we'll know that you'll be getting what you need, and that's the most important thing to us."

Mordy started crying then, and the three of us huddled around him, trying to contain our own tears, Aharon and I each holding one of his hands and Dr. Cohen's arm wrapped around his shoulders. I mentally stepped back for a minute then and marveled that even though he was saddled with such severe health problems, Mordy was lucky to be surrounded by so much love.

But then of course I had to break it up, because too much emotion at one time made me nervous. "Okay, Mordy, that's enough for tonight. How about we get you back to bed? It's almost time to get up." He looked at me slyly with an expression I knew very well from the other young man in my life. "Can I have some hot chocolate first?" he asked, the picture of innocence.

I smiled. "Of course."

That look again. "With marshmallows?"

Aharon and I started laughing while Dr. Cohen looked confused.

"He's picked up some tips from his brother," Aharon explained.

"Aha," said Dr. Cohen. "Street smarts."

"Something like that," I said. "Let's go."

I got up and wheeled Mordy out of the room, leaving Aharon and Dr. Cohen to finish the conversation. I didn't want to miss a minute of it because I knew there were things that still needed to be said. I left the door to the kitchen open so I could overhear, just in case.

"You handled that really well," said Dr. Cohen. "I can see that Mordy really trusts the two of you."

Aharon's voice came back muffled and I knew he was covering his face with his hands as he spoke. I could see his image in my mind.

"We tried," he said.

Then he surprised me. "I know my wife feels very guilty," Aharon said.

"I'm sure you do too," said Dr. Cohen.

"No." Now his voice was clear and strong. "I don't. It was terrible, what happened, but I was not acting on my own. I was guided by people I trust. That's number one."

Aharon with his numbers. I listened carefully for number two. Mordy was nudging me for his hot chocolate, but there was no way I was going to miss the rest.

"And number two, I've learned a very important lesson from all of this."

But it seemed I was going to miss it, because Mordy started banging on the table to get my attention, another trick from Ephraim Baruch's repertoire. I poured the hot chocolate from the thermos I kept it in on Shabbos into a big cup and dumped a handful of mini-marshmallows on top. I'd have to ask Aharon about his important lesson later.

CHAPTER 65

DEVORAH

I found out about Aharon's big lesson only later on, and it was a good thing. If I'd heard about it then, I might not have believed him and that would not have been good.

We had agreed that Mordy would move into the group home once it was ready to receive its residents, but there was one thing I wanted to do before he left us. I wanted to take Mordy to see my parents.

Aharon did not think it was a good idea. "How are you going to get him there all by yourself?" he asked. His voice cracked a little so I knew he was really upset.

My parents had been keeping up on developments by phone, almost daily, waiting for the green light to come meet Mordy. I'd been holding them off, thinking that by the time they came for the bar mitzvah everything would be settled and I could show him — and us — off proudly.

My mother was on to me right away, though. "Devorah'le, you don't need to make everything perfect," she'd said. "We're your parents."

"I know, Ma, but just give me a little more time to get my act together," I had told her, which, as time passed, seemed to be moving further and further away.

"Your mother sees him every day," I said to Aharon, which was by the way one of the true miracles of this story. The transformation of my mother-in-law could be written up in a psychology textbook, though the premise was simple: We all need to be needed. The fact that Mordy had gained a best friend and teacher as well as a loving bubby made the miracle that much sweeter.

"That's your argument?" said Aharon. "Have you considered the logistics? Why can't you just tell them to come here?"

Now that was the million-dollar question. It had been my plan to have them meet Mordy when they came for the bar mitzvah, but now that it wasn't going to happen I realized what a bad idea it was. How would they be able to spend time with him and get to know him with all that would be going on at a *simchah*, for one thing? And it wouldn't be fair to Ephraim Baruch either, if all the attention was focused on Mordy. He was already behaving like a tzaddik, willing to share the spotlight with his brother.

"Their house isn't even accessible," Aharon added, throwing the last bucket of water on the fire of my great idea. Accessible had become a code word in our house. Everywhere we turned, we could see how accessible our house was now. But Aharon was right. My parents' house had twelve steep steps leading up to the front door, and it didn't get better after that. There were pitfalls everywhere, and I kind of wondered how I'd grown up safely there.

When I told my mother that visiting wouldn't be possible, she was, as usual, one step ahead of me. "Let us worry about that," she said. "Just come."

I eventually wore Aharon down and he agreed to let us make the trip. He wanted to come with us but I told him I needed him to stay home with the kids, that I would manage and that if I needed him I'd call. He looked at me skeptically but eventually he gave us his blessing. Getting Mordy on the plane was a challenge, but what they lacked in accessibility they made up for in helpfulness. We managed. The flight was about two hours, the limit Mordy could handle, and before we knew it I was flying into my mother's open arms. I felt ridiculous, a grown woman clinging to her mommy like a five-year-old, but neither she nor I held back. We were so busy hugging that I forgot about Mordy for a moment.

My father had in the meantime already engaged him and had him smiling. Moments after saying hello he was already pulling quarters out of Mordy's ears, to my son's delight. Ephraim would have rolled his eyes right away but Mordy was a fresh audience, able to enjoy all kinds of things without judgment or embarrassment.

"Hello, Mordy," said my mother, gently disentangling from me and turning to greet her grandson. She'd asked me on the phone whether she should bend down to talk to him while he was in his wheelchair or if she should remain standing. Pleased by her sensitivity, I had told her to do whatever felt right.

"What felt right" to my mother meant bringing along to the airport a small folding stool and setting it up next to his chair! When she sat down she was so precisely at his eye level that it was almost as if she had measured it.

"Should I have a gift ready for him?" she'd asked. I had told her to do whatever felt right.

As she greeted him, she removed a small package from her pocket and handed it to him.

"These are for you," she said. "It gets cold in Ohio." He opened the box and pulled out a beautiful pair of lined, leather gloves. They were soft as butter on the outside, and after putting them on, you felt like your hands were wrapped in silken buttercups. I know this because I couldn't resist trying them on. Mordy was clearly charmed; my mother, as usual, had done exactly the right thing. How does she do it? Again, I realized I should pay more attention. Learn from others... Yeah, one of these days...

My parents had rented a wheelchair-accessible van and had made sure they knew how to use it, and the trip home went smoothly. I wondered how they'd solved all the accessibility problems but was afraid to ask.

I should have known better than to doubt them. There was a ramp leading up to the front door. They had refitted the entire first floor of the house, including the entrance, to accommodate Mordy.

I could visualize my father planning the whole thing, sitting at his desk, drawing diagrams, taking measurements, making trip after trip to the hardware store and the lumber-yard. The solutions he'd come up with were simple, inexpensive, sturdy and ingenious, going so far as to lower the bathroom sink so Mordy could reach it from his wheelchair. My mother had followed after my father and blew her beauty dust over everything so you could barely tell how much had been altered. I noticed, too, that these preparations had not been done overnight. They'd clearly been working on this for a while, maybe even from the moment we'd brought Mordy home. It wouldn't have surprised me.

I recalled our conversation with Dr. Cohen when he'd been explaining to Mordy that parents made mistakes and sometimes said things they didn't really mean. I looked at my parents and wondered how I could possibly be a product of these two outstanding people. I felt honored and a little ashamed.

Until it all fell apart.

CHAPTER 66

DEVORAH

I t was after dinner on our second night in Ohio. We were going to stay only five days, so the past two had been a whirlwind of activity. My parents had planned an amazing schedule, and Mordy was having the time of his life.

So, after dinner, when my mother did not get up and immediately start clearing the table, I got suspicious. I had already helped Mordy to bed, and my mother started serving coffee at 9 p.m. More warning bells.

"Is this decaf?" I asked, leaving it on the saucer. "You know I don't like decaf."

"No, it's regular," she said, taking a sip. "Fresh."

I looked at my father for a clue, but he was expressionless, which was an almost impossible feat for him.

"Devorah'le," my mother started slowly. This was what she said when there was a confrontation ahead. She started out speaking softly and revved up as she went along.

"Your father and I have been talking." She looked at me for a response, but I did not give one. I was listening to my heart pounding.

"We love Mordy," she said. "Just love him. *Nebach*. He's had such a hard life."

"We're making up for it," I said. "Or at least we're trying."

Bad thoughts were entering my head like a heavy fog rolling in. Since Mordy's return, memories had been coming at me thick and fast, heavy waves knocking me off my feet. One was headed my way at that moment.

"Mom," I said tentatively. Did I really want to spoil the visit with ugly thoughts? Shouldn't I wait to hear what they had to say? But once impulsive, always impulsive. "Mom, where were you when Aharon and everyone were making arrangements to take Mordy away from me?"

My mother looked straight at me, unflinching. I knew this part of her too, because it was one of the few things we had in common: mama bear syndrome.

"That's part of what we want to talk to you about," she said, her back an icy steel rod.

I said nothing.

"We never told you, but we turned over heaven and earth to get custody of Mordy."

I sat up straight in my chair, as if someone had yanked me up with a rope. "What are you talking about?"

"Well, when we heard what happened, you know, Mordy's birth, we wanted to take the first flight to New York, but Aharon asked us to wait. He said that you were not well and that we would not want to see you like that. As if that would have kept me away! But you and Aharon were so newly married, your father and I didn't want to get in the middle, so we respected his wishes."

This was all news to me. I, like Mordy, was also surrounded by love, but this type of love teetered dangerously over the border into betrayal. "I was pretty out of it," was all I could say.

"By the time Aharon let us into the picture, Mordy was already with that terrible foster family. We spoke to everyone, begging them to let us have Mordy, and we were answered with every excuse in the book. 'He would never survive at home,' they told us. We were too close to him and to you to take care of him properly — he needed a family that was uninvolved, they said. But you know me, Devorah'le. I was not going to take no for an answer."

"So, what happened?" I asked, shaking. "Obviously it didn't work out. Why didn't you just ask Aharon?"

She sighed heavily. "You know we love Aharon, and we've never held it against him. But he had already signed away parental rights, and once he did that our hands were tied. There was nothing we could do except daven for this day to come. And it did. We never gave up hope. Not for a second."

"Why did you never tell me this?"

"Well, you didn't ask, practically speaking, and anyway, what would have been the point? You had to move forward, and we didn't want you to blame Aharon. He did everything right, followed the advice of his *rabbanim* and made the best decisions he could have under the circumstances. We have no issue with him and we didn't want you to have any, either."

"And when I came to stay with you after Ephraim was born?" I was almost whimpering now, remembering that awful time in my life.

"Honey," said my father, "I don't know if you realize what shape you were in back then. Mommy and I were very worried about you."

I actually had very little memory of that period of time. All I remembered was a feeling of being wrapped in heavy gray wool that made it very hard to move or breathe.

"We had to do everything for you. You were incapacitated with grief, and you had a baby to take care of, a healthy baby who needed you. Would you have liked us to throw fuel on the fire and tell you how hard we tried to save your other son?"

"Well, you didn't," I said woodenly. "Save him."

"Look how much *nachas* you have," my mother said. "We were so glad to be able to help then, and we'd like to help now."

I looked back and forth between the two of them, and figured it out just moments before they dropped their bomb.

She turned to my father and he nodded, urging her on. "Your father and I want to offer, to suggest, that rather than sending Mordy to that group home, with strangers and a gentile staff, and who knows what else, we think you should send him here to live with us."

Of all the things I expected her to say, this was not one of them. So many emotions and responses were at the tip of my tongue that I wasn't able to say a word.

My mother watched my face carefully — "Your face is like a traffic light," she always said — waiting for the green light to continue.

"It's a perfect solution," she said. "We have all the time in the world to devote to him, and we'll make sure he gets the best care. And don't forget, he needs to go to school and catch up — there's so much to do. He needs tutors and therapists and medical supervision. We know you're busy, and we understand why you want to send him to the group home, but your father and I..." again, looking at him for encouragement, "honestly believe he'd be better off here with us."

CHAPTER 67

DEVORAH

My mother continued talking, listing all the many reasons why they thought it was such a good idea to let Mordy live with them, but all I could hear was a rushing noise in my ears.

More than half the things she mentioned hadn't even occurred to me. Why, for example, had I left Mordy to vegetate in the living room of our house all this time when he should have been going to school, or at least learning with tutors? Why hadn't I insisted that Aharon take him swimming after

Dr. Cohen had suggested how good it would be for him?

I'd been so self-absorbed that I had once again done nothing about Mordy while I licked my wounds. There's nothing like going home again to be reminded of who you really are.

I sat with them for a short while longer, as long as I could, nodding sadly, until I saw that my mother was running out of steam. She always spoke for the two of them, and now it was my father's face I studied.

He was the only person I knew who could convey several, often conflicting, emotions at once, and as I observed him now, I sensed that he was clearly of two minds. He agreed with my mother wholeheartedly, as he had surely proven with his meticulous attention to refitting the house to accommodate Mordy.

Although he was always thorough no matter what he did, anyone could see that this had been a labor of love that no amount of prodding from my mother could disguise. Aharon was a wonderful father, but my father was outstanding. I knew he'd be able to work wonders with Mordy, because, besides his many gifts, he and my mother simply had more time to devote to Mordy.

Yet a part of him was with me totally, sympathizing with my plight, understanding how hard it would be for me, and also how hard it had already been for me starting from the day of Mordy's birth. My father was a man of few words and many deeds, and I knew if he could have found a way to take my pain away, he'd surely have done it.

I wondered if they were trying to make up for their inability to rescue Mordy from the arms of strangers when he was a baby, but it didn't really matter. Sending Mordy to live with them was probably the right thing to do. All the points my mother laid out were absolutely on target, but it was the unsaid things that made me cringe, as we both knew that despite my many talents, I was in way over my head.

I stood up, feigning exhaustion when in reality I was shaking with a surfeit of adrenaline. My heart was pounding, the rushing in my ears wouldn't stop, and I really needed some quiet time to think.

"Mom, Dad, I can't tell you how much I appreciate all the care and thought you've put into this. You are both incredible, and I hear everything you're saying. I just...can't give you an answer right now..."

"But you agree on principle?" my mother asked.

"You know I need to speak to Aharon and our *rav*, and of course to Mordy. This is not the kind of decision I can make on my own."

My mother sat back, pressing her lips together to hold back the next thing she wanted to say. My mother was a genius at knowing when to rest her case.

"Do you need anything, sweetheart?" she said now, standing with me as I started to make my way upstairs. "Would you like a hot drink?"

I did, actually, but I couldn't talk. I simply shook my head and climbed heavily up the stairs. It wasn't too late to call Aharon, so I picked up the extension in my old room where I was sleeping — it was the same phone my parents had installed when I was a teenager because they knew, without my saying so, that I was at an age when I needed some privacy. I'd been grateful for their sensitivity then, and their foresight now.

I tried to calm down as I listened to the phone ringing unanswered in Brooklyn. Finally, after about ten rings a breathless Aharon picked up the phone.

"Hi," I said, gathering my strength and attempting to sound normal.

"How *are* you?" he asked, emphasizing the word *are*.

I took a deep breath. "You're not going to believe this," I said, and he listened quietly as I told him the latest developments.

"I had a feeling something like this was going to happen," he said when I'd finished. I'd managed to hold back my sobs while I was speaking, but something in his soft reply broke me up.

"You did?" I wailed. "I didn't. Why do I never see these things coming?"

"That's what husbands are for," he said gently. I could hear him chuckling, but I wasn't upset. He knew how to make heavy things lighter, and it was something I deeply appreciated.

"It just seemed obvious to me," he continued. "They wouldn't have fixed up the house the way they did if they weren't thinking long term."

"Well, what do you think? They're right, aren't they? Wouldn't he really be better off with them than in the group home?"

Aharon let me ramble on a bit before he gently headed me off. "It's not a question of right or wrong, Devorah. It's not black and white. I know you like to put things in those little boxes of yours in your head, but this time that won't work."

"But don't we have to do what's best for Mordy?"

"Yes, we do, but first we have to define what's best."

We spoke a bit longer, until I could barely keep my eyes open. I knew that nothing was going to be resolved that night. I wasn't so sure I agreed with him that it *wasn't* black and white. I loved Mordy and wanted him to be with us, but once I heard my mother's arguments, and especially the unspoken understanding that I was incapable of truly taking over Mordy's care, it didn't sound so far-fetched.

If we were thinking of placing Mordy in the group home in any case, didn't it make more sense to place him in my parents' loving care, even if it meant I wouldn't be able to see him as often as I'd like? My mother saying, in her nice way, "*Treif, treif, treif,* how could we do that to him?" would ring in my ears for a long time.

CHAPTER 68

DEVORAH

My visit to my parents with Mordy ended on a high note. We spent our last day in Ohio at the aquarium, which Mordy absolutely loved. When he had first come to us for Pesach, Dr. Cohen had asked us to get him some colorful books on wildlife, so I knew Mordy took an interest in animals, birds, and fish. What I didn't realize was how knowledgeable he was. He could identify most of the fish, their natural habitats and eating habits. He had then done the same on our visit to the zoo, where he'd found a partner in my father, who was just as well-informed. The two of them had swapped facts and figures, talking over each other excitedly and debating the fine points of lion maintenance. My parents had been *kvelling*, so proud of Mordy were they, and my mother was giving me a look that said, "Look how much potential he has." I knew. I did not need to be told.

On the way home I'd asked Mordy what he had enjoyed the most about the outing. Without missing a beat he had said, "Zeidy." That didn't surprise me either. I knew that when he said "Zeidy," he meant both my father and my mother, only it was my father who made the stronger impression. The two of them together formed an indivisible unit. I could only imagine what, together, they could do for Mordy. I wondered if Aharon and I were now, or if we would ever be, as formidable and as effective a team as my parents.

When we deplaned back in New York and walked out through the arrivals gate, I was surprised to see Aharon and all the children waiting for us. Even Bubby Yitta was on hand for the occasion. They held little welcome signs. For a moment I was overcome, observing the scene through both my own and Mordy's eyes. He was beaming, smiling and laughing at the warm reception, but I felt a knot form in my insides. If I sent Mordy to my parents, this part of his life — the siblings, the camaraderie and warmth of a large family — would be left for special occasions only. I had already begun a mental for-and-against list that had yet to see the light of day, and while the "against" side was a respectable size, there was no denying the "for" side was much longer.

We all drove home in Mordy's special van, stopping off for some Chinese take-out food on the way. Mordy loved

Chinese food. We all thought it was amusing how much he enjoyed it. The first time we'd served it to him it had taken him a few minutes to absorb the new flavors and make sense of the textures. Then his eyes opened wide and all he could say was, "What is this? What *is* this?" We didn't make a habit of eating take-out food or eating out at restaurants, but we all loved seeing Mordy enjoy himself so much that we did it a bit more often than we used to.

Later that night, after everyone was settled, Aharon and I sat down to talk. I gave him a much fuller version of the discussion with my parents and the subsequent conversations we'd had until the end of the visit. As I spoke, my voice grew lower and heavier, until it was filled with tears like an overburdened rain cloud.

"We don't have to do it, you know," said Aharon. "There's no law saying that a child must reach his 'full' potential to the exclusion of all else. The potential for giving and receiving love must also be considered. Likewise the growth of emotional intelligence and the development of relationships. The potential to feel safe and protected, the potential to be part of a loving family, are also important."

I heard what he was saying, but it was hard for me to take it in. According to my parents, the most important thing was to give Mordy *every* opportunity to strengthen his body and his mind. This way he could go on and live independently and enjoy a meaningful life without being dependent on anyone else. But Aharon was saying something else now.

"What if he reached 75% of his physical potential, 82% of his intellectual potential, and 99.9% of his emotional and spiritual potential?" Aharon continued. "Would that make him a success or a failure? What if he didn't do math so well but was an amazing big brother to Maya? Who determines what makes a person a success?"

"Aharon, come on. He can learn all of that stuff later. The most important thing is to use the time now, while he is young, to strengthen him as much as possible."

Aharon got up and started clearing away our plates and coffee cups, as he does when he's bringing a conversation to a close. "I'm not so sure, Devorah. He can learn plenty — not as much maybe, but certainly enough — right here with us."

"Aharon, you wouldn't even take him swimming," I blurted. That had been one of the sore points about keeping Mordy at home. "How do you expect us to build him up from so many angles if we can't even get him to the pool?"

Aharon smiled. "I see you've been thinking about this. I'm sorry I haven't taken Mordy to the pool, Devorah. I'll do *teshuvah* on that, but I think part of the problem is that we never sat down to make an organized treatment plan. Once we know what to do, who does what and when, it will be much easier. We're both responsible people. We're not going to shirk our responsibilities once we know what they are."

I couldn't believe what I was hearing and I wanted to confirm it. "Are you saying that we *shouldn't* send Mordy to my parents? Are you actually advocating for him staying with us?"

He turned to look at me, his face drawn and serious. "Are you saying we *should* send him away?"

"I'm confused," I said. "If we were already considering sending him to the group home, doesn't it make more sense for him to live with my parents, in a *frum* home, with kosher food, with people who love him?"

"When you put it that way, of course it makes more sense. But you are leaving out a very important part of the equation."

"What's that?"

"Us."

CHAPTER 69

Before Mordy came back into their lives, Devorah thought she knew Aharon inside and out. She could finish his sentences, predict his reactions, and they barely had to discuss things because they were so frequently on the same page. But she had learned more about him these past few months than she had in all the time they were married.

While she thought it was obviously the right decision to send Mordy to her parents, Aharon clearly thought otherwise, and they spent most of the night arguing back and forth and generally getting nowhere. Devorah didn't understand how Aharon could think there was anything more important than keeping Mordy in a religious environment and ensuring his intellectual as well as his physical development, and he didn't understand how she could think there was anything more important than being near family.

"But my parents *are* family. It's the perfect combination," she said. "The best of both worlds."

"I know, Devorah. But there is something about being part of your immediate, nuclear family, parents and brothers and sisters, that is irreplaceable. Grandparents are wonderful, but if Hashem wanted children to be raised by their grandparents, that is how it would be."

"Where is this coming from, Aharon? You don't have such a close relationship with your mother. How would you know—" She stopped herself.

Aharon nodded sadly. "You never knew my father," he said. "My mother was a different person when he was alive. The chemistry between them was perfectly balanced, they complemented each other to perfection, but once he passed away, her sparkle and energy drained away. When they were together, we had a marvelous relationship between us all. Yes, I sometimes find it difficult now interacting with my mother, but we both remember what we had before, and the shared memory gives us strength."

Devorah listened quietly, imagining her mother-in-law smiling and laughing with her family around her, and she realized Yitta had been doing much more of that lately. "Is there anything about Mordy that reminds you of your father?" she asked.

Aharon nodded. "A lot of little things — the way he pronounces certain words, the way he turns his palms up in the air when he speaks, like someone is going to put something amazing in his hand any second. His smile, of course, is purely my father. But that isn't the point, Devorah."

"I know. I'm just trying to understand. You're a practical person. And we know the group home would be a big problem with kashrus and possible or probable exposure to bad influences."

"But we can visit constantly, supporting and encouraging him. I've said this to you before, Devorah, but maybe I didn't say it strongly enough. Fathers and siblings are important, but a kid really needs his mother. There is no replacement for it."

"Not even grandparents?" she asked.

"No. Not even grandparents. Mordy needs us even if he can't handle us as a family right now. How will he feel if we ship him away again? That would be a mistake we wouldn't be able to fix."

This conversation was not going the way Devorah had intended. She thought that sending Mordy to her parents' house would solve all the problems they'd have with the group home and also expose Mordy to *Yiddishkeit* in a calmer, softer way. Now Aharon was saying that the problems in the group home could be overcome because the most important thing for Mordy was a stable family in close contact, even if he didn't live with them.

"Who says Dr. Cohen is going to let us spend that much time with him? Maybe he'll try to pull him away from us again."

Aharon finally smiled. "I think Dr. Cohen has learned his lesson, and so have we. The only way this will work is if we all cooperate, and we all know that now. That's the least of my concerns."

They kept going around in circles, like dust eddies swirling in a strong wind, until they finally agreed to table the subject until the following day.

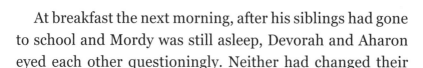

At breakfast the next morning, after his siblings had gone to school and Mordy was still asleep, Devorah and Aharon eyed each other questioningly. Neither had changed their opinion, but Devorah had one more thing to say.

"I'm worried that this is making me sound like I don't want Mordy. You know that's not true, right? Like we said, I want what's best for him, not for me."

Aharon sighed. "Of course I know that, Devorah. I just think you're selling yourself extremely short. But you know what?" he asked. "Since when are we independent operators? Let's ask the *rebbe*. I'll make an appointment."

Aharon called later to let Devorah know that the *rebbe* would see them that evening. She lost no time sitting down and bringing her pros-and-cons list to life. Her thoughts, finally given free rein, spilled out so quickly her pen could barely keep up. She tried to ignore all that Aharon had said and concentrate on her own feelings, but she couldn't get his words out of her head.

Sitting across from the *rebbe* that evening, Devorah held the list in shaky hands, prepared to read it out loud and prove her point once and for all. Aharon filled him in on the background, most of which the *rebbe* already knew since he had been guiding them throughout, and presented the new dilemma in his orderly, methodical way, careful not to interject his own opinion and inadvertently present it as fact.

The *rebbe* listened carefully, nodding his head, tapping his pen so lightly on the desk that it didn't make a sound. Then he turned to Devorah. "If I understand Reb Aharon correctly, you are in favor of sending the boy to be raised by your parents. Is that right?"

"Yes. I am in favor of that. If I could just read the *rebbe* my concerns..." She held up her list but he raised one hand to stop her.

"You must think very highly of your mother," he continued.

"I do!" replied Devorah. "She is amazing. She would raise Mordy like he was her own child."

"Tell me, Mrs. Landau, without going into details so as not to damage your mother's *kavod*, but in general, would you say your mother is a person without flaws or faults?"

"What difference does that make? I don't care if she has flaws — she's my mother." Devorah looked quickly over at Aharon, suddenly unsure where the *rebbe* was taking the conversation, and was surprised to see his eyes light up.

"Did you hear what you just said?" Aharon asked. He flashed a quick glance at the *rebbe*, silently requesting permission to speak. The *rebbe* nodded.

"It makes no difference whether she has flaws or not, she's your loving mother. Just as you are 'qualified' to raise Mordy, whether you have flaws or not. You're his mother, and spending time with you and being with you and just sitting quietly listening to you talk to a friend on the telephone can do more for him than all the physical therapy in the world. Am I not right, Reb Aharon?

CHAPTER 70

T he *rebbe* sat quietly, thinking a little longer before he spoke. "From what you've told me, while your son has blossomed beautifully considering his circumstances, he still needs quite a lot of care, physically, mentally, and emotionally. There must be no stone left unturned for the child to reach his full potential."

Devorah couldn't hold herself back and she gave Aharon a strong "I told you so" look, certain that the issue was turning her way.

"On the other hand, which is really the cornerstone, a child belongs with his mother. Nothing and no one can replace her presence in his life."

"Even if we send him to the group home?" asked Devorah.

"How far away is the group home? How often would you see him?" asked the *rebbe*.

Aharon intercepted at this point, saying, "We live about half an hour away by car. I think I can safely say that one of us would see him every day, and he'd come home for Shabbos."

"But what about the kashrus?" Devorah wailed. "That is a major issue! It's bad enough he's been eating *treif* all his life. There's no way we can let that continue. My parents' house is glatt kosher."

The *rebbe* and Aharon exchanged a glance. "I think we might have a solution for that," said Aharon.

"What is it? How can there be a solution? Dr. Cohen isn't going to make the place kosher."

"Don't be so sure about that," said Aharon. "We can talk more about it later, but let's assume the kashrus is not an issue."

They both looked at the *rebbe*, waiting for his verdict. "This is *not* a *psak*," he said firmly. "This is an *eitzah*. That means that if you decide to do differently, there will be no issue of 'going against *da'as Torah*.' Is that understood?"

"Yes," said Aharon.

Devorah grumbled her assent, arms crossed firmly as though to ward off whatever was about to come.

"It is my opinion that you should keep the boy with you, but in the group home, for now. A child needs his mother, as well as his father and siblings, even if he doesn't live in the house with you. And from what I understand, the move is temporary until he gets acclimated. How often would you see him if he lived with your in-laws?" he asked Aharon.

"We could move there to be near him," Devorah exclaimed.

"I can't say that would be a practical solution. I'm sure you want the best for your child — what mother wouldn't? But the truth is that *you* are the best for your child — your love, your attention, your presence. *Never* underestimate your value as a mother."

The *rebbe* stood up then, ready to show them out, but Devorah was crying too hard to stand up.

———————————————

Later on, in the car, Devorah's tears started and stopped a few times more before they finally slowed to a trickle.

"So we're doing this?" she said.

"Yes," said Aharon. "We most certainly are."

"How will I break it to my parents?"

"I don't mind telling them," said Aharon. "I'm sure they'll understand."

"I'm not sure they will. Thank you for your offer, but it's something I'll have to do myself. But do you understand, Aharon? I just want to be Mordy's mother, like the *rebbe* said. I don't know if I can be his nurse or his teacher or teach him multiplication—"

"He already knows how to multiply," said Aharon. "And divide."

"You know what I mean," said Devorah, but with a smile. "I know other mothers can do it all. I can't do it *all*, but I can still do a lot. Are you sure though?" she asked. "Are you sure he's going to be okay?"

"You heard the *rav*. Inside the *eitzah* is the *berachah*. Mordy's going to be fine. But he did say we had to do everything in our power to help him reach this mysterious thing called potential. We'll have to work it out with Dr. Cohen and his team."

"What about the other boys? What if they're a bad influence on him?" asked Devorah.

"I talked to Dr. Cohen about that. This first round of boys he chose are all from Ravensfield. Mordy knows all of them."

"Right. I should have realized that. I guess whatever influence they had on him already hasn't been too bad if Mordy turned out so nicely. Oh Aharon, isn't he lovely? Isn't our Mordy just the most wonderful child?"

"He's cute," said Aharon, understated as usual. "Yeah, I guess he's okay."

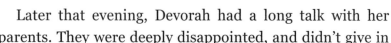

Later that evening, Devorah had a long talk with her parents. They were deeply disappointed, and didn't give in so easily, but who more than they, such exceptionally loving parents, could understand Devorah's desire to be near her son? "He was gone so many years, Mom," Devorah said softly after her father hung up the extension. "So many years."

"I know, sweetheart. Just remember, if it gets too difficult you can always change your mind."

"Thank you, Mom, for everything. It's your strength that's giving me strength."

"I love you, honey. Good luck."

"Thanks, Mom. I love you too."

Devorah hung up and, when she turned around, she realized she had company.

"So Mordy's not going to Grandma's?" said Ephraim Baruch.

"No, he's not," said Devorah. "But he is going to the group home."

"Okay, I can live with that. But he's gonna get bored there pretty quick, even if Bubby is there all day."

"Bubby?" Devorah said. "What does Bubby have to do with it?"

Ephraim made his face go completely blank, a trick he had that Devorah wished she had as well and often tried to copy — with no success. "I don't know," he said.

"Ephraim Baruch Landau, tell me what's going on right now!"

"I can't," he said.

"Why not?"

"Because I was eavesdropping on that conversation also!"

Devorah looked at him, exasperated. "We'll get to that afterward, and I will *not* forget about it. Now, tell me what you heard about Bubby and the group home."

"Are you sure I won't get in trouble?"

"No, you will get in trouble, but not for telling me. Now talk!"

Ephraim raised his eyebrows in sly supplication, which Devorah was normally immune to, but she knew that now was not the time for *chinuch*. She reached into the cabinet and pulled out a bag of potato chips, Ephraim's favorite. He reached out for it and that was when she hesitated.

What am I doing?

"You're a tzaddik," she said. "I almost stumbled into forcing you to tell me something you know without the person's permission, even though it was ill-gotten gains. Shame on you, but I can't make you tell me. That's what the chips are for. But I can still punish you for eavesdropping. It's a terrible thing to do."

As she spoke to him, she could see on his face that it was one of those rare moments when what she said was actually getting through.

"I can't say I won't ever do it again," he said frankly. "But I can say that I will try."

"Fair enough," said Devorah, and they shook hands.

Ephraim smiled, made a loud *berachah*, and stuffed a handful of chips into his mouth.

"Lovely," she said, smiling. "Now, where's your father?"

CHAPTER 71

Not one to sit quietly by, Bubby Yitta was one step ahead of everyone else. Once she'd heard about Mordy's possible move to the group home, she gave Dr. Cohen a call.

"Let's say," she started out abruptly before identifying herself. Anyone else would have been taken aback, but Dr. Cohen knew immediately who it was. Love came in all different packages, he thought.

"Let's say Mordy moves into your group home. We have a kashrus problem."

"A what?" Jeremy asked.

"Kashrus...a 'kosher' problem. Mordy won't be able to eat anything there. Have you thought about that?" she asked.

"I have, actually," said Jeremy. "I was thinking I'd order something like those kosher airplane meals for him, supplemented by whatever food your daughter-in-law chooses to supply."

"I beg your pardon. You don't intend my grandson to survive on those prepackaged meals, do you? And what about the other Jewish boys? I have a much better idea."

And that's how Bubby Yitta became the housemother/cook/housekeeper at Jeremy Cohen's group home, with the only cost to him being her carfare and a small room for her to sleep over if need be.

When Aharon heard this, a weight rolled off his shoulders. Now he knew that Mordy would not only be in good hands, but the right hands. Kosher hands.

It was a strange, soggy day when they packed Mordy up and set out for his new lodgings. Included in his luggage were all the books and games and medical devices they had bought for him since he'd come home, along with some new ones as well.

"Mommy, Tatty, I don't need all this stuff! I won't even have place for it in my room!" Mordy remonstrated. "I'll be fine on my own. What could go wrong with Bubby Yitta there? Do you think she would ever let anything happen to me?"

Aharon and Devorah laughed.

"Hardly. It's just that we'll miss you, here at home," said Devorah.

Ephraim rolled his eyes, perhaps a bit insulted at being usurped by Mordy as Bubby Yitta's favorite. Not too upset, though, because he and his bubby had already concocted some secret plans. "We're coming to see you on Shabbos and it's already Tuesday," he said. He and Mordy slapped a forceful high-five, almost tilting Mordy out of his chair.

"Ephraim!" Devorah scolded.

"Don't worry, Ma, he can take it, right, Mordy?"

"You bet!"

Mordy, in his wheelchair, rose up on the lift into the van, and he waved at his siblings seeing him off. "So, Mordy, you okay?" said Devorah.

"I'm fine." He was already engrossed in the book Ephraim Baruch had just given him, *Avraham ben Avraham*. He felt a little bit like the *ger tzeddek* of the book, but luckily hadn't reached the end yet.

They were warmly welcomed at the residence by Dr. Cohen, Bubby Yitta, three staff members, and the other young residents of the home. One of the boys gladly helped Aharon schlep Mordy's luggage to his room, to be lovingly unpacked by Bubby Yitta. It was obvious she'd already established herself there as a firm but kind presence. The boys had clearly taken to her, and Dr. Cohen was no less smitten.

Devorah was about to sit herself down on the couch in the common room but was gently directed toward the door by her mother-in-law. "Time to go, *mammele*. Let him get settled."

"But I want to make sure he's comfortable and that he has everything he needs!" She was serious, but everyone laughed. She'd gone over the list a hundred times, and they'd even, with Jeremy's approval, put up mezuzos in the apartment and had a small *chanukas habayis* the day before. She grudgingly admitted that the time had come to leave him. She knew it was temporary and realized that she'd be able to really focus on him now instead of herself. He'd get the care he needed, and he'd go to school now as well. What more could she ask for?

"We're really lucky, you know," said Mordy suddenly.

"I know we are," said Aharon. "But in what way do you think?"

He looked around at the disparate group surrounding him, gazing at him with tremendous fondness.

"We all found each other. Isn't that great?"

Tears welled in four pairs of eyes, as well as those of some of the staff. They all knew that with Mordy as the center, they'd been drawn together in a loving circle around him. He'd pierced the heart of each one of them, and they were all the better for it. Every ray of sunshine, every shy smile, every new experience had awakened their own joy and bonded them together. They really were lucky.

Aharon crouched in front of Mordy in his wheelchair. "You know the drill. Whenever you want to come home, we're waiting for you. And you can come home every Shabbos but you don't have to. We can also come and make Shabbos here. Got it?"

Mordy rolled his eyes in perfect imitation of Ephraim. "Got it."

Aharon stood and shook hands with Dr. Cohen. "Thank you," he said simply.

"Thank you," Jeremy replied.

Yitta led Devorah gently by the arm, and stopped just next to the door. "You're so brave," she said, cupping her daughter-in-law's cheek with a thin, warm hand. "This will be for the best. He'll grow in both places, and somewhere down the road the paths will cross. I promise you that."

"I know," she sobbed softly.

Yitta gave her a hug, the first of many more. "It's not true that home is where the heart is."

Devorah pulled back. "What do you mean?"

"It's *narishkeit*. Home is not where the heart is. It's not even where the house is. Home is where Hashem is." She gave Devorah the softest, kindest push.

Then with one hand resting lightly on her grandson's shoulder, Yitta and Mordy watched Aharon and Devorah leave, making sure they were safely on their way before turning around and closing the door behind them.